HOT

Living close to ... adores shoes, her kids, cats, gardening and tall men, although not necessarily in that order. Constantly torn between being a born-again sex kitten – it's never too late – and cleaning out the litter tray, Gemma enjoys photography, long lazy suppers with friends and being old enough to be taken seriously in shops.

GEMMA FOX

Hot Pursuit

HarperCollins*Publishers*

HarperCollins*Publishers*
77–85 Fulham Palace Road,
Hammersmith, London W6 8JB

www.harpercollins.co.uk

A Paperback Original 2004

A catalogue record for this book
is available from the British Library

ISBN 978-0-00-718302-9
ISBN 978-0-00-784192-9

Typeset in Sabon by Palimpsest Book Production Limited,
Polmont, Stirlingshire

Printed and bound in Great Britain by
Clays Limited, St Ives plc

To my friends and family – you know who you are – but most of all to my youngest son Sam for putting up with a mother who hasn't got a proper job.

'The name of a man is a numbing blow from which he never recovers.'
Marshall McLuhan.

1

'Oh my God, *oh my God*. I think the baby's coming. I want to push. Oh no, oh God, it can't be – oh, oh . . .' squealed the woman, desperately trying to grit her teeth and hold on tight to her dignity.

Bernie Fielding stood his paint kettle down on the grey civil-service carpet and sighed.

'No, yer don't. Come on now, love, don't get yourself in a state. You'll be all right. Breathe, pant. I know what I'm talking about. I was in the Falklands, me. Paramedic, yomped into Goose Green, Iran, Iraq – you just want to take it steady, darlin' – it's probably only wind. Do you want me to go and get you something? A nice glass of water – what about a pillow?'

As he turned, the large ginger-haired woman dropped down onto her haunches and bit the desk, while droplets of sweat glistened and rolled slowly into the rising swell of her ample cleavage. She groaned and then as Bernie watched very, very elegantly rolled backwards onto the floor as the contraction passed, her floral pink sundress tight as clingfilm across her creamy-white flesh. She looked like a *Homes & Gardens* beach ball.

'Ring Linda in security, will you?' she hissed between tortured breaths and clenched teeth, waving wildly towards the phone. 'Or Anthea in Human Resources. Oh, my God, I think there's another one coming. I thought that it was a false alarm; the baby isn't due for another fortnight . . . Oh my Godddddddd.'

The woman's face contorted into a hideous snarling mask while Bernie stared, overwhelmed, at the switchboard beside her computer. One little light flashed and then another, and another. It looked like some bizarre children's puzzle. It was no good; he had no idea which key to press. He looked down at the woman, desperately clutching her distended Laura Ashley abdomen – it was obvious that she wasn't going to be any help at all. Bernie stepped over her with some care, and opened the office door.

Outside in the corridor, a fey-looking boy in a cheap blue suit was busy pushing a trolley along the linoleum. Bernie beckoned him over.

'S'cuse me, mate, but there's a woman in here having a baby. I really think that you ought to go and get someone to give her a hand.' He glanced back over his shoulder as the woman heaved herself over onto her side, panting furiously, her face flame red with effort and exertion. 'And you'd better make it snappy.'

The boy's face turned ashen. 'What? Really? Who? Not Ms Hargreaves? Oh my goodness, oh my . . . Wait here, I'll go and fetch someone.' He looked down at his watch. 'God, it's nearly lunchtime, everyone will be leaving soon – His last words were snatched away as Ms Hargreaves let out an unearthly screech and the terrified boy broke into a run.

Bernie leant back against the wall; all in all it had been a funny sort of morning so far. He had been roped in by a friend with a painting and decorating business to help him with a little job, cash in hand, no names, no pack drill – a bit of easy money – and Bernie most definitely needed the money. He had had a couple of bad years, when nothing had gone right. The Inland Revenue were after him, national insurance, VAT, the bank, the finance company, two ex-wives – not to mention the council-tax people and the bloody rent man: in fact you name it and they had Bernie's name top of the list.

He thought his mate was taking the piss when they'd turned up in the works van at this place out on the Colmore Road, and that maybe he'd been set up. It was obvious, though there were no signs up outside, that the offices were government. The whole place reeked of tax returns and little men in grey suits with beady eyes hunched over columns of figures that didn't quite add up. Just pulling into the car park had made him feel a bit queasy, but it had been okay – until now.

Ms Hargreaves wailed again.

Within a few seconds two middle-aged women in suits appeared, bustling down the corridor pursued by the boy, whose complexion had turned from grey to bright crimson.

'In my opinion it's best if we get her downstairs to First Aid,' said one woman, elbowing her way past Bernie.

'Shouldn't we leave her where she is, Audrey? If we could just get her into the recovery position – I don't think you should move a casualty –'

'But that is exactly my point, Lucinda, she *isn't* a casualty *is she*? She is in labour –'

'But I read –'

On the floor between them Ms Hargreaves let out a terrifying grunt as the women rolled her over onto her back and the boy slammed the trolley into the newly painted skirting board where, by some unspoken consensus, it was decided it would make a superb impromptu stretcher. One suited woman peered at Bernie from behind her wire-rimmed spectacles, then glanced down at his paint-splattered overalls.

'Just keep an eye on the office, will you. Don't touch anything. I'll send someone up to – to –'

'Oh, please hurry,' snorted Ms Hargreaves,

easing herself onto the trolley. 'I don't think I can hang on very much longer. I want to push –'

Seconds later there was an unpleasant wet sound and a great tidal wave of steaming liquid swamped the pile of manila folders on the trolley. The boy looked as if he might faint. Manfully, one woman braced herself behind the handles of the trolley and guided it and Ms Hargreaves back out into the corridor. She glared furiously at the boy.

'Get a grip, Hemmingway; it's all perfectly natural. Run downstairs and keep an eye out for the ambulance.'

After they vanished through the swing doors Bernie blew his lips out thoughtfully and stepped back into Ms Hargreaves' office. Keep an eye on things they'd said. He pushed the door to and lit a cigarette in spite of the little notice on Ms Hargreaves' desk thanking him not to. The clock ticked; the computer hummed. He ran his fingers idly across the contents of the in-tray. Shouldn't be long before someone showed up, always assuming they'd remembered to tell anyone he was there. Bernie sighed and looked around the spartan interior of the little office before glancing out of the window.

Below him, outside the main doors, Ms Hargreaves was struggling to get off the trolley while the two women were doing their level best to ensure she stayed on it. The boy was throwing up into a bin, while from somewhere in the distance Bernie could just make out the wail of an ambulance siren. He puffed again, lowering himself into the swivel chair.

Despite Bernie's initial apprehension and the distinct sense that he was walking into an ambush, the ample Ms Hargreaves had barely given Bernie a second look when he'd opened her office door first thing that morning and waved the paint pot in her direction. She had grunted on and off for most of the morning, but not at him.

Bernie put his feet up on her desk, thinking that he should be painting, really – as the boy had so rightly pointed out, it was almost lunchtime. He stubbed out his roll-up in Ms Hargreaves' pot-pourri and glanced without much interest at the computer screen. Probably a requisition order for park benches and paving slabs.

The screen swirled with random dots until he moved the mouse. Instantly it cleared and an animated cartoon character ran across it on what appeared to be some sort of title page. Below the little bearded sprite the text read:

'RUN STILTSKIN . . .?'

The words flashed enticingly. Bernie glanced over his shoulder into the empty office. Why the hell not? Who would ever know? Maybe he could top her best score.

He'd had a nice little PC until the bailiffs had been round to repossess it. Bernie clicked the mouse and the picture on the screen unfolded like an origami flower to an altogether more official-looking document. He leant closer to read the closely spaced lines of text and then grinned with pure delight. Maybe there was a God after all.

Very, very slowly, Bernie Fielding unpeeled himself from Ms Hargreaves' ergonomically designed vinyl chair and closed the door of her office. He took the bentwood coat stand from against the wall and wedged it tight up under the door handle.

'Bingo,' he whispered as he sat down again, and typed his full name, address, and date of birth into the spaces provided.

Downstairs in another part of the building, Nick Lucas took a seat and the cup of coffee the woman offered him. He smiled his thanks. She nodded and screwed her mouth up into a little moue of professional pleasantness that may or may not have been a smile, Nick really wasn't certain and didn't intend pushing to find out. She had jet-black hair, pulled back like curtains off her angular face, and looked as if she had been constructed from white chamois leather stretched tight over a wire coat-hanger.

'Now,' said the woman in a soft Scots accent, turning the computer screen so that he couldn't see what she was typing, 'it's all very simple. We will be getting your new details through any minute . . . oh, here they come.'

Beside her, a printer spluttered into life and started to dart back and forth across a roll of white paper.

Nick coughed nervously and took a sip of coffee. It tasted like sweet tar. 'I'm still not sure about this, Ms Crow . . .' he began. To say that the name suited her was going way beyond stating the obvious. 'I know that you said that it would all be fine, but I –'

Before he could spill his fears and anxieties out all over the grey institutional carpet, Ms Crow nailed him with her icy blue stare, strangling his confidence into an unmanly falsetto, and then rolled her eyes and pursed her lips again. 'I'm sorry? Did you say something?' she growled.

Nick swallowed hard. 'I'm worried about this – I mean, will I be safe? With this Stiltskin thing; will I be all right?'

Her face rearranged itself back into what passed for a smile. 'We've been through all this before, Mr Lucas, our witness relocation plan is extremely secure. We operate one of the premier services in the world. Our record speaks for itself. A complete new identity at the press of a button.' She pressed a button on her keyboard to emphasise the point.

'Just don't audition for *Blind Date,* and I'd steer well clear of *Big Brother* if I were you,' said a distinguished-looking, thick-set man stepping into the office. He sounded cheerful in a brisk no-nonsense way.

Nick got to his feet. 'And you are?'

'Coleman, Danny Coleman. Senior liaison officer on the Stiltskin team. You're high priority, Mr Lucas; trust me, you'll be just fine. Ms Crow here is my assistant. My right-hand woman. I don't know what we'd do without her.' He smiled, and extended a hand to take Nick's. 'From now on, whatever you want, whatever you need, I'm your man.'

Nick noticed that the smile on Coleman's face only warmed his mouth; his marble grey eyes remained resolutely cool. Nevertheless, Nick shook the man's hand firmly and then said, 'I'm still really not sure about all this.'

'Everyone feels the same way,' Coleman said. 'Don't you worry, believe me, it'll be just fine.'

Ms Crow got up from the keyboard to let Coleman take her place. Nick tried to look relaxed but knew he was failing miserably.

'So who am I now?' he tried with forced good humour.

Coleman looked up from the screen. 'Just hang on a mo', we'll have to wait for this to finish the run.' He glanced up at his assistant who was hovering by the door like a prim, Viyella-wrapped bird. 'Ms Crow, if you'd like to go into the other office and get someone to transfer all this stuff onto Mr Lucas's new documents, please?'

She screwed up her face again and left.

'New documents?' said Nick haltingly.

Coleman nodded. 'Uh huh. It's very simple – all the same documents you've got now only they'll be in your new name. Passport, driver's licence, national insurance number, credit cards, bank accounts. We can do them all from here but we'll need some photos before we take you to your new address. You haven't had any photos taken yet, have you?'

Nick shook his head.

'Okay, well that won't take too long, and it says here that you're divorced; I'll just buzz through and make sure they knock you up a decree absolute while they're at it.' Coleman grinned, the warmth once again only reaching the equator of his rotund features: his eyes stayed ice cold. 'Never know when you might need it – and besides, a damned sight cheaper than the real thing, eh? As I said, if you have any problems all you have to do is phone in. It's our job to see that the transition goes nice and smoothly. It normally doesn't take our clients too long to adapt. Obviously these things aren't always as simple as we'd like, but we've got all kind of experts on the payroll who can help if you have any problems. I think you'll be fine once you've got yourself a proper home again, and a job, obviously – gives you a sense of belonging. What do you do?'

On the desk the printer ground to a whining halt and Danny Coleman tore off a sheet of paper.

'I was a chef,' said Nick, realising with a start

that he had used the past tense, but Coleman seemed oblivious, his attention on the documents.

'Oh really? Shouldn't be too hard to find work then, we'll sort out your certificates and some references,' said Coleman, and then, 'Here we are.' He presented the printout to Nick Lucas. 'Mr Bernard Fielding, this is your life. Or should I say, this is your new life.'

Nick took one look at the sheet of paper and felt sick.

In a little village, deep in the heart of rural Norfolk, Maggie Morgan slammed her ageing Golf into reverse and teased the car back up along the narrow lane that led to her cottage. It complained bitterly. Overhanging branches scratched the already scarred paintwork.

'Sit down, Joe, I can't see.'

'You heard what Mum said,' added Ben, dragging his little brother down into the footwell. Joe shrieked.

'Oh for God's sake, will you two stop it. I haven't got the energy for this. Now both of you shut up and sit down.' Her headache was making her even more ratty.

'But he started it,' whined Ben, as the car crunched over the weed-fringed gravel.

'I don't care who started it – just be quiet.' She glared at them crossly in the rear-view mirror.

'Ben, can you nip round and open the boot and help get the cases out, please? I'll go and open up. Joe, don't just sit there, honey. You can go and tell Mrs Eliot that we're home safe and sound and see if she got the milk in.'

As the boys clambered out of the car Maggie eased herself out of the driving seat. It felt so nice to be home. She was so tired that her body ached right through to her bones. She stretched and looked around. The little pantiled cottage basked like a big ginger cat in the summer sunshine; the climbing rose over the door weighed heavy with scented creamy-pink flowers. It looked wonderful, so why was her fickle mind so eager to point out that the lawn desperately needed cutting and the bay hedge ought to be trimmed back?

Maggie grimaced. This was what the summer holidays were for. No marking or lesson planning for a few weeks; just the kids and the house. The hedge and the lawn and all the other jobs on the list would get done another day in some glorious unspecified *mañana*. Once she'd got the mower fixed and found the hedge trimmer, obviously. Maggie sighed. There were days when doing it all alone seemed like a cruel joke. In quiet moments on holiday Maggie had yearned for a change. She pined for a little excitement.

She groaned and headed inside. The drive back up from Somerset had taken forever and, roses or no roses, excitement or no excitement, if she didn't have a decent cup of tea and a pee soon she might just die.

Joe, who had just turned six, trotted round from the next door neighbour's carrying two pints of milk in his arms. He grinned, as behind him their elderly neighbour followed.

'Nice to see you're home, Maggie. Nothing very much has happened while you've been away. Did you have a good holiday? Joe looks like he caught the sun – look at his hair, all bleached blond at the front.' The old lady ruffled it affectionately.

Maggie smiled, taking the milk from Joe. 'It was wonderful, exactly what we needed; lots of sun, sea, and sleep. Everything been all right here?'

Mrs Eliot nodded. 'Oh yes, fine. No problems at all. Oh, and the gasman turned up to mend your boiler at long last. I gave him the keys like you said.'

Maggie smiled. 'And not before time. Great, look, I'm just going to get in and get things sorted out. I'll pop round later and tell you all about the holiday.' She nodded towards the boys. 'The kids have bought you a little present.'

The elderly woman smiled. 'How lovely. I got their postcard, it was nice of them to think of me. I've put it on the mantelpiece; pride of place. You'll have to come and have a look, boys.'

Ben, with a red face, hefted one of the suitcases up onto the front step.

'Why did you have to tell her that?' he hissed

13

as Mrs Eliot made her way back inside. 'You bought her that vase.' At nine he was beginning to see himself as the man of the house.

'Shush. Here, let me have that. You go and help Joe with the black bags; and be careful, they've got all the blankets from the beach hut in them – they'll be heavy,' she called as Ben headed back down the path. Maggie slipped the key into the lock and pushed open the door with her foot.

Inside the hallway it was still and cool. Maggie let out a sigh of relief. She always enjoyed the first few seconds when she arrived home, when the house seemed slightly unfamiliar and she could view it with new eyes; except that this time the sensation lingered a second or two longer than usual. There was something wrong, something out of kilter that Maggie couldn't quite put her finger on. The two boys, bearing black bags, pushed in behind her and dropped them on the flagstone floor.

Ben picked up the milk. 'Is it all right if I have some cereal, I'm starving.'

'Of course, love, there should be some in the cupboard. Can you put the kettle on while you're in the kitchen?'

Joe bolted upstairs to add his new holiday dinosaur to the collection on his bedroom windowsill. Still the strange feeling remained. Maggie shook her head. It was probably just that she was exhausted; the traffic on the way home had been terrible.

Ben came out of the kitchen as she piled the rest of the bags up in the hall.

'Mum,' he said accusingly, holding out a box towards her. 'Somebody's been eating my cereal.'

A split second later Joe glared at her over the banister. 'And somebody's been sleeping in my bed,' he said before vanishing.

Maggie laughed and threw her handbag onto the hall stand.

'Oh my God,' she said, clutching her chest theatrically. 'Don't tell me. We've accidentally wandered into a police reconstruction of Goldilocks and the Three Bears.'

As she spoke, the door to the study opened very, very slowly and a tall, rangy man wrapped in a bath towel stepped, dripping, into the hall.

'Who the hell are you?' he said, clutching the skimpy towel tight around his belly.

Maggie blinked, once, twice, strangling the scream that threatened. 'I'm sorry?' she mumbled. Her first thoughts were muddled; this couldn't be happening. Next come shock, then fear, then surprise; a startled, bright, primary palette of emotions.

'What are you doing in my house?' he barked furiously.

Maggie settled on outrage, an unfamiliar scarlet glow, and looked round for something to defend herself and the boys with. Everything seemed to be happening in slow motion, everything sharp and clear and crisp.

Across the hall the man's face contorted, and his body, already wound tight, hunched as if he meant to spring. 'I said –' he began.

'I heard what you said,' Maggie snapped, easing herself towards the hall stand. Her heart began to tango under her tee shirt. She could hear the reverberation in her ears as if reassuring her she was still alive and well. But for how long? She was acutely aware that Ben's baseball bat stood amongst the umbrellas no more than an arm's length away.

'Well?' demanded the man, the colour rising on his face and chest.

Maggie nodded towards her eldest son. 'Quickly, love, go into the kitchen and phone the police,' she called, and, as the man turned to watch Ben scurry away, she lunged forward. Grabbing the bat, she hefted it up to shoulder height.

The man took a step back, lifting one hand to ward her off, as Maggie settled into a batter's stance.

'For God's sake,' he yelped, as she took a practise swing in his direction, his other hand still clutching at the towel. 'Are you mad? You nearly hit me with that. And there's no point ringing the police.'

What did he mean? Was he going to kill them?

Had he cut off the phone lines? Maggie narrowed her eyes, wondering just how hard she would have to hit him to subdue him. 'I don't know who you are, or what you want, but this is my house –' She swung the bat again. 'And I want you out. Now.'

Ben appeared in the doorway with the phone and began to tap in the number.

'There has to have been some sort of mistake' the man said, his voice still tight. 'They brought me here.'

'They? Who's they? Little green men?' Maggie said, more aggressively now, the adrenaline coursing through her veins like molten lava. She gestured towards the door. 'Come on. Out.'

'What?' he said.

'You heard me,' she said, sidestepping towards the front door.

'What? Like this?' He sounded incredulous.

Maggie nodded. Once he was out she could lock the door, and throw his clothes out of a window. Let the police sort him out. Ideas spiralled through her mind like crows.

'Here Mum,' said Ben, waving the phone at her.

'I've already told you, there's no point ringing the police,' the man protested.

Maggie felt another little plume of fear rising, her stomach contracting sharply as her fingers tightened around the hickory shaft.

'Why not?' she said, licking bone-dry lips, watching his every move. 'Did you cut the wires?'

He sighed and ran his fingers back through his wet hair. 'No, of course I didn't cut the wires – don't be so melodramatic. It's just that the police know that I'm here already, they were the ones who brought me here in the first place,' he said quietly. 'How many burglars do you know who break in to take a shower, for God's sake?'

Joe thundered halfway down the stairs two at a time and then froze when he spotted their unexpected guest. Maggie shooed him towards the kitchen. 'Keep back, Joe. It's all right – don't worry. He's just leaving.'

The man groaned. There was a look of total disbelief on his face. 'Look, I'm not going to hurt anyone. There has to have been some sort of mix-up somewhere –'

Maggie balanced herself on the balls of her feet. She was ready for him if he made a move. 'So what are you doing in my house?'

'As far as I was – am – concerned, this is *my* house. The lady next door gave me the key –' He waved towards Mrs Eliot's house.

Maggie suddenly understood. 'That's because she thought you were the gasman.'

The man looked hurt. 'She said that she was expecting me.'

Maggie swung the head of the bat back and forth speculatively. 'She was – at least she was expecting someone from the gas board. It's taken them six weeks to get around to repairing my boiler, although actually – unless you *are* the gasman, they still haven't made it.' The bat was getting heavy. 'Now, can you explain what's going on?'

'They've never been the same since they were privatised,' he said.

'That wasn't what I meant and you know it,' Maggie hissed. She was having trouble sustaining her sense of outrage.

The man looked down at his damp belly. 'Would you mind very much if I just nipped back upstairs and got dressed? I was getting out of the shower when the car pulled up and as I wasn't expecting anyone I came down to see who it was.'

'And then I opened the door?'

'Yes – I thought I'd better hide. I wasn't sure who you were. I won't be a minute –'

Maggie watched him turn and hurry upstairs still clutching one of her best fluffy white towels around his midriff. He wasn't the only one who wasn't sure who was who.

Ben, still carrying the cordless phone, looked at her from the kitchen doorway. 'Do you still want me to ring the police, Mum?'

Maggie shook her head, feeling vaguely ridiculous standing in the hall brandishing a baseball bat, all wound up and ready to go.

'No, love – just go into the kitchen and make us some tea, will you?'

'Oh, go on, Mum, let me, please,' Ben whined. 'I know the number and everything.'

'No,' Maggie snapped.

Standing beside Ben, Joe pulled a face. 'You told Mrs Eliot that you were going to go round hers for tea. You promised and she's got chocolate biscuits.'

Maggie sighed. 'I did, didn't I? Just nip across the garden and tell her the gasman is still here and I'll try and get round later if I can. And then come straight back.'

It didn't take the honorary gasman more than ten minutes to reappear, dressed in faded jeans and a sun-bleached blue cotton shirt. Maggie couldn't help but notice that his shirt had four odd buttons. One wasn't sewn on in quite the right place, revealing an interesting glimpse of tanned, hairy chest. His feet were bare, his dark hair slick and damp. He was still rolling up his sleeves as he loped into the kitchen.

'Now,' she said, across the kitchen table, still holding the baseball bat as she handed him a mug. 'How about we take this from the beginning? Is tea all right?' she asked, thawing slightly.

The man looked uncomfortable but pulled out a chair. 'Tea's fine. I don't know what to say really.' He bit his lip thoughtfully. 'As far as I'm concerned this was – my new start,' he said. 'I belong here. I don't understand what's happened. This is my place –'

Maggie tucked the bat under her arm and opened the biscuit tin. There was a two-week-old Jammy Dodger and a half-eaten Wagon Wheel inside.

'No,' she said firmly, closing the lid and looking up to meet his gaze. 'That's where you're wrong. You don't belong here. If you belonged here I'm quite certain I would have remembered. Tell you what, let's start with something simple, shall we? How about you tell me your name?'

He pulled another face and then said, 'Hang on a minute,' extricated a wallet from the back pocket of his jeans and opened it. 'Oh yes,' he said brightly, taking out a driving licence and handing it to her. 'There we are, I'm Bernie Fielding.'

Maggie suddenly felt dizzy, as if somehow she had managed to wander into a waking dream – or perhaps a nightmare.

'No,' she said again, but more firmly this time. 'That isn't true either. You see, I was married to Bernie Fielding for eight years and believe me, unless he's had a personality transplant and a lot of plastic surgery you are most definitely not him.'

The man glanced back into the hall, where Ben was watching him with all the concentration of a trained sniper. 'Bloody hell – the boys, your boys, I mean, are they *my* boys, too?'

Maggie took a long pull on her tea. 'No, that's something else I'm sure I would have remembered, and no, before you ask, they're not Bernie's either. I married Bernie when I was eighteen, which seems like a very long time ago now. I've been married again since then.'

'Oh my God, this is a total bloody disaster,' said the man uneasily, clambering to his feet, his colour draining rapidly. 'Where is he? Is he parking the car, walking the dog? On his way home from work? Oh my God. Bloody hell, this is such a mess.'

Maggie waved the bat in his direction, encouraging him back to his seat. 'Relax, I've got the most terrible taste in men. I asked him to leave a couple of years ago and, surprise, surprise, he did.'

The man ran his fingers back through his dark wavy, still damp-hair. 'Thank God for that.'

Maggie sniffed. 'I know. I don't understand what I ever saw in him,' she said, and then, smiling, continued briskly, 'Right, I'm going to get the kids some crisps and fruit out of the car. Then I'm going to park them in front of the TV, and while I'm away –' she glanced at her watch '– that gives you about five minutes. I'd like you to come up with a persuasive and, if possible, plausible argument for exactly what you're doing in my house and why I shouldn't call the law and have you dragged out of here.'

Maggie picked up her car keys. 'Oh, and it had better be good, Ben's still got the mobile phone with him. One squeak from me and the Old Bill will be round here before you can pack your shower gel.'

'Actually, I think I've probably been using yours. I thought it was really odd that the house had so many personal things in it. I was going to get some boxes, pack it all away – the policeman said I should just chuck out what I didn't want.'

Maggie shivered, wondering what might have happened to her possessions if she had been gone another week.

Meanwhile, in a small sub-post office in an Oxfordshire village, the real Bernie Fielding was busy pushing a large pile of envelopes across the counter.

The woman smiled up at him. 'Wedding?'

Bernie, dragged away from an entirely different train of thought, peered at her.

'Sorry? What? Whose wedding?' he said.

The envelopes contained a bevy of application forms for all the documents he'd need for his new identity, everything from a birth certificate through to a duplicate driving licence and American Express card. Numbers and account details all courtesy of Stiltskin. Courtesy of Stiltskin, James Cook also had a very healthy bank balance. Bernie had already been to the bank in Banbury to pick up his temporary cheque book and some cash.

'Yours?' she asked, nodding down at the thick

bundle over the top of her horn-rimmed spectacles. 'Or are you throwing a party?'

Bernie sighed. God save him from women with tongues.

'Change of address actually. Can I have a dozen, er . . .' he peered at the handful of change he had in his hand. 'Second class, please.'

The woman opened the stamp book and counted them out.

'Not local, are you?'

Bernie puffed thoughtfully and looked at his inquisitor. She had a great tumble of teased blonde hair, while behind the horn-rims, rather attractive fiery conker-brown eyes watched him with barely concealed curiosity. What the hell, he had nothing to hide, at least not now he didn't.

Bernie warmed up his smile a degree or two. 'No, actually I've just moved onto the caravan site at the back of the Old Dairy.' He saw the fleeting glint of disapproval in her eyes as he plummeted earthwards in her estimation.

'Although,' he added hastily, clawing himself back from the brink of social-security oblivion, 'it's only temporary, obviously, just until I can find myself a decent house to buy. I was pipped at the post for the last one – I've already sold mine and needed somewhere to stay fast, you know how it is. I've been to see several others but . . .' Bernie hesitated, tangled up in the strings of his own lie. He backtracked, wondering if he

24

was finally losing his touch. He really needed to concentrate more.

Over the counter the woman was watching him wriggle like a cat watches a baby bird that's fallen from the nest.

'To be perfectly honest I haven't seen anything else that's quite me yet. You need to like the feel of a place – feel like it could be home – you know what I'm saying? One man's inglenook is another man's naff old fireplace.' The lie dropped down a gear and accelerated away so fast that Bernie could barely keep up with it.

'And besides, I'm looking for something a little bit special, double garage for the BMW and my four-by-four, obviously. Stables would be nice; livery is so expensive. But there's just nothing on the market at the moment that really takes my fancy. Trouble is I have to move around a lot with my job and I've always hated hotels. I was going to rent a house, but all the fuss –' Bernie lifted his hands to imply some enormous complex puzzle that he hadn't the time to unravel. 'Whereas I could just walk into a caravan, no problem, pay the deposit pick up the key and wham bam, thank you, ma'am – there we are, in like Flynn. And they're fun, aren't they – caravans?'

Bernie knew he was waffling but he didn't seem able to stem the flow. 'My new contract starts next week, so it all fell into place. Hadn't got time to hang about. Nice secure little number, three years . . . bloody good salary.' Lungs empty, right down to the red line Bernie hastily drew in a long, calming breath.

Thoughtfully, Conker-eyes tipped her head on one side and looked him up and down.

'Sounds interesting,' she said in a low voice. 'My name's Stella; Stella Ramsey.' She left a little breathy pause at the end of the introduction, a pause that invited a wild variety of possibilities.

Bernie coughed. 'I'm new to this area, I was really hoping to find someone to show me all the sights.'

Stella smiled lazily. 'There's not a lot to see in Renham, to be honest.'

He grinned. 'Well, how about we go out for a little drink instead, then?'

She lifted her eyebrows. 'The local pub is a right dump.'

He leant on the counter, enjoying the show of token resistance. 'Well, in that case, perhaps you'd like to show me another one, somewhere . . .' he hesitated, 'somewhere nice, tasteful, and expensive. I've always had *very expensive* tastes.'

Conker-eyes ran her tongue around the end of her well-chewed Biro. 'Oh, have you?' she said slyly. 'Well, in that case, there's always the Lark and Buzzard over at Highwell. They do a lovely chilli con carne, chicken in a basket, tikka marsala – very international cuisine, is the Lark.'

Bernie grinned, feeling a nice little buzz in the

bottom of his belly as their eyes met. 'Really? I don't suppose I could tempt you to show me where this place is, could I? Only I'm at a loose end this evening –'

This time she hesitated, batting long eyelashes coquettishly. 'But I don't even know your name.'

Bernie smiled, pausing long enough to check that he remembered his new name before wheeling out a well-worn 007 impression. 'Cook,' he said, in a very poor imitation of Sean Connery, 'James Cook.'

Conker-eyes blushed furiously. 'Well, Mr James Cook, in that case, what time do you want to pick me up?' she asked.

Bernie glanced up at the clock above the counter. 'Shall we say about eight?'

She nodded. 'Why not? I'll meet you out the front.'

Bernie smiled, and without another word made his way to the door, opened it and lifted his hand in salute. As the shop bell rang to announce his departure, Stella Ramsey was licking his stamps and putting them on the envelopes that would secure all the things he needed for his new life. Her tongue was very, very pink.

In Maggie Morgan's kitchen, the new Bernie Fielding, alias Nick Lucas, was watching with fascination as the woman who had burst into what he had truly believed was his new life and new home, went about cooking him and the boys supper. As she worked, the two lads ran a relay race of surveillance between the cottage kitchen and the sitting room.

Maggie had set the baseball bat down alongside the chopping board and was busily hacking an onion into uneven lumps with a large kitchen knife.

'So, you can have some supper with us,' she was saying, 'and then you can go home.'

Nick sighed. 'I've already explained to you, I can't go home. I haven't got anywhere else to go.'

She turned towards him, waving her knife like a conductor's baton. He flinched. 'You haven't explained anything, and what you have told me is total baloney. What sort of an idiot do you take me for? You didn't get here by magic, you came from somewhere. And everyone has somewhere they can go, even if they don't want to. A sofa, a friend's floor – back to their parents.' She crushed a couple of cloves of garlic under the heel of the knife and shuffled them into the pan. 'This just isn't good enough. It won't do. I need an explanation.'

Nick shook his head. 'I can't tell you anything else.'

'What do you mean, you can't tell me? Why not? How about name, rank and serial number? Me Maggie – you?'

He looked at her again. She was still smiling

despite a sense of growing frustration. Casually dressed in a grey tee shirt and jeans, thick dark hair pushed back behind her ears, baseball bat within easy reach, Maggie almost looked as if she was enjoying herself.

'You're funny – I can't imagine my ex-,' Nick began and then stopped, an instant before he coughed his ex-wife's name out onto the kitchen table. It stuck in his throat, a cold, grief-stricken, misery-laden lump. The pain caught him unaware, like cramp.

Maggie pushed her fringe back off her face and took a tomato out of one of the carrier bags on the work surface. 'So,' she said casually, 'you were married, then?'

Nick reddened furiously. 'Yes – but I'm divorced now – about a year.'

Maggie nodded. 'Right. And so how does that relate to my finding you naked in my hall, exactly?'

'It doesn't. What I was going to say was are you always this unflappable? I can't imagine my ex being – being so – so –.' He couldn't think of a word to end the sentence but fortunately for him Maggie could.

'Accommodating? Calm under fire? My mother calls it robust good humour but trust me, it only lasts for so long and then poof –' she gestured an explosion, '– it goes, just like that, to be replaced by raging fury.'

Nick sighed. 'Look, Maggie, I am sorry about this – can't you just pretend that I'm Bernie Fielding?' he said miserably. 'It would make life so much simpler.'

Maggie grimaced, plunging the knife deep into the heart of an innocent-looking red pepper. 'No, I'm afraid that's one of the things I most definitely can't do. I've spent God knows how many years trying to persuade myself that all men *aren't* Bernie Fielding. Why don't you just give in gracefully and tell me what the hell's going on here and then we can call you a cab. How hard can it be? How about we start with your real name –'

Nick groaned. 'I can't tell you – the thing is, if I could tell you that then I could tell you everything else. It's just not possible. You have to believe me, there is a very good explanation for all this. I just can't tell you about it.' It sounded lame even to him.

'Nice try,' Maggie said. Instead of concentrating on de-seeding the pepper she was watching his face as he spoke.

'Careful,' said Nick anxiously. 'You'll cut yourself. Look, I'm good with food, would you like me to do that for you?' he asked.

Maggie looked down thoughtfully at the long thin knife-blade and then slowly back at him. 'Very kind but I think I can manage, thank you. Besides, you still haven't answered my question.'

Nick sighed. There had to have been some kind

of mistake. Surely Bernie Fielding wasn't supposed to be a real person? Unless of course he was dead. 'Is Bernie still alive?' he asked hopefully.

Maggie lifted her eyebrows. 'As far as I know, although after a night up the pub it was sometimes extremely difficult to tell. Except for the snoring and the scratching, obviously.'

'Okay, okay – so what does he do?'

'Bernie?' Maggie wiped her hand across the chopping board guiding the great heap of mangled vegetables into a big saucepan and then looked skyward as if trying to frame a thought. 'Gynaecology,' she said, slamming the pan down onto the stove and lighting the gas. 'He was always very good with his hands was Bernie.'

Nick felt his colour draining away. 'Oh my God, are you saying that Bernie Fielding is a doctor?'

Maggie shook her head. 'No, unfortunately not – just a keen amateur, which was a shame because we could have done with the money.'

Nick stared at her and then reddened as comprehension dawned. 'God, I'm so sorry – I thought – sorry –' he stammered.

Maggie waved the remark away. 'What? It's not your fault, is it? I'm assuming you've just got his name and not his moral outlook? What is it you know about food?'

'Food? Oh, right, well I used to run a restaurant, before –' said Nick, struggling to regain his composure. 'Before all this happened.'

'There, see, now we're getting somewhere. It wasn't all that painful, was it? And how about now?'

'Now? Now I'm – I'm on holiday,' he stalled.

Maggie snorted. 'Don't be silly. You can't be on the run and be on holiday.'

'I'm not exactly on the run, I'm . . .' Nick squirmed. He couldn't see how the hell he could go on with this and so he raised his arms in surrender. 'Okay – the things I'm about to tell you are secret but under the circumstances I don't see what else I can do. My real name is Nick Lucas and I'm in a witness protection and relocation programme. Bernie Fielding is, *was*, supposed to be my new name, my new assumed identity. The thing is there has to have been some sort of mix up, because I'm certain that I'm supposed to have a ficticious identity, not take over the tail end of somebody else's life. The only problem is I'm not sure what I can do to sort out any of this at the moment. I genuinely haven't got anywhere else to go – at least not straight away. I thought I'd ring the number they gave me –'

Maggie grinned, slapping the lid on the pan with a flourish.

'You don't hold up very well under pressure, do you?' she said, pouring them both a glass of wine.

2

There had to have been some kind of mistake, except of course that that was impossible. Stiltskin didn't make mistakes. In the neat, well-ordered, air-conditioned government offices deep in the bowels of Colmore Road the clerk tapped at the keyboard of the computer keeping one eye on the door.

'RUN STILTSKIN . . .?' flashed up on the screen again. She had already run it twice and something strange had happened. Very strange. It was her responsibility to do the back-up files on those people her department took under its protective wing. Normally it only took a few minutes, but she had been working on this one for the best part of half an hour.

First of all she'd needed to check up on the client's new name and address. Except when she'd fed his name in, the computer kept coming up with two new names. Two sets of fictitious details scrolling merrily down the screen, side by side. Now, having repeated the process, the same unlikely combination of information rolled out again and again, like digital schizophrenia.

According to the notes that went with the case, Nick Lucas *should* have become James Cook. That was what was supposed to have happened, that was what she had expected to have happened, except that somewhere in the wiry underbelly of the computer on Colmore Road a third name had entered the equation: Bernie Fielding. It was all very odd. She had never come across anything like it before, even on the trouble-shooting training course she'd been on at Cheltenham.

Somehow, Bernie Fielding had become James Cook, and Nick Lucas had become Bernie Fielding.

The girl sniffed and glanced up at the office door, licked her lips and then stared at the screen. She'd only come in as a favour because the girl who usually worked on Stiltskin had shingles and no one else had the right security clearance.

Who would ever know? Surely one imaginary new life was much the same as any other? The girl looked over her shoulder to see if anyone else was looking. If her boss found out he'd make them stay behind to unravel what had happened and she'd booked up for ballroom-dancing lessons after work. An intensive five-night course, 'Learn to Rhumba with Marj Cuthbertson', accompanied by Barry Telling on his electric organ. She'd been looking forward to it for weeks.

One keystroke, that was all it would take. The girl took another look through the information. They'd printed up a whole new set of documents in the name of Bernie Fielding so that had to be the right one, didn't it? There was even the docket to say he had been delivered to his new safe house. So why was it that James Cook's bank account kept coming up as being active. She scrolled down. Very active by the look of it. Here was a computer error that loved shoes apparently. Bugger.

The girl hesitated, weighing up the options – one pearly-pink nail-polished finger hovering above the delete key as she wrestled with her thoughts. The tea lady opening the office door made her jump and before she had time to really consider what she was doing the girl pushed delete, and James Cook's name vanished forever from Nick Lucas's file.

Just like that. She hadn't planned it exactly but it seemed that by an act of God, Nick Lucas was officially Bernie Fielding. She remembered him now – sexy-looking guy with dark wavy hair and big blue eyes. She bit her lip – he didn't really look like a Bernie, but then again it was too late to change things now. Wasn't it?

'I thought you told me that you'd got a BMW?' complained Stella tartly as she squeezed herself past Bernie's guiding arm and into the passenger seat of a battered sunshine-yellow 2CV.

Bernie had reasoned that Ms Hargreaves was hardly likely to need her car for a few days, having just been whisked off in an ambulance to deliver her new infant. He'd found the keys in her desk drawer and cheerfully arranged – via Stiltskin – for the car to be re-registered in his name. His new name. As he whiled away the hours until he had to pick Stella up from the post office, Bernie had given the absence of the fictional BMW some thought – not that it normally took him much effort to come up with a plausible-sounding excuse.

He slipped in beside her and looked down, feigning grief.

'I'm sorry, I suppose I should have told you earlier. My wife died last year.' He spoke in a gruff monotone. 'This was her runabout. I didn't like to get rid of it – at least not yet. This car was like a pet to her. I try to give it a run out now and again. She would have wanted me to use it and it seemed – well – I wanted to take you out in it. She would want me to start over – and it felt right. "Bernie," she used to say,' he said, staring unseeing into the middle distance, '"I don't want you moping around once I'm gone – I want you to get out and on with your life."' He looked at Stella to see how he was doing and then smiled bravely. 'She was a good woman.'

Stella touched his hand. 'Oh God, I'm so sorry, you poor, poor thing, you,' she said softly. 'You must think I'm ever so tactless, but why did she call you Bernie?'

He stiffened. Bugger, he was going to have to watch that. 'Um – um – pet name,' Bernie said after a bit of struggle. 'She always reckoned I looked like that bloke out of *Boys From the Black Stuff*, you know – he reached around inside his memory discarding all manner of Bernards till he got to the right one. 'Bernard Hill; the dark bloke with the moustache.'

Stella looked him up and down and nodded. 'So you do, now that you come to mention it.'

Bernie sighed with relief. 'God I miss her,' he added as an afterthought, wiping away a phantom tear. 'It's all right. You had no way of knowing. But she loved this little car.'

Stella Ramsey's eyes filled, too. 'Oh, James.' She was wearing a pink leather mini-skirt with matching high heels and a little sleeveless white cotton top, her bleached blonde hair sculptured in a great corona of curls and waves. For a post-mistress she was an absolute cracker, Bernie thought.

Bernie brightened visibly. 'Now, whereabouts did you say this pub is that you were going to take me to?' he said, sliding his hand down over his back pocket to check he had his wallet.

'James?'

It took Bernie a second or two to register that Stella meant him; he would really have to start thinking of himself as James Cook.

'Yes?' he said, relieved that Stella had taken his hesitancy for tearful reflection.

She leant closer, resting her hand very lightly on his thigh. 'I want you to know that if you need to talk about your wife I perfectly understand. I mean, I don't want you to feel you have to hold anything back. It's good to talk about these things.'

Bernie nodded. 'Thank you – not everyone understands. Her name was Maggie,' he said unsteadily. 'She was such a lovely girl . . .' And as he spoke, the old Bernie Fielding faded slowly into oblivion to be replaced by James Anthony Cook; sensitive, caring widower.

While the old Bernie Fielding slipped seamlessly into his new persona and the new Bernie Fielding waited for Maggie Morgan to finish cooking the bolognaise sauce, an aircraft was landing at London Heathrow and out at Elstree a small television production company was busy finalising the details of its midweek schedule.

Aboard the aircraft two tall, good-looking, suntanned men in mirrored shades and expensive charcoal-grey suits waited for the cabin doors to open. Cain Vale tucked a newspaper into his flight bag.

'What d'ya think then, Nimrod?'

Nimrod Brewster, sucking on a Minto, grinned the cool, even smile of a basking shark and glanced out of the window at the clear blue sky.

'No problems, my son,' he said in an undertone. 'In. Out. We'll be back in Marbella by teatime tomorra.' He mimed a sharp-shooter's draw with his index finger and then blew away a phantom wisp of smoke so real that he could almost smell the cordite. They had been offered a nice fat fee to cream a nobody. Nimrod would have done it for nothing if it wasn't for the fact that he liked to maintain his professional status.

Cain cheered visibly. 'Right, so in that case can I have the window seat on the way back?'

Nimrod considered for a moment or two. 'I'll toss you for it. Afterwards.'

'All right. Where's the business happening?'

Nimrod tapped the side of his nose conspiratorially. 'You worry too much, Cain, we'll know the details all in good time. It's all arranged. We'll be met at the hotel with the rest of the stuff – we already know the who, we just need to know the where and when.'

Nimrod patted the computer printout in his jacket pocket.

'What's his name again?' asked Cain.

'Nick Lucas.'

Cain nodded as if fixing the information somewhere deep in his mind.

'Maybe we should ring him,' said Nimrod with a sly grin. 'Tell him he ought to kiss his ass goodbye while he still has the opportunity.'

Cain giggled.

Robbie Hughes, sitting in a darkened office in Elstree, had been chasing Bernie Fielding for a very long time – years, in fact. First as a researcher for the BBC and now as a presenter for *Gotcha*, a twice-weekly, prime-time, consumer TV programme. He had never had any problems filling the available airspace with the public's worst fears. But for Robbie the hunt for Bernie Fielding had become something of a personal vendetta. He was Robbie's very own Holy Grail.

The blinds in the upstairs office were closed to cut out the early evening sunlight. At the front of the room one of the younger researchers was busy showing everyone his latest PowerPoint presentation, pitching an idea to the show's boss for his very own one-off special. A whole show devoted to one person, one topic, one major crime was the brass ring that everyone on the *Gotcha* team was aiming for. Their baby, broadcast to the nation.

The boy clicked onto the next image. 'Potential here for some great visuals,' he was saying as the camera panned around what looked like a normal suburban living room. There was a murmur from the assembled audience although Robbie wasn't sure whether it was of agreement or boredom.

There was a glitch in the air conditioning and the room was unpleasantly warm. People were stripped down to shirtsleeves and strappy tops, sipping Evian, iced tea and coffee frappé, trying to ignore the growing miasma of antiperspirant battling with Mother Nature, while still looking cool and interested – after all, it might just be their turn next.

Robbie sat at the back, a little apart from the crowd as befitting his status as cohost, letting the puppies play. All of a certain age, four of them rotated the job as studio anchor – two old hacks, a female newscaster and him. If not in the studio the presenters would be out in the field just like the good old days. It was his turn today to ride shotgun on the *Gotcha* creative crèche to make sure there weren't too many stories about fake designer tee shirts and imported DVDs.

Robbie had his own idea for a *Gotcha* special but now was not the time. He certainly had no intention of making his pitch in front of the children.

It had always seemed, in the great scheme of things, that he and Bernie Fielding had been destined to meet again and again – star-crossed consumer synchronicity. Bernie Fielding's name, if not his face, had haunted Robbie night and day for years; an ever-present name amongst a flurry of other directors on a dozen dodgy letterheads, that signposted sharp practice, deceit and cheap

41

Asian imports. It seemed to Robbie that Bernie saw himself as King-Con.

First it had been the floral sun-lounger that had nearly disembowelled Robbie on a south coast beach; Bernie's company name was there on the instruction slip. Later there had been the conservatory that had spontaneously combusted when his mother-in-law turned on the spotlights. Robbie's dodgy second-hand Merc that had turned out to be two cars welded together, his sons' radio-controlled exploding cars, his sister's garden swing – Bernie Fielding had – it miraculously seemed – had a hand in them all.

And when, just before Christmas one year, Robbie Hughes's wife had said she'd put a deposit down on a time-share villa in Tenerife as a surprise present, Robbie knew, even before he opened the phoney letter of receipt, whose name would be there up above the date. Oh yes, he had an idea for a special all right. Bernie might have been quiet for a while but Robbie's senses were tingling; something was up and he planned to find out what. He was going to nail Bernie Fielding's arse to the mast on prime-time TV – and he was going to do it soon.

3

While supper cooked, Nick Lucas nipped the phone between cheek and shoulder and hung on as instructed, waiting for someone, anyone, to talk to him.

'Your call is currently in a queue,' repeated a cool synthetic female voice. 'All calls are being answered in strict rotation. If you would like to hold the line, one of our operators will be with you as soon as they are free . . . Your call is currently in a queue . . .'

Nick sighed with frustration and glanced out of the upstairs window in Maggie Morgan's country cottage, wishing there was some way that it could still be his. Roses crept stealthily up over the sill, framing the view. The long summer's day was fading fast into shades of old gold. Here and there, sunlight reflected off windows in houses on the far side of the common, tinting them with a fiery glow. Across the unkempt lawn a swing under an apple tree struggled to take advantage of the evening breeze. It was the most glorious summer's evening.

Nick sighed again. Maybe it had been too good to be true after all. Hadn't his first impression been that the house was too far from any where, too exposed to be safe? Even though Nick had been amazed and relieved when Coleman's men dropped him off at the cottage, in the back of his mind, wasn't there a part of him that would have felt safer in the anonymity of a city? He was used to London. He had wondered what would happen next, and now he knew.

'. . . one of our operators will be with you as soon as they are free . . .'

Nick Lucas closed his eyes. His unguarded thoughts were fragmented and disordered; for months now there had been no peaceful place inside his head. But oddly, however disruptive and unexpected, there was a part of him that felt more comfortable now that Maggie and her kids were there with him. Nick had been uneasy about being alone after months and months of longing for his privacy. It had felt so odd to have a house to himself, and unnerving, too, almost as if he had been forgotten. Like everyone had moved on without him. For the last year or so Nick had had police protection twenty-four hours a day. Shifts of police officers coming and going, a stream of constantly changing faces who were sometimes there day after day for months but occasionally were there only for a few hours – whoever it was, there had always been someone close by.

Since he'd arrived at the cottage he'd toyed with the idea of buying a dog. It felt wonderful to be able to walk outside again, to amble down to the shops for a paper – but frightening, too, as if at any moment something terrible might happen. For what had to be the hundred-thousandth time Nick wondered if he would ever feel truly safe again.

'. . . Your call is currently in a queue . . .'

'Oh for God's sake, come on,' Nick muttered, tapping his fingers impatiently on the windowsill.

Finally, at the far end of the line there was a man's voice – although not Coleman's – and with that Nick tried to explain how his brand-new life had already turned sour.

'So,' Nick said, after a five-minute unbroken monologue, 'I'm in the shit really. It's complete madness. You promised that I would be safe here, but a whole family apparently lives here already – I mean what the hell's going on? Would it be possible for me to talk to Danny Coleman?'

'Ummm,' said the disembodied voice thoughtfully after a second or two's reflection. 'I'm afraid not, your handler isn't on duty at the moment but I'll see to it that he gets a full briefing regarding your current situation. It's all a bit odd, isn't it, eh?' The man sounded unreasonably cheerful. 'We don't usually get problems this early on. Not that we get many problems at all really,' he added hastily. 'It does sound very strange. But don't you worry, just leave it with me and I'll get back to you. A.S.A.P. My advice – if the woman who owns the house is agreeable – is to stay where you are for the time being, keep a low profile, and we'll sort something out,' and with that the man hung up.

'My handler?' snapped Nick into the empty, burring line. 'What do you mean my bloody handler? And what do you mean you'll sort something out? What about the family whose life I've just walked into, for God's sake?' he shouted angrily. 'Not to mention your bloody fail-safe, extremely secure, sodding . . . low profile my arse.' From the bottom of the stairs the younger of Maggie's boys watched him suspiciously from behind big blue eyes. Nick reddened under his unflinching stare and struggled to control the great rip of fury nestling in his belly. He tried out a smile; the child didn't move a muscle.

Wafting up the stairs came the rich smell of tomatoes, peppers, onions and garlic, all simmering away. The aroma made his mouth water, a sensation that took Nick totally by surprise. He took a longer, deeper breath, savouring the smell. It seemed like a long, long time since he had been truly hungry. God, how bad was that for a man who had made his living by cooking? Had he been so lost, so far away from himself . . . Nick stopped and let the sensation roll through him. Over the last few months his guts had been crocheted into a tight uneasy knot, so hunger, strangely enough, felt like a good omen. Dropping the receiver back into its cradle, Nick hurried downstairs. The little boy scuttled away from him before he was even halfway down.

By the time he reached the kitchen Nick's new ready-made family were sitting around the table and turned to look at him as one as he crossed the threshold. He stopped mid-stride, uncomfortable under the gaze of the two small boys. Nick noticed that alongside the salad and the cutlery, Ben still had Maggie's mobile phone close to hand.

Maggie, at the sink straining the spaghetti through a huge stainless-steel colander, nodded towards the nearest chair. 'You'd better sit down, take the weight off your alibi. How did you get on?'

'It didn't go quite how I imagined, if that's what you mean.'

Maggie laughed. At least she had disposed of the baseball bat. As Nick pulled out a chair Ben's hand hovered over the phone like a gun fighter waiting to make a quick draw.

Maggie shook her head. 'No, love. It's all right. Why don't you go and get some apple juice for you and Joe?' she said gently. Ben sniffed imperiously, eyes not leaving Nick as he went to get the glasses out of the kitchen cupboard.

* * *

Fifteen minutes later Maggie mopped up the last of the pasta sauce from her plate with a rip of french bread. Ben and Joe, hunger having finally overcome suspicion, had eaten their supper with the unbridled passion of the young and were now preparing, very reluctantly, to go to bed.

'Right,' said Maggie to Nick, shovelling the last remnants of supper into her mouth as she got to her feet. 'I want it all and I want it now. The whole sordid story. You can tell me all about it while I make us some coffee.'

Nick groaned. 'Look, I'm sorry, Maggie, but I can't – I'm not supposed to tell anybody. Not anything. Not a word,' he added lamely, pushing his plate away. Despite Maggie's cavalier approach to preparation the pasta sauce had been delicious and had tasted as good as it smelt. 'You know too much already. If you knew any more you could be at risk, too.'

Maggie snorted, stacking the dirty crockery in the dishwasher. 'So, dropping a complete stranger into my life with my ex-husband's name wasn't just a little bit risky, then?'

Nick puffed out his cheeks. 'I've already said that I'm sorry, I don't know what else to say to you – and I can't explain how this has happened because I've got no idea. But don't worry, the people who brought me here know now. I'm sure it'll all be sorted out soon. They said that they would speak to Coleman, the man who's dealing

48

with my case, and get back in touch. A.S.A.P.' Nick reddened. Said aloud it all sounded pretty pathetic.

Maggie lifted an eyebrow, observing his growing discomfort. The born-again Bernie Fielding was either very naïve or very desperate, although whichever it was, it was quite endearing; he probably still believed in the tooth fairy, too. As she studied him he pushed his fringe back up over his forehead and smiled. If he was a puppy in a pound no woman on earth could have resisted him bringing him home.

Maggie sighed. Her mother always said she was a soft touch.

'I hope you'll forgive me if I don't look altogether convinced, Nick. What I mean is I'm not planning to hold my breath until the cavalry show up. I'll make you up a bed in the spare room for tonight; Joe wants his bed back, and then tomorrow I'm afraid you'll have to hit the road. Okay? Why did you sleep in Joe's room anyway? You look more like a double-bed man to me.' As she said it Maggie blushed and cursed the bit of her brain that let her say what she was thinking without considering the consequences.

But it's true, protested her brain. Worse still, Nick Lucas looked like the kind of man that she had always hankered after but never quite found. He was tall, with broad shoulders, a strong gentle face – nice eyes. Beautiful hands too, kind of good looking in a lived-in way. Under other circumstances . . . Maggie stopped herself from thinking the whole thought and shook her brain into submission. These were not 'other circumstances' and being taken for a ride by a total stranger was just the kind of thing you warned your children about. Even so, her mystery guest most definitely had the air of a man who preferred not to sleep alone if he could possibly help it, the kind of man who liked life best if there was a woman in it.

Maggie took two mugs down off the shelf and then forced herself to concentrate on spooning coffee into the filter, hoping that he couldn't read her mind.

'What I meant to say is that as you're quite tall, a double bed has to be more comfortable –' Maggie continued, as smoothly as she could manage, attempting to cover her tracks. He had amazing blue eyes, the corners crosshatched with humour.

Maggie tightened her grip on the rogue thoughts that chattered busily through her mind, reminding herself that she didn't know a thing about Nick Lucas except what he'd told her – which wasn't much – and that he lied very badly, and that her track record was pretty terrible when it came to men. Her first impression of the real Bernie Fielding had been that he was a really nice man, too. It was a salutary thought, as effective as a cold shower.

Why was it exactly that Nick Lucas had turned up at her house with Bernie's name? It wasn't the first time that the idea had gone through her mind but it was the first time Maggie had let it settle. Why here, why now? Surely Bernie wasn't big enough to have had a hand in this? In which case, why did every instinct tell her that this had the real Bernie Fielding's paw-prints all over it?

Across the table Nick Lucas said nothing, staring blankly ahead as if collecting his thoughts. Finally he turned to look at her, lifting his hands to encompass the room. 'I've already said that I'm sorry about all this. I don't know what else to say to you. It's totally crazy.' He looked uncomfortable, as if he'd been caught out.

Maggie, chewing on the nub end of the French stick, said, 'Just how crazy is that, then, Nick?'

He continued almost as if she hadn't spoken. 'Things like this shouldn't happen to people like me. I used to run a great little restaurant, you know. Good food, reasonable prices, in an up-and-coming area. We were beginning to build a reputation, getting to be well-known locally. They even did a feature on us in the *Evening Standard*. It's ridiculous – why did I think for a moment that this would come good?' He sounded increasingly upset. 'What the hell am I supposed to do now?' As he spoke his gaze met Maggie's, looking at her as if she might have the answers.

Maggie stood the coffeepot down between them on the kitchen table and slapped two mugs alongside it.

'You could tell me what's going on. Maybe I could help?' Her tone was gentle and conspiratorial. 'After all,' she grinned mischievously, 'we *were* married.'

Nick groaned and dropped his head into his hands.

She pushed a mug towards him. 'Don't worry, I'm good in a crisis. What was it exactly that you witnessed?'

Nick ran his fingers nervously through his hair. 'To be honest I wish to God I knew. It seemed such a small thing really. As far as I was concerned they were just regular customers. Vegetarian lasagne, green salad, home-made game pie with vegetables of the day –'

'I'm sorry?' said Maggie, wondering if the bottle of Italian red that they'd shared over supper had confused the issue. 'Are these the cryptic clues?'

Nick looked up. 'No, no, that's what the two of them always had when they came into my restaurant. Nice safe choices. They usually came in once, sometimes twice a week.' He looked uneasy. 'I thought they were just the sort of clientele we wanted, you know. Respectable, regular business customers. Nice, quiet, appreciative; something off the sweet trolley, two cappuccinos and they always tipped well – no fuss, never complained. Ideal customers.'

Maggie sniffed. 'Whoa there. Hang on a minute. I think I've lost the plot here somewhere. You have been relocated, renamed, given a completely new identity, because of two nice regular respectable lunchtime diners? I don't understand, Nick – I thought you must have seen something really – you know – awful, terrible.' Maggie paused as the images of innumerable TV crime shows, police reconstructions and photo-fit pictures trickled through her mind in a gory slide show. 'Messy, murderous, violent.'

Nick, still deep in thought, glanced up. 'Sorry?'

'What I'm saying is that I thought you must have seen something, you know, really ghastly to put you in so much danger that they needed to relocate you.'

He nodded. 'Me, too, but it seems you don't have to witness something messy for it to be dangerous. One morning two guys turned up at the restaurant with official-looking bits of paper and asked if I'd give my permission to have my regulars' table bugged. I was totally amazed. My two nice tidy customers turned out to be up to their eyebrows in God knows what. The fraud squad had been on their trail for months trying to tie the pair of them together.'

'So what was it?' said Maggie leaning closer, while trying hard not to look too eager or too pleased with herself. She knew that she'd cracked it. She could tell by the look on Nick's face that he'd made up his mind to tell her everything.

He shook his head. 'To be perfectly honest I still don't have any clear idea. Something to do with stocks and shares – some sort of international computer fraud, I think.'

Maggie stared at him, feeling totally deflated. 'What? Is that it? But you *were* a witness, weren't you?'

Nick nodded. 'Uh huh, I suppose so, but not in a Perry Mason big courtroom drama kind of a way. All I had to do was to identify them as the two people in question, give a few details from my bookings diary. When they'd met, how often – and of course it was me who gave permission for the bug to be planted at their table in the first place –'

'And they relocated you for that?' Maggie knew she sounded slightly incredulous.

Nick's face reddened. 'Yes. The unfortunate thing was the two of them came from different sides of the tracks. One was a highly respected financier in the city of London and the other one was something very, very iffy in organised crime.'

There was a long pause. 'And?' prompted Maggie. It was like pulling teeth.

Nick sucked his bottom lip and slowly turned the coffee mug between his long fingers. 'And after they were arrested the two of them tried to persuade me not to testify.' His voice was low now and very controlled as he turned the mug around and around. 'It got very nasty very quickly once they'd been picked up. They're not the sort of people you mess with. They threatened to rearrange my anatomy so I could bear children, they firebombed my restaurant and filled my basement with raw sewage. Not them personally, of course, but their hired help.

By the time the case came to court they'd blown up my car, ruined my business, destroyed my marriage, terrorised my staff and driven me to breaking point.' He sighed heavily. 'The pair of them systematically destroyed everything I had built to try and stop me from taking the stand. The authorities extradited one of them to the States. The police had already decided by that time that I was at long-term risk from reprisals.' He drained the dregs of his coffee. 'So there we are, now you know, Maggie. That's what I'm doing here.'

She stared at him, not quite sure, now that she had dragged the story out of him, what to say. 'My God. So what happened to the two men?'

Nick shook his head, uncomprehendingly. 'I don't know what you mean. Which two men?'

Maggie looked heavenwards. Nice eyes but not too bright obviously. 'The two men you gave evidence against? *Your two regulars*? Mr Vegetarian Lasagne and Mr Home-made Game Pie.'

Nick shook his head. 'Oh no, you've got it wrong. It wasn't two men I testified against, it was two women – and if they find me they'll have me killed.'

Maggie swallowed hard. 'Two women?' she whispered.

Nick nodded.

'Oh bugger,' murmured Maggie, 'You really *are* in trouble.'

Nimrod Brewster and Cain Vale had booked into the large anonymous hotel adjoining the airport. They had shed their suit jackets, turned on the TV and raided the mini-bar by the time their contact arrived. He was a man so undistinguished, so grey that he managed to render himself practically invisible. He stepped quietly into their hotel room and smiled without warmth.

'All set then, are we, lads?'

Nimrod nodded and removed his mirrored shades to reveal the palest ice-blue eyes rimmed with piggy-white lashes. Outside, beyond the triple glazing, a silver jet rose noiselessly into the late evening sky.

'Yeah, all fired up and ready to go. Brought everything we need, have yer?' he asked, tucking his shades into the top pocket of his immaculately pressed shirt.

The man nodded and dropped a large manila envelope on one of the single beds.

'There we are. Half now and half on completion, all expenses paid, as agreed. Oh and I thought you might like this.' He pulled out a radio scanner and set it on the bed alongside the envelope. 'You know how to use it?'

Nimrod nodded. 'Nice touch. I always like to keep an ear out for the feds.'

The man paused and then looked at Nimrod thoughtfully as if weighing up just how much to tell him. 'I want you to be especially careful with this one, Nimrod,' he said in a low, unremarkable monotone.

'Of course. We always are,' said Nimrod, slightly affronted by the slur on his professionalism.

'I know, I know, but just hear me out. Is your friend here with us?' he said, stony-faced. Across the room Cain was stretched out on the other bed, his attention firmly fixed on the TV screen.

'Don't mind Cain, he loves all them crime reconstruction programmes, CCTV footage, anything like that, watches them all the time in case he sees someone we know. Saw his dad on there once. But when it comes down to the job, we're there, you know that. Totally focused – one-hundred-and-ten per cent or nothing at all. It's just that the planning side of it isn't his forte.' Nimrod's tone was icy.

The little man nodded his head. 'Sorry. I'm most certainly not implying that you're normally careless. We wouldn't have hired you if we thought that was the case.' He paused. 'It's just that I think that somebody somewhere out there may already have got a sniff that something's going down.'

Nimrod raised an eyebrow. He liked violence; he didn't like unnecessary risks involving the law.

'Yeah? What makes you say that, then?'

'My clients are very insistent that Mr Lucas pays for his faux pas, and if you don't take the hit someone else will, but what I'm saying is that if you don't want it, it's not too late to pull out.' The man sucked his teeth, waiting for Nimrod's reaction.

'Go on,' encouraged Nimrod. 'Cough it up. We're here now.'

'My sources at Stiltskin have informed us that our friend, Mr Lucas, was all set to be relocated as one James Anthony Cook. Three days later and James Cook Esquire has vanished completely from their computer records only to reappear as one Mr Bernard Fielding.'

Nimrod nodded knowingly although he hadn't got a clue what the man was going on about, his only real experience of computers involved creaming countless hoards of screaming aliens, but he did know when to keep schtum.

The little man continued. 'My instincts tell me this may well be a complex double-bluff to throw us off the scent. I'm still convinced that James Cook is our man. The powers-that-be have just tried to dig him in a little bit deeper, added a *soupçon* more camouflage. Made it a little more difficult for anyone to find him. Maybe they suspect someone is hacking into their database, maybe they suspect a leak, who knows? One thing is for sure: if they knew for certain it was us then the likelihood is we would have been pulled in by now.' He pointed towards the envelope on Nimrod's bed. 'We've already turned up several bank transactions in Banbury for our Mr Cook. New suit, good shoes –' He grinned and tapped his nose. 'Don't ever doubt that Big Brother has his eye on you, lads.'

Nimrod grimaced. He sincerely hoped not; he had kneecapped his big brother back in '86.

Across the room Cain was flicking through the channels while delicately stirring a maraschino cherry on a cocktail stick through the froth on the top of his Advocat snowball.

'So, you're saying that Nick Lucas is definitely now this James Cook bloke, then?' Cain said slowly, suddenly looking up at their undistinguished visitor. 'You're certain? Only it could get very messy if you've got it wrong.'

The man sniffed, his smile opening up like an icy fissure.

'Yes, absolutely. His new address is in the envelope, courtesy of the bank's computer, then there's photos, all the usual stuff that you need. He's holed up in a caravan site near Banbury apparently, presumably sitting tight until they find him a house. So there we have it, lads. Your mission if you choose to accept it.'

Nimrod looked at Cain. For a moment their eyes met and Cain gave a barely perceivable nod.

Nimrod picked up the money. 'Seems like the deal is on, then,' he said.

'Good,' said their contact. 'I knew you two wouldn't let me down.' He paused as he got to the door. 'Ring me when it's all over. And don't blow it, lads. I don't have to tell you that my clients are very influential people. Mr Lucas is to be made an example of. We can't have people of their calibre being screwed over by some moronic little gimp in a pinny, now can we?'

Over the years Bernie Fielding had developed a sure-fire way to get women into bed; he led them to believe that he was impotent. It always worked like a charm. A few veiled references to things not being quite right. A murmur of regret at being unable to take a relationship any further. A tender plea not to get involved because he could never give a woman what they truly wanted or needed and could only bring them heartbreak and he was in like Flynn. It seemed that a plea for under-standing and consideration brought out the Florence Nightingale in them all.

Women, he had realised early on in life, loved a challenge; loved to feel that they were special, different, needed. It didn't take very much to have them thinking that perhaps they were that special someone, the one to provide the sexual elixir that would miraculously cure him of his tragic affliction – and of course, as it turned out, they always were.

Stella Conker-eyes was proving no exception. Snuggled up beside him in a quiet corner of the lounge bar in the Lark and Buzzard, compassion was her middle name. She had delicately teased out of him the full story of his poor dead wife, wiped away a tear as he spun her a long and complicated yarn with many thoughtful pauses – which Stella took to be grief, but which were actually Bernie trying to think up something heart-rendingly tragic. It was only halfway through the evening and already Bernie had successfully wiped out his wife, the family Labrador and his sex drive. Not bad going for a slow night.

And now, after four large gin and lemons and something greasy in a basket, Stella's little leather skirt was riding higher up her thighs than Bernie thought physically possible. Her dark eyes glistened as she leant towards him, her floral perfume so strong it was making his nose run.

'Oh, James, you poor, poor man,' she purred, easing herself closer still so that they were sitting thigh to thigh. 'Life really hasn't been very kind to you at all, has it? No wonder you're always on the move. I can understand it. It must be so hard to put down roots after everything that's happened; you're afraid of getting hurt all over again, aren't you?'

Bernie sighed theatrically. 'Not everyone sees it like that. You're a very perceptive woman, Stella,' he said, damp-eyed. 'You've made me realise just . . .' he paused for added emphasis, '. . . just how empty and pointless my life has been for the past two years.' He let his hand rest lightly on her knee.

Stella let out a strangled throaty sob. 'Oh, James,' she said softly and guided his head down into the cleft between her expansive breasts.

Bernie shivered, drinking in her warmth and the scent of her skin as she held him tight against her. Shit, the way he was going he'd have her knickers off before closing time.

Meanwhile, in the *Gotcha* production office, now that the creative kindergarten had all gone home, Robbie Hughes was pitching his story to the show's producer. He had waited patiently for this moment. Bernie Fielding was far too important a pearl to be cast before the rest of the *Gotcha* swine. Robbie was hoping, if he played it right, that his boss would let him have that magic one-off special – a whole programme devoted to the machinations of Mr Bernie Fielding. She had given him ten minutes.

'Double glazing,' he said, stabbing a pile of

brochures with one doughy finger. 'Conservatories, pyramid selling, security alarms, pension plans, time-share. Jesus, what more do we want? What more do we need? He's quiet at the moment – probably regrouping, going for the big one. I think now is the perfect time to get him. Bernie Fielding has been into every money-grabbing, stitch 'em up cowboy con trick you can think of, and more besides. The man is a real menace, a social evil, he needs putting away. *We have to put him away*. We've got complaints, affidavits, reports, letters, photographs. We've got all the evidence we'll ever need to nail him.' Robbie picked up a letter at random from the pile. 'Eighty-year-old pensioner lost her entire life savings in one of his pyramid scams. He took her for every penny she'd got and then backed over her cat in his Jag –'

His boss leant back in her swivel chair and peered for a moment or two at her long scarlet-tipped fingernails. He could sense that she was deliberating; Robbie held his breath.

'We've been here before Robbie so I'll cut right to the chase. This isn't research; it's a personal vendetta. It's an obsession. A hobby gone bad. I have heard this damned story dozens of times. I'm sorry to disappoint you, Robbie, but it's old news, darling. Stale. Let's face it, these days everyone is bored shitless by all this sort of stuff. It would be different if you could prove that this guy had actually killed somebody. Even maiming is better than nothing –'

The smell of her perfume, the odour as memorable as sulphur, permeated the entire room. She picked up her pen and pointed at the rows of hessian-covered pin-boards that dominated the office walls. Each one was a précis of a story that they were currently working up for broadcast.

'Organs. That's really hot at the moment. Unwashed proles being hoicked in to have their tonsils out and waking up to find someone's whipped out a kidney. Nineteen-year-old mother of four goes in to have her appendix out, wakes up with an eye gone – emotive stuff.'

She swivelled a little further round on her chair, pen aimed at the pin-boards like the staff of Moses. 'What have we got – toxic teddies, some guy poisoning toddlers, that's always a good angle. Family pets into fun furs, tabby tote bags. Dodgy doctors, a nun selling smack outside an orphanage. It's all ground-breaking stuff. Pyramids are very passé, Robbie, very passé. Does your man do organs?'

Robbie looked down and closed the bulging dossier he had on Bernie Fielding.

'Just give me a little bit longer,' he said. 'I'll see what I can come up with.'

4

Once he had been dismissed Robbie hurried back downstairs to his own office. The lights were still on although the rest of the floor was in darkness. Inside his assistant looked up expectantly.

'How did it go?' she asked, and then the words and the smile faded as she saw Robbie's expression. 'Oh no. Was it that bad?'

Robbie threw out his chest and stapled on a happy face. 'No, no, not at all. Don't worry. Just a little set-back. It's nothing that can't be sorted out.' He made an effort to sound brisk and businesslike. 'What we need is to find the focus, the hook for one good Bernie Fielding special. Madam Upstairs was worried that the thrust of our programme was perhaps a little too broad – maybe even a little dated – but as I told her it's nothing that can't be put right with a bit of old-fashioned dedication, research and midnight oil. We just need to find out what Bernie's up to now.'

Lesley smiled. 'It sounds quite promising then?'

Robbie nodded. 'Absolutely,' he said, not quite meeting her eyes. 'Now, I know it's late, but I want to pull out everything that we've got on our Mr Fielding: old addresses, old haunts, old ties, any little clue that we can come up with as to where he is now and what he's up to. This is all-out war. I want to get that bastard put away before Madam Upstairs decides to pull the plug on the whole bloody project. You know how fickle she can be at times,' he added hastily in answer to Lesley's startled expression. 'I can't believe that Bernie isn't up to his old tricks somewhere. We just have to track him down and nail his hairy little arse to the mast, and we have to do it soon.' There was just a hint of Winston Churchill in his delivery. As Robbie Hughes spoke he stared up at the pictures and notes on the pin-boards above his desk. Some had been there so long that they were brittle and yellow with age. He and Bernie Fielding went back a long, long way.

His entire office wall looked like the presentation of evidence for a serial killer. Passé; he'd show that bloody bitch passé. Still mumbling to himself Robbie started rummaging through the filing cabinets pulling out great wads of paper, photocopied sheets and all manner of advertising fliers. 'Right, let's see what we've got –'

'Oh God, I love it when it's like this, Robbie,' said Lesley breathlessly, taking down a row of box files from one of the stationery cupboards. 'It feels like we're at war, you know – like we are really making a difference.'

'But we do, Lesley, we do.' Robbie smiled indulgently in her direction and opened the first of the box files.

They were labelled by date with *Bernie Fielding 1–5* along the spine. Lesley had stayed behind to lend him moral support. A couple of years out of university she was still a little overwhelmed by the whole set-up at *Gotcha,* and for some reason by Robbie Hughes in particular. Maybe because he had personally plucked her out of a backwater in the company to join his personal staff. Unconsciously, under her adoring limpid gaze Robbie puffed out his chest further.

'That's exactly what this is – war. It's this kind of dedication that brings in the awards year after year: ITV viewers' Community Service Award three years running, Senior Citizen's 'We're Fighting Crime' special award for five years on the trot, Senior Ladies' Circle best programme award. This is the cutting edge, but we mustn't get complacent. Oh no – we need to continue with the good work, we must track these con men down, sniff them out wherever they're hiding. We have a duty to the people of this country.' Robbie allowed himself the ghost of a smile and turned up the Winston Churchill just a smidgen. He pulled himself up to his full five-foot-two-and-a-half inches while holding tight to his lapel and tucking his elbow firmly into his side in his favourite 'leader of men' stance. Shame they weren't filming him, really.

Lesley nodded enthusiastically – Robbie thought for one glorious moment she might actually burst into spontaneous applause, but no, she just blushed furiously and pushed her glasses back up onto the bridge of her nose with her index finger. It was an endearing little habit Lesley had, and sometimes when they were in bed together he noticed that she would do it even though she hadn't got her glasses on and would then giggle self-consciously. Robbie smiled indulgently for a few seconds, coming over all soft and sentimental; what a precious little thing she was.

Lesley understood of course that Robbie would never leave his wife for her: he'd made that perfectly plain right from the very start. Robbie had decided that Lesley probably saw herself as the latest in a long line of valiant, self-sacrificing, much-overlooked women who attempted to sleep their way to the top and eventually settled for a place in the shadow of great men. The wind beneath his wings. Not that someone like Lesley was actually destined for the top, but even so he wasn't the sort of man to disillusion a girl, particularly not one who was a natural blonde and so pleasantly perky and eager to please. No, Robbie Hughes was genuinely fond of Lesley, and she hadn't said a word nor batted an eyelid when he'd slipped on her tights one night after work and suggested she might like to let him try on her shoes some time. Oh yes, as a personal assistant Lesley was perfect in lots of ways.

'Would you like some coffee?' she asked, as he opened up the first of the files. 'It might help us to concentrate?'

'Thanks, but no thanks. Not really a good idea, Lesley, not with my prostrate the way it is, I'd be up and down all night, but you have one by all means. We're both in for a long hard session.'

She giggled although Robbie decided not to pick up on the double entendre; it wouldn't do for them to get distracted when there was work to be done.

'How about a mug of Cup-a-Soup instead, then?' she suggested, padding over to the side table where the kettle, mugs and drinks were kept.

Robbie nodded, all the while surveying the notes he had piled on his desk. 'Why not. I'll have one of the ones with croutons. Now what we have to do is to imagine that we are big game hunters, Lesley. It's important to understand our quarry if we stand any chance of catching him. So how do we find this man – where do we start?' It was a rhetorical question and one that Robbie would try and work into the commentary if they ever managed to track Bernie Fielding to earth.

'Let's start with what we know, shall we? How about his background, his family?'

Waiting for the kettle to boil, Lesley gazed up at the ceiling and recited from memory, 'Born 1952 to Shirley Elizabeth Fielding. His father Ernest Charles left when Bernard was just four years old, under a cloud of suspicion about his relationship with Lily Smith from the chip shop, to name just one of his numerous liaisons, and the whereabouts of the Glee Club Christmas money. Bernie left school at fifteen and has had various jobs since, including working on a market stall, delivery driver for *Sunblessed*, taxi driver and window cleaner – although he likes to tell people he was a paramedic in the Army or served undercover in the SAS. In 1972 he opened his first shop, importing cheap electrical goods, and he has been married twice; to Doreen Jean Parker in 1972, and in 1982 to Margaret Ann Morgan. Divorced twice, 1980 and 1990, a string of lovers and live-in girlfriends in between and on occasions at the same time, no children – or at least none that he pays maintenance for.'

Thoughtfully, Lesley stirred a heaped teaspoon of Nescafé into her mug, although her attention still seemed to be focused somewhere in the middle of the office ceiling. It disturbed Robbie a bit when she looked like that; it was as if Lesley could see something that he couldn't, and then she turned and said thoughtfully, 'You know, Robbie, if I'd have been married to Bernie Fielding I'd jump at the chance to stitch him up, once and for all. I

70

mean I can't see him playing straight with his wives any more than he did with any of the other punters.'

Robbie nodded. Lesley had picked up a certain streetwise patois since working at *Gotcha*, a little at odds with her nicely clipped Home Counties accent. She hadn't quite got a real grasp of mockney yet but Robbie noticed with some pride that she was really giving it her best shot.

'So you think we should start with his ex-wives, do you?' he said hesitantly. It sounded a bit too close to home.

She nodded. 'Uh huh, and previous lovers. I'll go right back to the beginning, that way we won't miss any potential leads; we've got lots of his old addresses on file. I'll chase up all the Fieldings as well. I've got a copy of the electoral roll on the computer –'

Lesley handed him a mug of Cup-a-Soup and as she did Robbie engineered it so their fingertips touched for just an instant. She blushed deliciously, giggled and went to pick up another of the files.

'It's a real shame that we haven't got a decent photo of him,' she said, although Robbie could see that her mind – like his – had at least momentarily moved away from Bernie Fielding and onto something more carnal, more pressing, more immediate. They both knew that moral support wasn't the only thing that Lesley had stayed behind for.

'It is, isn't it?' he said in a low purr.

Eyes glittering like a feral cat, Robbie took the file out of her chubby little fingers and set it down alongside her coffee. A grainy press cutting of Bernie Fielding's second marriage to some poor unsuspecting girl in Norfolk slipped out onto the desk top. The dots that made up the image were so blurred that it looked as if a giant hat was marrying an Afro with a Mexican bandito moustache. The clipping fluttered with surprising grace into the puddle around the bottom of Robbie's mug and sucked up the liquid like a parched man, tinting the bride and groom a not unattractive sunbed beige.

Not that Robbie took a lot of notice. If they were going to pull an all-nighter what was half an hour between friends on the office couch? He picked up his digital camera from the desk and pointed it at her. 'How about I get a few good close-up shots of you for the album?' he purred, in what he liked to think was a deep, seductive tone.

'Oh Robbie,' Lesley giggled furiously as he leant closer and unbuttoned the top of her blouse. As she wriggled like a fish, he pulled her down onto his lap.

'You are such an animal,' she gasped, as Robbie focused the camera on her cleavage.

'Why don't you take the rest of your clothes off,' he said. 'Get yourself nice and comfortable?'

Lesley put her hand over the lens, while with the other hand she tried to undo his trousers. 'No publicity,' she whispered thickly as the buckle gave way.

In the small but snug sitting room of a residential caravan at the back of the Old Dairy in Renham, Stella Conker-eyes had pulled off a miracle comparable only to the raising of Lazarus; and so far she had managed it twice. Although it would have been a considerably more erotic encounter if she hadn't cried the first time and kept telling Bernie what a dear, sweet man he was.

Not that Bernie had too many problems with the idea of being a charity case in this particular instance, although when she managed it a third time even he was surprised.

Holding her tight up against him in case she stopped her ministrations, Bernie said, 'It's been a long time since I've felt this – this relaxed and happy, Stella. It's been a fantastic evening. You have no idea how good it's been –'

'Oh James,' she whispered thickly.

Bernie froze for an instant, feeling as if he had caught her out in some act of betrayal until it struck him that he was, of course, now James Cook. He really had to get used to the idea, before his face gave him away, although fortunately for him, Stella wasn't looking at his face at that particular moment.

On the drive home from the pub he had floated the idea of dropping in for a coffee.

'Oh all right, then,' Stella said with a giggle. 'If you insist.'

Bernie, who, as he was driving had only had a pint of bitter and then gone on to orange juice and was as sober as a Methodist Minister, smiled. 'Your place or mine?'

'It'd better be yours. Mum will probably still be up. She's a very light sleeper – get's a lot of gyp with her back and her sciatica and her water-works – and besides there's the two West Highland whites, Nancy and Ronald, and that bloody parrot of hers. The row them three make if she isn't awake when we get in she soon will be.'

Bernie nodded and turned off towards the caravan site. The night was dark and warm, the wind rustling through the treetops like indolent fingers.

'Don't get me wrong, it's not that I don't like animals,' Stella was saying, her speech slurred with drink, 'but them bloody little dogs make such a row, yap-yap-yapping, and the parrot is so messy, seed and bits everywhere. No, as soon Mum passes away, God bless her, or goes into a home, they'll have to go.'

Bernie nodded. He knew better than to inter-rupt a woman when she was rambling. 'Okay,' he said when he was certain that she'd finished. 'Although I have to warn you that the caravan's a bit of a mess at the moment, but at least it's nice and quiet and it is only temporary.'

Stella looked at him slyly and said that she quite understood that it was only temporary, and no, she didn't mind the mess at all. No, really. It was fine, after all things would be different when he got his new house, wouldn't they? Maybe she could drop by with a copy of the local paper later in the week; they had a big pull-out housing section at the back and she had always liked house-hunting.

So here they were, stretched out half-naked on the hearth rug in front of the gas fire, in the wee small hours. Stella moaned softly and crept up towards him.

'Would you like to go to bed, James, only I'm getting terrible carpet burns on my knees.'

Bernie did his best to look tender and serene, although he did wonder just how much she could see without her glasses. 'You know, Stella, this really is the best evening I've had in – in –' he began, wondering what constituted a suitable measure of time.

Fortunately he was saved by Stella pressing her fingertips tightly to his lips. 'Don't. It's perfectly all right. There really is no need to say anything, James,' she murmured in a low throaty mewl. 'Let's not dwell on the past, this is not the time. Why don't we just go to bed instead?'

Bernie grinned. It suited him fine; this way he

wouldn't have to try and make up some plausible story for the last best time he'd had; and after the bottle of wine they'd drunk since arriving back at the caravan he'd forgotten his poor dead wife's name anyway. At the door to the bedroom, while looking back at him over one large creamy-white shoulder, Stella said, 'Although maybe I ought to go home; I haven't got a towel or a toothbrush with me.'

'Don't worry, sweetie. I'm sure I can find you something,' he said, flicking off the lights.

'Thank you,' Stella murmured, sounding genuinely touched.

Bernie grinned. He couldn't give a stuff whether she brushed her teeth or not.

It might be very late, but in his office Danny Coleman was still seated at his desk, caught in a jaundiced arc of lamplight and staring fixedly at the computer screen wondering what the hell was going on.

He was in two minds over what to do; there were all manner of protocols in place within Stiltskin for a variety of situations, but not this one. In theory Nick Lucas's cover had been compromised, but how and when and by whom? Should Coleman arrange for a Stiltskin recovery team to go in and pick him up, bring him in? Was he in any immediate danger? Or could the joins be papered over and things left as they were?

Coleman turned a pen between his fingers, still staring at the screen. At this stage he was reluctant to draw attention to Nick Lucas by renaming and moving him. Some part of him still hoped that Bernie Fielding might turn out to be a secure identity after all. Change always made ripples, and ripples, however small, always showed up on the surface. And changes made too hastily – well there was no telling how big those ripples might get if there was a knee-jerk reaction to the Nick Lucas situation. That was the official line from the guys upstairs.

Coleman puffed out his cheeks thoughtfully; maybe if Lucas just moved area, he mused, doodling on his phone pad, all the while instinctively knowing that there was no way the answer was ever going to be that simple.

Something was horribly wrong, something was leaking somewhere. His superiors had suspected it for some time. But how, and where? In his gut Coleman knew that things would only get worse, probably much worse before they got any better. The problem with the whole Nick Lucas thing was that it didn't fit into any pattern that made sense. Stiltskin had never coughed up a real person before. Coleman ran his fingers back through his thinning hair and looked at Nick's call as it had been transcribed alongside the details of the new identity that had been set up for him.

Surely it made more sense for anyone who had

infiltrated the system to just expose Nick Lucas and shoot him, rather than put him into a house with a real family. Or perhaps he was meant to be linked to . . . Coleman glanced down at the notes to check the names . . . Maggie Morgan, or Bernie Fielding, but why, for God's sake? He made a mental note to run the pair of them through the computer to see if anything came up. Unless they weren't after Nick Lucas at all but had bigger plans pinned up on the drawing board. Perhaps someone wanted to compromise the whole relocation procedure and Nick Lucas was involved purely by chance.

Trouble was that Coleman couldn't get any kind of handle on how that was possible from this piece of nonsense. He closed his eyes, trying to glimpse the big picture, but any connections totally eluded him. He'd get Ms Crow to take a look at the data trail to see if they could find out what had gone wrong, but from where he was sitting this didn't feel like a leak, it felt more like a total cock-up. Coleman pulled a nasal spray from his inside pocket, squeezed once, twice, sniffing hard as he did, waiting for the moist chemical hit to clear his sinuses and from there his head. First thing in the morning he'd get Ms Crow on the case, and meanwhile he just hoped that the wheel didn't come off.

The cold splintery taste of the nasal spray ran down the back of his throat and flooded his taste buds.

'I reckon you're addicted to them things, you know, Mr Coleman,' said the security guard, pushing the door to Coleman's office open a little wider. 'They rot your nostrils you know, burn through the septum – that little bit in the middle – you'll end up with a snout like a pillar-box. Saw it in the paper.'

'That's cocaine, George; you had too many years on the force, you think everything's bad for you.'

The older man smiled. 'In my experience, if you enjoy it, it most probably is. I was about to lock this floor up for the night –' There was a question hidden in the statement.

Coleman nodded and stretched, feeling tired bones grate and rub in his back and shoulders. 'Right-o, I'm on my way then. I know when I'm not wanted.'

'Me, too,' said the security man. 'That's why I'm out here on the bloody night shift, and not tucked up safe and sound in front of the TV or in me bed. Now I'm retired my missus can't abide me being under her feet messing the place up.' He sniffed. 'Working on something important are you?' The man spoke casually, his gaze apparently without any real intention drawn towards the neat rows of names and addresses currently displayed on Coleman's machine.

Coleman smiled indulgently and then, unhurriedly, leant forward and switched his terminal off before getting stiffly to his feet. 'No, George, just another bloody glitch in the admin, too many light bulbs and toilet rolls again, you know how it is.'

The old man laughed. 'I'll have to start taking more home, then.'

Stiffly Coleman got to his feet and pulled on his jacket. The trouble with a leak was that everyone got wet.

Maggie Morgan couldn't sleep either. Uneasy now the night had fallen. She had wedged a chair up under the handle of her bedroom door and then thought better of it. What if the man currently tucked up in the back bedroom was waiting until everyone was asleep and then got up and attacked the boys and she couldn't get to them fast enough? Maybe she should have them in her bed, or maybe she should have gone and slept in theirs.

'Or maybe you should go and get in with him,' whispered a wicked little voice somewhere in the back of her head. 'What? What did I say?' the voice protested when Maggie growled at it. 'I only meant then at least you would know for certain exactly where he was.' There was a pause and then the voice added, 'And what he was doing.'

Maggie blushed and pulled the duvet up over her head while her brain continued to torment her. 'He's good-looking in a nicely rumpled kind of way; and let's face it, it's been a long, long time, Maggie. Think about it. How many times have you said if only someone nice would turn up, just drop into your life. He's a gift. It would be a terrible shame – rude even – to turn him down. He's like manna from heaven. It's fate, he was delivered right to your door – into your hall, for God's sake, what more do you want?'

Maggie groaned, rolled over and glanced again at the bedside clock with eyes that felt as if they had been back filled with fine sand and wood ash. It was nearly half past two in the morning. What had seemed reasonable two or three hours earlier – Nick Lucas's heartfelt plea to stay for a couple of days until he could get himself sorted out – now seemed like taking the pen from the devil and signing her soul away.

It was totally crazy. Madness. Maggie knew absolutely nothing about the man. She had no idea who he was or what he was or where he came from; his story could be a complete fabrication. If only she had thought of those things earlier – like when she had met the other Bernie Fielding – her life might have turned out very differently. Talking of which, why *was* he using Bernie's name, of all names? Maybe the voices in *his* head had told him to do it. What if Nick Lucas was really an axe murderer, what if he had escaped from an asylum or worse? Maggie's mind, ever helpful, scurried around the dusty corners of her skull trying to come up with something worse, much worse.

Finally conceding defeat, Maggie sat up. Outside in the garden the wind had steadily begun to rise, bringing with it the promise of a summer storm. The ropes on the swing hummed out the harmonies. Maggie grimaced, resisting the temptation to put her fingers in her ears as a gust whined melodramatically in and out of the chimney pots; trust Mother Nature to cash in on her paranoia.

In the distance through the windows she saw the first white-hot glow of lightning illuminate the night sky, followed moments later by a drum roll of thunder and then something, somewhere close by, creaked.

Maggie shuddered and then held her breath. She had been straining so hard to pick out the sounds of Nick Lucas creeping across the landing carrying a carving knife, drooling, his eyes wide and vacant, that she had given herself a terrible headache. And now she really could hear something. There it was again, louder now.

Cold and nervous and wrapped tight with unspeakable fear and panic, Maggie crept out of bed, tiptoed across the bedroom floor and pressed her ear to the door. There. There it was again, something low and ominous rattling right there on the periphery of her hearing. Was it bare feet creeping across the floorboards? Or the sound of a door creaking murderously on its hinges?

Maggie's mind reached out through the darkness,

feeling its way around the sound to try and hear more clearly. And then all at once she knew exactly what it was and pulled back in disgust. It was someone snoring. A man, a grown man, snoring contentedly, curled up fast asleep, totally unaware of the storm or her spiralling terror.

Like water draining out of a bath, the tension trickled out of her shoulders and stomach. Exhausted now and on the edge of tears, Maggie stumbled back to bed and dragged the duvet up over her head. Typical that while she fretted and tossed and turned, the axe murderer down the corridor was sound asleep. It was instincts like that which had got her tangled up with the real Bernie Fielding in the first place. Outside, it began to rain furiously.

In the hotel near Heathrow, Nimrod was also tucked up in bed. 'You gonna turn that bleeding TV off soon, then, are yer?' he growled wearily. 'Only we ought to make an early start in the morning, I want to miss the worst of the traffic. Makes me very tense getting snarled up in a jam and you know that I like to be calm. Zen; deep breaths, at one with all things.'

Turning his palms uppermost Nimrod pressed the thumb and index finger of each hand together to form a yoga-style circle gesture, although he drew the line at actually chanting in front of Cain who tended to laugh and pull faces.

Cain sniffed. 'I won't be long; I like this pro-celebrity fishing.'

'Well at least turn the bloody sound down then and God help you if you can't get up in the morning. When that alarm goes off I want you up; bright, sharp and on the ball – got that?'

Caught in the flickering light from the TV screen, Cain – sipping a piña colada – nodded just as someone from Slade pulled a fish the size of a corgi up over the side of a boat.

Nimrod groaned, closed his eyes and pulled the pillow over his head. Within minutes he was sound asleep.

While Robbie Hughes snored peacefully on the *Gotcha* office sofa Lesley poured over the tele-phone directories she'd brought up from the in-house library and busied herself making lists from the books and the database she'd pulled up on the computer, as well as from the Internet. Lesley had always been very good at cryptic clues and puzzles and games of logic – so far she had made all sorts of connections to all sorts of names on her list. First thing tomorrow she'd start ringing round to see how many more pieces she could slot into place. She liked puzzles. Maggie Morgan's name was right up under Bernie's mum and his first wife.

Lesley looked over at Robbie. His mouth was open, head thrown back, a little trail of drool glistening on his chin. She smiled indulgently. He wasn't an easy man to work with but then was anyone of his calibre?

Some days she saw Robbie Hughes as a natural leader; fiery, quixotic, one of life's visionaries, while on others he struck her as a grumpy little man with an ego the size of an emerging African nation. She suspected, with a wisdom far beyond her years, that he most probably was a subtle combination of the two and that one side fuelled the other. Whichever it was, working with Robbie had to hold more of a future than answering phone calls from women worried about the brown mould on their pot plants on the family channel. Getting up from the desk, Lesley very carefully pulled a woolly blanket off one of the chairs and covered Robbie up. Couldn't have him getting cold, now, could she?

5

'So here we go, then. Photos, gloves, guns, Mintos.' Nimrod, talking aloud to himself, ran through his mental checklist one more time, although he had been repeating it over and over in his head like a mantra for most of the morning. He and Cain had managed to get up early, showered, had a coffee, even fitted in fifty sit-ups. Life was sweet, the traffic was light and Nimrod had got everything on his list.

If anyone had ever asked Nimrod Brewster for his tips for success in the hit man business, they would have included a clear sense of purpose about what he was trying to achieve, good photos of the target, precise information, an accurate to-do list, a sharp suit, comfy shoes and a good selection of boiled sweets for the journey.

Tucked away under the CD player, the radio scanner that the Invisible Man had left them was tuned into the police frequency. It burbled and bipped and peeped away in the background, snatches of police messages adding a rather piquant soundtrack to Nimrod's thoughts.

Nimrod slipped the envelope of photos out of the glove compartment of the undistinguished silver-grey hire car and took one final long hard look at Nick Lucas's face, fixing the features in his mind.

Nimrod was good at his job, and when it was a hit, not a beating-up or a frightening or something just for fun – which to be frank, as he got older, Nimrod was less and less keen to be involved in – he prided himself on a certain swiftness of execution. These days he preferred to specialise. There was no mess, no unnecessary pain or fuss if he could possibly help it, just in and out and all over. Cool, steely, clinical. Nimrod saw himself as an emissary of death, not that he would ever say that to Cain, or any of his clients. He tugged his lapels straight. He was death's personal postboy.

It was an easy drive – M25, M40 all the way – empty roads, good weather. Nimrod stretched. Beside him, Cain drove; he always drove just under the speed limit, carefully, considerately, with gear changes as smooth as oiled glass. Broad-shouldered, newly shaved and dressed in their neat charcoal-grey suits and crisply tailored macs the two of them could easily pass for Mormons or off-duty police officers. Invisible, low-key, discreet, that's what Nimrod liked best. He made a mental note to add this to the checklist in case anyone ever asked him to appear on a *This is Your Life* Villains' Special.

The little Oxfordshire village of Renham was still early-morning quiet, with just the odd car or two pulling out of driveways, exhaust fumes spiralling away in the new dawn air. Sunlight reflected on the morning dew, birds busy in the horse chestnut trees that sheltered the caravan site behind the Old Dairy. All in all it was a lovely morning.

'So,' Nimrod said, as they parked up under a tall hawthorn hedge close to the caravans; not so close as to draw any unwanted attention to themselves but not so far away that they had to cross a lot of open ground to reach their target. 'Number fourteen, here we come. In, out, over and home in time for tea and buns.'

Cain pulled a face. 'What, buns, for breakfast? I was hoping we could stop off for egg and bacon somewhere when we're finished.'

'It's just a turn of phrase.'

Cain thought for a few seconds and then said, 'Oh okay. So can I have the window seat when we go home, then?'

Nimrod pulled a face. 'No. What the hell brought that up? It isn't a done deal yet.' He nodded towards the regimented row of vans.

'Oh come on. How much trouble do you think one chef's going to give us?'

Nimrod surreptitiously slipped a hand around his well-toned belly to check the butt of the gun concealed in the small of his back, tucked away neatly in its custom-built holster. Warmed by the heat of his body, he still liked to make sure it was there, always afraid – in the way of bad dreams – that one day he would reach for it and find it gone.

He took a deep breath to calm himself. Photos, gloves, guns, Mintoes. Today's mantra.

'I wasn't talking about Mr Lucas, I was talking about the bloody window seat,' said Nimrod. 'Anyway, yer never know, I might fancy it.' He shot his cuffs and then pulled his jacket straight.

'The window seat? Oh, yeah right,' snorted Cain. 'You always say that but you hate looking out of the window. I've seen you with your eyes closed when we're taking off, pretending to read the instructions on them cards. You don't fool me for a minute.'

They were out of the car now and walking without apparent hurry through the crisp early morning light of a brand new summer's day, every sense alive, sniffing the air like feral dogs.

'But you promised,' said Cain petulantly.

'I did not promise,' said Nimrod, all the while his eyes working over the little numbered plaques stuck into the verge beside each of the plots.

Just before they got to number fourteen the two men fell silent. They paused for an instant, other older animal senses picking up the smells, the sights and signs that couldn't be explained in words, and that ordinary men, those not amongst life's natural predators, might very easily miss. An instant later they moved off simultaneously in an unspoken agreement to get the job over and done with. It was time.

As he stepped over the knee-high fence surrounding plot fourteen, Nimrod took a deep cleansing breath; only the mad or those with no imagination would ever assume that this job was easy or simple, their senses blunted by one too many Hollywood blockbusters. The reality was hot and raw and fierce and terrifying, a moment of absolute power mixed with absolute dread.

Those who live by the sword shall die by the sword was another mantra that Nimrod Brewster had tucked away in one of those dark foetid little rooms behind his eyes. Some days the words were clearer and closer than others and they were never sharper or louder than when Nimrod was sprung and ready and waiting for the off.

In those last few seconds before the hit, when everything went into slow motion, when time stretched out into aeons, when every heartbeat hung in the air like a roll of thunder, he could see the words blazing in neon somewhere deep inside his skull. In and out, in and out, each breath rising in his chest seemed to take a week to run its course.

The two of them took up positions either side of the caravan door. Pressing himself tight up against the bodywork, Nimrod gave an almost imperceptable nod and an instant later Cain slipped a jemmy bar down his sleeve and prised the flimsy metal door open. There was barely any noise, certainly no fuss, just a faint, satisfying thunk as the lock popped under the pressure. As it did there was the sensation of time rushing forward to meet them, catching them like elastic snapping back.

Silent as cats, despite their bulk, the two men sprung inside, filling the tiny space, covering each other's backs with the guns that had appeared in their hands without any apparent effort like the dark doves of a malevolent magician.

Scanning left and right Nimrod's senses burnt white-hot, the adrenaline rush shutting out everything except for the moment; it was pure Zen. His breath roared through his chest now, as loud as an express train, his pulse screaming in his ears.

The kitchen was clear; corridor, second bedroom, bathroom, too. The whole place smelt of frying and cheap perfume.

Cain pressed his ear to what had to be the master-bedroom door and with a quick glance at his partner kicked it open, covered by Nimrod, who then strode inside, his gun ahead of him like some dark divining rod.

'What the fuck,' grunted a sleepy voice from under a duvet.

Later, Nimrod Brewster would say it was prescience that stopped him from opening fire there and then, although actually what did it was the sight of one large, perfect creamy-white breast framed by a greasy grey ruck of grubby duvet cover.

A fraction of a second later a woman with a mane of crunchy, scrunchy bleached-blonde hair sat up and having tried to focus on their faces, fumbled around on the bedside table for her glasses. 'James, what on earth is going on?' she mumbled thickly. 'There's a man in the room.'

As she spoke Cain whipped back the bedclothes.

Wrapped around the woman like the rind on a rasher of bacon was a long thin hairy man. His flesh was the colour of skimmed milk, with an infill of coarse dark curls that covered him like a moth-eaten pelt.

'James Cook?' Nimrod barked in the tone he copied from the armed-response unit that had called just often enough at his various homes to encourage him to move permanently to Spain.

'Yeah, that's right,' said the man after a second or two, 'I'm James Cook, what's it to you?' all the while scrabbling to pull the duvet back up over what, it had to be said, was not the most impressive of bodies, while blinking and rubbing his eyes. 'Who the hell are you anyway and what are you doing in my bedroom?' The voice was thick and crusty with sleep.

Cain looked at Nimrod and sniffed, his gun already tucked back in its holster. 'It's not him, is it?' he said.

Nimrod shook his head. 'No.'

James Cook was nearly wide awake now and fast beginning to collect his thoughts. 'What the fuck *is* going on here?' he growled.

Nimrod slipped his gun away.

'Gas board, Sir,' he said. 'There's no need to panic. Someone rang in and reported a leak.' And then before either of the figures in the bed could say another word Cain and Nimrod backed out of the room as quickly and quietly as mist, closing the door tight behind them.

'Did that bloke have a gun?' asked Bernie, totally bemused.

Stella slipped on her glasses and shook her head. 'No, I don't think so, it looked like it was some kind of detector thing to me. Although when they came to mine last year, they knocked. It must be a real emergency if they're bursting straight into places.'

Bernie got out of bed, pulled on a tee shirt and – still a little muddled – retraced the intruders' steps. There was no sign of them at all except that the caravan door-lock had been neatly sprung, and there was an indentation to one side that suggested force. Neatly done though, thought Bernie; the bailiffs who had broken into his last house had ripped the door clean off the hinges.

Barefoot, Bernie clambered down the steps onto the dewy grass. From somewhere close by he could hear the sound of a car engine firing up and driving away. He looked into the distance trying to work out what the hell had just happened and what it was he had missed. As Bernie mulled it over it struck him that surely the caravan site only had bottled gas. But before he could slot all the pieces together, Stella, in a low, dreamy, little-girl-lost voice, called, 'Why don't you come back to bed Jamesie. It feels ever so big and lonely and cold in here all on my own.'

'But what about the post office?' he said. 'I thought you said you'd got to be –' The words dried in his throat as he climbed back into the caravan.

She was standing in the open bedroom doorway, naked except for a sly smile and her horn-rimmed glasses. 'I have, but it's early yet,' she purred. 'I've got a couple of hours before I've got to go over and open up. Any ideas? Or are you too tired?' she said, and then after a second or two added, 'I mean, no pressure; if you don't want to we could always just snuggle up and talk.

They say that's the worst thing, don't they? You know, the pressure to perform.'

For a few moments Bernie tried to work out what the hell she was talking about and then it came back to him: impotence. It seemed that Stella Ramsey was still on a one-woman mission to heal him.

'Let's just see what happens, shall we?' he said in an undertone and followed her back into the bedroom, all thoughts of the gasmen receding under a tidal wave of lust.

'So can I have the window seat, then?'

Nimrod looked across at Cain. 'Can't you think about anything else?' he snapped, throwing his hands up in frustration. 'How does this look on the score sheet, eh? What does it do for our reputation? One nil to the opposition. Bugger. How could we have got the wrong man?'

'It could have been worse. At least we didn't shoot him,' said Cain, drawing a gloved finger across his throat miming mixed metaphors.

Nimrod nodded. 'I suppose you're right, it's not our fault we got bad intelligence. Have you got any of those mint humbugs left over there in the door pocket?'

'Uh huh.' Cain nodded. 'What are we going to do now, then?' he asked, taking one and then passing Nimrod the packet.

'Go back to the hotel I suppose. I'll have to

phone our man to tell him that it was a no ball.'
Nimrod pulled the envelope out of the glove
compartment just to check. He ran a gloved finger
under the line of type: James Cook, number fourteen, The Old Dairy, Renham. He sighed; at the
least they had got the wrong man and not the
wrong address.

It was well after nine when Maggie Morgan finally
woke up and for a moment, as she lay looking
up at the cobwebs clinging to the coving above
the wardrobe, she marvelled on just how amazing
the human brain was. Amazing what it could come
up with, really complex and ridiculous dreams,
so detailed, so convinc—

'Gooooooal-lazio!' screamed Joe, the distant
words cutting through her thoughts like a Stanley
knife. 'He shoots, he scores. Oh yes – did you
see the curve on that? We are the champions –
we are the champions,' he sung at the top of his
voice.

'Oh come off it. That was offside,' protested
Ben. 'Wasn't that offside? Tell Joe it was offside.'

'I'm not sure. How about we call it a draw,
lads, and go in and get some breakfast?' said a
distinctive male voice that Maggie seemed to
remember featuring rather heavily in last night's
ridiculous and extremely complex dream.

It was all coming back now. Maggie rolled over
and clambered out of bed. Pulling on a dressing

gown she looked out of the bedroom window. There below her on the dew-damp, overgrown grass, in amongst the holiday washing, two boys were playing footie with someone who may or may not be a lunatic. It was a great way to start the day.

An instant later the phone rang and Maggie felt a strange flicker of relief, of at least being temporarily excused the dilemma of what to do with a good-looking lunatic and her children. Almost anything had to be better than that.

'Hello?'

'Oh good morning,' said a cultured female voice. 'Could I speak to Margaret Morgan, please?'

'Speaking,' Maggie said guardedly, not exactly sure what might follow; being a teacher she had toyed on more than one occasion with the idea of going ex-directory.

The woman sounded relieved. 'I'm sorry to ring you so early but I wondered if you could help me. I'm trying to track down Bernie Fielding – and I –'

'Oh right. Good,' Maggie said, cutting the woman short. Down in the garden they had finally agreed to settle the problem with a penalty shoot-out. 'He was expecting someone to be in touch – if you can just hang on a minute I'll go and get him for you.'

'Get him? What he's there?' said the woman incredulously. 'With you?'

'Well, of course he is, I could hardly throw him

out on the street, could I? Although I have to admit the idea crossed my mind. I'm certain he'll be incredibly relieved once all of this is sorted out.'

The woman took a breath. 'Really? Are you saying that Bernie is prepared to talk to us?'

Maggie laughed. 'Well of course he is, what other option does he have? You know where he is, you know what he's been up to. Hang on, I'll just go and fetch him for you –'

'No, no, there's no need,' said the woman quickly. 'By the way, could I just confirm who I am speaking to?'

'Maggie,' said Maggie, 'Maggie Morgan.'

'Bernie's ex-wife?'

'Well I suppose you could say that,' said Maggie, laughing nervously. This wasn't quite how she had expected the conversation to go.

'Right, well that's absolutely wonderful,' said the woman. 'We'd like to come round and talk to him today if that's possible.'

'I'm sure that will be just fine,' said Maggie. It didn't sound as if this woman knew what she was doing – no wonder Nick had ended up in such a mess. 'What time will you be here?'

The woman hesitated and then said, 'Shall we say after lunch? Around two? Will that be all right?'

'I'm sure it'll be perfectly okay – I don't think he's got any plans to go anywhere. I'll let him know you called.' Maggie glanced back out into the garden, and as she did so the bedroom clock caught her eye. It was nine. She smiled. Just another five hours and everything would be back to normal.

In the garden Joe had taken a dive – or at least that was what Ben said. Maggie hurried downstairs to tell Nick the news.

Lesley, Robbie Hughes' personal assistant, dropped the phone back into its cradle and smiled triumphantly. 'Gotcha,' she hissed in an undertone and then shook her head with amazement.

It seemed almost ridiculously easy now; it was only her third phone call of the morning. Bernie's mum had been taken away and put in a home or so the woman who was living in her bungalow reckoned. Although it had occurred to Lesley as she hung up that given Bernie's track record and the fact that he had to have got it from somewhere the woman could well have been lying.

His first wife had sworn and then hung up after suggesting exactly what Lesley might like to do to Bernie if she ever found him, and then bingo! *Voila*. Third time lucky. Lesley smiled.

It was hard to believe that after all these years Bernie Fielding was finally there, slap bang in their sights. Lesley chewed her lip, her heart fluttering; it almost felt like divine intervention. Surely it was meant to be.

For an instant she caught a glimpse of Robbie's face in her mind's eye. She imagined his gratitude, his delight and with it came a fantasy fast-forward of images clamouring for her attention, ending with a registry-office wedding and then a church blessing; with Robbie, resplendent in top hat and tails, making a speech at their reception in a creamy-white marquee pitched on her parents' lawn.

'It was when we were first working together at *Gotcha* that I realised that I really couldn't imagine spending the rest of my life without my dearest, darling, precious Lesley-kins,' said Robbie, holding up a champagne flute in a toast while looking deep into her eyes. 'I'm such a lucky, lucky man to have found such a perfect woman.'

Lesley sighed.

'You're in early this morning, you want something off the trolley, do ya chuck?' said the tea lady through the open office door. Lesley blushed furiously and hastily tidied her thoughts away in case the other woman could somehow see them.

'No, no I'm fine,' she said, 'but thank you for asking.'

'I hope you're on overtime,' said the woman, straightening her pinny.

Lesley made a noncommittal noise.

'Or at least getting some of the credit,' said the woman, settling herself behind the handle of the trolley. 'The last lassie worked with him was just the same. In here all hours of the day and night working her fingers to the bone for him, you know.' She nodded towards the desk in case there was some mistake about who she meant.

Lesley looked up sharply and then chose to let it pass. Unlike the last lassie, whoever the hell that might be, *she* had tracked down Bernie Fielding. And she knew that Robbie would be delighted, although just how delighted remained to be seen.

Lesley stared up at the clock; it wasn't going to be easy to pull the film crew together by two. Robbie normally didn't get in till around eleven, sometimes later. She took it as a compliment, as if he trusted her, leaving his baby in safe hands. Not that Lesley ever told anyone that, oh no she was a loyal little bunny and if anyone ever asked she said Robbie had nipped out to get a sandwich or to chase up an important lead. But this morning things were different; they were on the home run. She needed his clout to order up the away team and knew instinctively that now Bernie was in the crosshairs Robbie would want to be at the helm.

Lesley picked up the phone; if they could just get the footage and get it edited, with a bit of luck they could air Bernie Fielding's interview or, better still, perhaps his confession on this evening's show. Finally the Bernie Fielding special was in their sights. Lesley considered the options one more time and then broke one of the unwritten rules

of both a good mistress and good PA. She phoned
Robbie at home.

In Norfolk, Nick was wandering around Maggie's
back garden, turning over the things he wanted
to say to Coleman, not that there were that many
of them if you cut out the swearing, the anger
and the statements of total disbelief.

Through the windows he could see Maggie
washing up and fussing round the boys, busy
pretending not to be keeping an eye on him. She
was lovely. He stopped and imagined for a few
moments what it might be like to have the three
of them as a family. His family. He smiled to
himself – Maggie Morgan would be a good woman
to come home to. She was warm and funny; sexy
in an easy unselfconscious way and . . . Nick
stopped himself and sighed before looking down
at his watch; it was pointless dreaming. Coleman
and his merry men should be there soon, although
the minutes seemed to be dragging by like hours.

Nick took another turn around the lawn. The
grass desperately needed cutting. Had Maggie not
shown up he had planned to mow it over the
weekend, and he realised as the thought perco-
lated through his head that he had been looking
forward to doing the garden: it felt like a talisman,
an offering to the gods of simple domesticity.

He had hoped that somewhere, out on the
distant horizon, he might just eventually be safe.

At the cottage over the last few days Nick had briefly caught a fleeting glimpse of how things might be – not immediately, but some time in an uncharted, unspecified future, when life began to unfold simply and without the sense of fear that had followed him around like a dog for the last few months. For a moment Nick had had a feeling that things were going to be all right after all and that he wouldn't be running forever . . . and now look at it. Back to square one.

Maybe it still would be all right, maybe this really was just a glitch. Mind wandering, Nick caught his foot in a tussock and barely saved himself from pitching head first into the compost heap. Yeah and maybe pigs would fly.

He caught Maggie looking at him again. She grinned and then looked away. Nick stuffed his hands in his pockets and did another lap. What would become of him now? Where would Coleman and his merry men cart him off to? Who would he be next? The thought made Nick sick to the pit of his stomach. If they couldn't do this properly what hope was there?

He took another look at his watch and took a deep breath; he was sick of the way his emotions seesawed from high to low and back. Another twenty minutes or so and, assuming Coleman was on time, everything would change all over again, his life no more than the coloured glass beads at the bottom of a kaleidoscope.

Maggie was still looking him through the window and this time Nick smiled back, after all she was the closest thing to family he had got for now.

6

Robbie Hughes glanced at his reflection in the rear-view mirror of the outside-broadcast van and made a few last minute adjustments to his appearance. He smoothed his hair and then licked a finger and tidied his eyebrows. He winked at his reflection, practising the warm reassuring twinkle that he was famous for. Robbie felt good, better than good, he felt great.

He was wearing black jeans, boots, and the shirt that Lesley had given him for Christmas, in a heavy jade-green silk. She said it made him look slimmer and slightly dangerous; like an avenging pirate, an image Robbie was only too happy to cultivate. He pulled on his favourite black leather jacket and then posed for a few seconds trying to get some glimpse of what his viewing public would see on screen. Perfect.

Robbie had mentioned to his wife over breakfast that he was thinking of getting his ear pierced and she had laughed, which wasn't nice, and then made some sarcastic comment about the onset of the male menopause. He sniffed; just showed what she knew. Robbie was a man in his prime.

The crew had already driven past Bernie Fielding's cottage several times in the last half-hour; once to get their bearings and then a few slow passes to get some decent long shots of the place, all snuggled up there in amongst hedgerows and roses and old fruit trees. It was a nice setting. It would make a good contrast to the main thrust of the piece; the menace of a viper curled up in a wedding bouquet. Oh yes, Robbie had got it all worked out.

Beside him Lesley looked up and smiled nervously. He had been in two minds whether to bring her along or not, but after all it had been her that had finally tracked Bernie down. It would have been churlish of him not to let her in at the kill.

Robbie checked his watch for the umpteenth time. It was almost a quarter to two. Arriving early was a ploy Robbie Hughes was very fond of using and as a tactic it had worked nicely over the years. He liked to catch his victims slightly off-guard, catch them while they were still pulling their pants up, or down, or doing some last minute tidying away of God only knows what. In the past he had caught people burning stuff, burying stuff and on one memorable occasion climbing off the next-door-neighbour's wife. Oh yes, early was good. Early and dangerous more or less summed him up; Robbie straightened his shoulders.

'Are we ready, then?' The crew looked up at him; it was a feeling he enjoyed. 'Let's go then, lads. Time to rock and roll – lock and load,' Robbie said, signalling a whirling rotor blade with one finger, and with that he opened the side door and dropped down out of the transit van. In his mind's eye he was storming the beachhead, charging ahead of his troops, leading them on to death or glory. Winston would have been proud of him.

'Now, you know what I want,' he called back over his shoulder to his troops as they headed briskly up the front path. 'Whatever else happens keep that camera rolling, keep it steady, and keep your cool, lads; as long as we've got the raw footage in the can we can cut it into shape when we get back to the shop. Capiche?'

The cameraman nodded.

'And Lesley?' She looked up at Robbie all dewy-eyed adoration and lust. 'I want you to stay back; if there's any chance of anyone getting hurt I don't want it to be you; you understand?' And then to the rest of the crew, 'Remember what I said guys, this man has taken years to track down, so we don't want to blow it now. He is unpredictable. We've finally got him cornered – on the one hand we don't want to let him go but what we don't know is why he wants to talk now. He could be ill, mad, suicidal – we've no idea – so watch your backs and let's be careful out there, okay?'

Everyone nodded. Robbie couldn't think of anything else to say so instead he gave them a double thumbs-up and marched smartly up to the front door, cued in the cameraman and rang the bell. The sound engineer was grinning but Robbie ignored him.

'Maggie Fielding?' he said to the attractive dark-haired woman who opened the door to him.

'Well, not really, not now, no,' she began, looking slightly bemused, but Robbie was on a roll, part jackhammer, part unctuous, fawning diplomat.

'So what name are you using now, then?' he said with affected warmth. It was important not to come across as too hard too early. The worst thing that could happen was that he lost the sympathy of his audience and they sided with the villains. No, it was important to come across as firm but fair, an avenging angel with impeccably good manners. He had been hoping that Bernie's ex-wife would turn out to be a bottle blonde with a face like a hatchet so he was more than a little disappointed to find out that she looked so respectable.

The woman looked from face to face, and then said. 'Maggie Morgan, but I'm not *using it*, that is my name. I'm sorry but I don't understand what's going on here,' she said nervously. 'What *is* going on?'

'Is Bernie in?' Robbie's smile held fast.

The woman stared past him towards the cameraman and sound crew. 'Well, yes, he's out in the garden at the moment, waiting for you, but he wasn't expecting all this. I thought this operation was meant to be a top secret. Low-profile. Invisible.'

Robbie laughed and then beckoned the camera to follow him. 'Is that what Bernie told you? Amazing, isn't it, what he can come up with? Still up to his old tricks, I see, even with his nearest and dearest. He has always had an over-active imagination has our Bernie; tells punters he's a Gulf-war veteran, a paramedic, anything to convince you he's on the level. But we both know better than that, don't we, Maggie?'

The woman's eyes widened.

'Oh yes,' Robbie continued. 'He likes to keep things under wraps, does our Mr Fielding. He's out in the garden now, waiting, is he?' Robbie's attention had already shifted onto the great anonymous viewing public who would witness this introduction, which, after a judicious bit of editing, would be great television. Investigative journalism at its best.

As they made their way through the cottage Robbie continued his conversation to camera, all the while composing and imagining the impact of the images in his mind; hardened conman in the great outdoors, playing happy families with his ex-wife.

On the stairs two small boys watched his progress with a combination of suspicion and interest and then, Robbie noted with a sense of delight, recognition. Ex-wife *and* children, things were getting better all the time.

'Mum,' said the older of the two trying to grab the woman's arm, 'Mum – that's – that's –' He pointed at Robbie but it was too late, he'd missed the boat – they were already through into the sitting room.

Throwing back his shoulders Robbie began another piece to camera. 'After years of rigorous investigation we have finally managed to track Bernie Fielding to earth. Finally it seems that he wants to come clean and talk to someone about his numerous exploits. That's right isn't it, Maggie?' He smiled wolfishly in her direction. 'Maggie,' he tried. 'Mags?' The woman didn't move a muscle. Her colour had changed to a strange angry shade of grey.

'Bernie Fielding is currently holed up in a tiny cottage deep in the heart of rural East Anglia. West Brayfield is a sleepy hamlet with a viper in its bosom.'

'What?' the woman spluttered furiously. 'What the hell do you mean, "a viper in its bosom"?' At which point a tall, good-looking man loped up to the French windows.

'I heard the bell,' he said, smiling pleasantly at Maggie, 'they're a bit early, aren't they?'

Robbie smiled with delight. He wasn't sure who Bernie and his woman had been expecting that afternoon but every instinct told him it sure as hell hadn't been the guys from *Gotcha*. Then there was a delicious moment when Bernie stepped in through the French windows and everything stopped.

The man looked from face to face, took a breath as if to speak and at that precise moment Robbie stepped forward and smiled. Robbie had to admit that his prey was somewhat better-looking and considerably more composed than he had expected, but then the bigger they are, the harder they fall.

'Here we at long last,' Robbie said, with an icy edge to his voice. 'So, Mr Fielding, where exactly shall we begin?'

The man sighed. 'To be perfectly honest I'm really worried about all the things that have been going on. It should have been so straightforward. That's what I was led to believe –' And then he looked round again, as if he was aware of the cameras for the first time. He stared at the dark-haired woman and then said, 'What exactly is going on here, Maggie – I wasn't expecting any of this.'

Before she could answer, Robbie snorted. 'Oh come on, Bernie, let's cut to the chase, shall we? There is no point playing Mr Innocent with us. We have all the evidence against you we need. We know what kind of man you are. Are you honestly planning to deny that you've tricked hundreds of people out of thousands of pounds? Narrowly missed killing and maiming God knows how many others with your cheap electrical imports and shoddy workmanship? Robbed dozens, if not hundreds, of their entire life savings? This is your day of reckoning, Bernie – the one chance you may have to have your say. Judgement day.' Robbie knew that it sounded a little melodramatic but it would be great once they'd played around with the close-ups.

The man stared at him in amazement. 'What? Yes, of course I deny it. I don't know what the hell you're talking about,' he blustered, looking from face to face in desperation. 'Where's Coleman?'

Robbie, to camera, ranted on, 'You are a menace, Bernie – a social pariah.'

'No, I'm not,' snapped the man.

'Well, of course we can hardly expect you to say otherwise, can we? In my experience the leopard never changes his spots. What can you say in your defence? That you didn't know anything about any of it? That you were framed? That it was a middleman – a big boy did it and ran away?' Robbie laughed sarcastically, the volume of his voice rising as his tone became increasingly incredulous.

The guy stared at him, mouth open. 'I have got absolutely no idea what you are talking about,' he said.

At which point Maggie leapt into action, trying to cover the camera lens with her hand. 'Look, there has been some sort of mistake. Get out,' she snapped. 'Now! You don't know what the hell you're doing. I don't know why you're here – can't you see that you've got the wrong man? I'm calling the police.'

'Really? Calling the police? That's rich with your boy Bernie's history.'

Maggie had picked up the phone and started to dial.

And then Robbie saw some parody of comprehension dawn on the man's face and he gasped and said, 'Oh you think that *I'm* Bernie Fielding –'

Robbie snorted; it was a masterly performance. 'Nice try, Bernie, but you don't fool me. I'll warn you now that *Gotcha* will never rest until justice is done. We're like the Mounties, we always get our man.'

Robbie felt a great wave of triumph, the expression on Bernie Fielding's face was pure gold. The film crew by some unspoken consensus were already backing slowly out of the cottage but Robbie sensed that it was Bernie who was on the run. If the crew got arrested so much the better.

The man was ashen. 'Look, you can't do this,' he stammered, hurrying after them. 'You don't know what you're doing – Jesus – look you can't use that film – stop this now, please,' he pleaded. 'There's been a terrible mistake, I thought you were – you were –' He stopped as if the words had dammed up in his throat. 'Somebody else.'

'That much is obvious, Bernie, but it's time that you had a little bit of your own medicine. We're going to get you –' snapped Robbie, jabbing a finger at his chest. 'If you won't talk to us today, well there's always another day. We'd like to hear your side of the story; you can have a chance to set the record straight.' Robbie's tone was heavy with irony – or maybe it was sarcasm? He always got those two muddled up.

The cameraman gave him an okay sign with thumb and forefinger. Robbie grinned and hurried down the path. They'd have the footage ready to broadcast on tonight's show; Robbie had been collecting evidence and statements on film for years. It was just a matter of cutting it into the segment; maybe it would make a whole show. Finally, the Bernie Fielding special. Robbie grinned. He'd show Madam Upstairs that he could bring home the bacon under pressure. *Passé* my arse.

'Don't you see, you're making a terrible mistake,' Maggie called after them.

Robbie smiled. 'I don't think so, Mrs Fielding, I plan to get your Bernie and hang him out to dry.'

'But you can't, you don't understand – they'll kill me if they find me,' her companion protested.

'And so they bloody well should,' said Robbie, as he and the crew scrambled back into the safety of the van.

'Where to now?' asked the driver.

Robbie grinned. 'Back to the studio, my good man. We've got a show to put on.'

Lesley looked up at him with those big liquid eyes of hers, and for a moment Robbie felt like a God.

Nick stood in the sitting room, his mouth open, his eyes glazed over, totally glued to the spot.

Maggie stared at him, realising that some part of her assumed he would know exactly what to do. She was trembling.

'He was that man off the telly,' said Ben.

'Are we going to be on the telly?' asked Joe brightly.

'Why didn't you tell me that Bernie Fielding was a crook?' Nick snapped.

Maggie watched his expression as he explored her face, trying to weigh her up. She didn't let her gaze drop; Bernie Fielding was history. 'Because it isn't important, Nick. I was a kid when I met him –' she began, aware that she sounded defensive. 'And it was a long time ago –'

'Not according to them –' Nick waved towards the door.

'What Bernie Fielding gets up to is nothing to do with me,' said Maggie.

Nick still hadn't moved. 'It is now,' he said, and then the ice melted. 'Do you know what just happened? Those mad bastards filmed me. Here. I was supposed to be *safe* here. They filmed me because they thought I was Bernie Fielding. If those women find me they'll kill me. Do you understand? They'll kill me.'

Maggie caught hold of Nick's arm; he was almost hysterical. 'Stop it; they won't. It'll be all right. I'll go and ring the TV station. I'll explain to them.'

'Explain what? If that film goes out I'm already as good as dead,' said Nick again.

Maggie looked at the boys anxiously, wishing that he would shut up in front of them. 'Why don't you go and ring the people who brought you here?'

'Fat lot of good that will do,' Nick hissed, and, stuffing his hands into his pockets, headed back out into the garden.

Maggie shook her head; she had to find some way to show Nick that salvation was possible. Directory enquiries had the number of the *Gotcha* studios, and she was connected on the second ring.

'Good afternoon, *Gotcha* Productions, how may I help you?' said a sing-song female voice.

Maggie took a deep breath. 'I've got a problem and I'm not exactly sure who I need to talk to.'

'Okay, well if you would like to tell me a little bit about the nature of your problem I can maybe redirect you to the right place,' said the girl helpfully. 'If you prefer to remain anonymous –'

'No, no, it's not that,' said Maggie. 'The thing is –'

A few minutes later Maggie hung up and almost at once Nick reappeared in the doorway. Maggie looked up at him, wondering where to begin. It felt hard to breathe, as if someone had made the air in her lungs thick and hot and heavy.

'Well?' he said, his expression tight as a drum skin.

'They said that under normal circumstances they need a court injunction to stop a film or any other material from being broadcast.' Maggie spoke slowly, frustration making her enunciate every word. 'To get them to stop the show we would need a judge. You have to talk to Coleman, Nick. Now.'

Nick shook his head. 'I would if I thought it would do any good. Why hasn't he contacted me, that's what I want to know. I feel like they've cut me adrift. Did you tell the TV company that it was a case of mistaken identity, that I'm not really Bernie Fielding?'

'Of course I bloody well did,' Maggie growled. 'They just said it wasn't the first time they'd heard that line. I even tried telling them about the witness relocation thing and the guy I talked to said that they'd heard that one before, too.' She looked up at him. 'What the hell are we going to do now?'

It was odd how it felt so very natural to say 'we' as if some part of her knew that her fate was already irrevocably tangled with Nick Lucas's.

Nick shook his head. 'If they find me, Maggie, they'll kill me.' He paused as if waiting until he had her full attention and then added in a low voice, 'And if they think you're involved they'll kill you, too.'

Cain and Nimrod sat in their hotel room near Heathrow, sipping Harvey Wallbangers and waiting for the phone to ring. Cain flicked through the TV channels, while Nimrod, sucking on the long candy-striped straw, trawled idly through a copy of *Homes & Gardens*.

'So what do you fancy, then?' said Cain.

'Anything as long as it hasn't got any bleeding fish in it.'

'How about this?' said Cain, settling himself down as the titles rolled.

'What is it?'

'*Gotcha*. I always watch it on Sky when I'm at home to see if I can spot any of the lads or pick up any good tips. You know you've gotta keep your finger on what's going down, where the pulse is. Oh bugger, it's only a trailer – damn.'

Nimrod sighed and then did a double-take, as a familiar face popped up on the screen.

'Wait, wait,' he snapped at Cain who was about to flick onto another channel. 'Hang on. Whoa. Look, does that remind you of anybody we know?'

'Tonight at half past seven on *Gotcha* we'll be talking face to face with Bernie Fielding, con man, thief and liar,' said the announcer.

Nimrod grinned and pulled the envelope of pictures out of his briefcase. It seemed that the gods had smiled on them after all. There on the screen was a close-up of their quarry; Mr Nick Lucas.

'Gotcha,' purred Nimrod. 'Well, well, well, so he's calling himself Bernie Fielding, is he.'

'So do you want to watch it later, then?' said Cain, sounding surprised and taking a long pull on his drink.

'Oh yes,' said Nimrod. 'I most certainly do.'

Cain turned towards him, his heavy eyebrows knitted together in a puzzled expression as if he couldn't quite place the face. 'Do we *know him*?' he asked quizzically, nodding towards the TV screen.

'Oh yes,' said Nimrod, picking up the phone with glee. 'We most certainly do,' and then into the handset, 'Operator, can I have an outside line, please?'

7

'What do you mean?' growled Coleman. 'I don't know what the hell you're talking about, we most certainly *did not* send a TV crew round to the safe house to film you. For fuck's sake, what do you take us for – some sort of circus act? It kind of defeats the whole complete anonymity thing, wouldn't you say?' He sounded annoyed, as if he thought Nick was totally crazy or possibly lying.

Standing in Maggie's kitchen, Nick was way out beyond annoyed in a cold numb place that made breathing hard and thinking almost unbearable. He felt as if he was on borrowed time. 'They said that they'd come looking for the real Bernie Fielding.'

Coleman snorted, his tone almost derisive. 'What do you mean the *real* Bernie Fielding? That's impossible; I've told you before there is no *real* Bernie Fielding. That's the whole point of the Stiltskin programme. We feed in your age and a few other non-negotiable details like race and height and it comes up with a whole new persona. Shazam, just like that. Trust me, this is just some weird glitch – a coincidence; *there is no real Bernie Fielding.*'

Maggie, who had been listening in on the extension, snapped angrily, 'Oh for God's sake, how much more proof do you need, Coleman? Who are you trying to kid? Do you seriously expect us to believe any of this stuff?'

'Who the hell is this?' snapped Coleman.

'The former Mrs Bernie Fielding,' Maggie snapped right back. 'Nick said I could listen and trust me, whatever you say about Bernie he really does exist.'

It had taken Nick most of what had remained of the afternoon to track Coleman down. Now that he was on the line they wanted answers. Lots and lots of answers.

'Look, the main thing,' said Coleman hastily, 'is not to panic. I want you to keep your head down. I've already pulled a crash team in to come and pick you up and my assistant is looking into what is going on here even as we speak.' Coleman sounded as if he was regaining his composure. 'Just hang tight in there; as I said it's only a glitch.'

'*Only a glitch?*' repeated Nick incredulously. 'What do you mean, only a glitch? Who's going to turn up next? The *This is Your Life* film crew?'

'Don't be so ridiculous. Calm down, you're over

reacting,' Coleman said in a low earnest voice, at which point Maggie's eldest son Ben came hurtling into the kitchen waving his arms about. He grabbed her hand, trying to pull her through into the sitting room.

'Mum, mum,' Ben said excitedly, 'come with me; we're on the telly, come and look. Come and look! We're on the TV –'

'What? What do you mean we're on the TV?' Maggie swung round and snatched up the remote for the little TV set that stood on the kitchen dresser, flicking furiously through the channels, and sure enough there they all were in glorious Technicolor. Her jaw dropped open.

'Oh my God. I don't believe it. There's a trailer for *Gotcha* on ITV,' she hissed in disbelief, turning to stare at Nick; her expression mirrored by her image on the TV. A line of text rolled along the bottom of the screen like ticker tape. 'They're doing a Bernie Fielding special,' Maggie whispered.

'Did you hear that?' roared Nick. 'There's your little glitch, Coleman. ITV, seven-thirty tonight –'

All Coleman could manage was a choked expletive before Nick continued, 'We're on TV for Christ's sake. You've got to get on to the television company now. I'm starring in tonight's show by the look of it. Maggie's already rung them but the production company won't listen to us. This is totally crazy; you and your department might

123

as well have taken out a full page in the tabloids with my bloody address on it.'

Right on cue Maggie hit the audio button in time to hear Robbie Hughes saying, '. . . currently holed up in a tiny cottage in the heart of East Anglia, West Brayfield is a sleepy hamlet with a viper in its bosom.' His voice-over was accompanied by film footage of her cottage – first a tracking shot down the lane and then a close-up of her front door, over which was superimposed a picture of Nick looking angry and waving the camera away. 'Tonight we explore the dark world of Bernie Fielding and those involved and entrapped by his cunning web of lies, trickery and deceit –'

Maggie felt her stomach contract sharply. 'For God's sake, Nick, he's telling people where I live. We have got to do something *now*. We can't wait for Coleman to ride in like the bloody cavalry and sort it all out. How many people do you think there are out there watching this?'

'I heard that. You stay exactly where you are,' growled Coleman furiously. 'We're sending a team in to pick you up; they're already on their way. Don't do anything silly, Nick, and I promise you'll be just fine.' If his tone was meant to be reassuring it failed miserably.

'Fine? You seriously expect us to believe any of that? You must think we're both totally and utterly stupid,' shouted Maggie and with that she hung up.

Nick gasped and then looked at her in amazement. 'What in God's name did you do that for?' he said, staring down at the dead phone in his hands. 'It took me bloody ages to get through to him. Now what are we going to do?'

Maggie sighed. 'Don't worry he was just telling you what he's been trained to say, Nick. He's doing it by the book – by numbers. How long is it going to take them to get someone down here? An hour? Two hours? And how many times do you think that ad's been on the TV already? I really, truly believe that we have to get out of here now, not when Coleman and his merry men show up, but *now*.'

She turned to Ben and Joe who were still standing staring at the TV. 'Go upstairs and get some toys. I'll be up in a minute.' She caught hold of Nick's arm and felt a tiny unexpected tingle of pleasure. Damn, now wasn't the moment. 'Go and get your things, too,' she said as calmly as she could. 'We have to get going.'

Nick looked down at her. 'I can't believe this is happening. I really thought I was going to be safe.'

Maggie looked up at him and smiled. 'Come on. Stop fretting. It'll be all right, trust me,' she said. Poor sod, Maggie thought, wishing that there was some way she could reassure him. After all, she didn't know what they were dealing with, maybe she should be more nervous than she was.

He moved a fraction closer and for a split second Maggie thought he was going to kiss her. She froze, wondering if she had got it wrong. Nick was gorgeous and dangerous and so close that Maggie could feel his breath on her cheek. She looked up and for an instant their eyes met and she felt her pulse quicken. Damn, damn, damn.

And then Nick reddened as if he wasn't quite sure and the moment passed.

'Go,' she said, waving him away, struggling to regain her composure. 'We need to be gone.'

Half way up the stairs Nick turned back to look at her 'Maggie, I'm sorry –' he began. 'I had no idea.'

She grinned. 'It's a bit late for that now, don't forget to pack your teddy and your tooth brush. I'll sort the boys out.'

In the offices on Colmore Road, Coleman slapped two files onto the desk alongside Ms Crow, who had been listening on the speaker phone.

'Okay. Nick Lucas, Bernard Fielding and James Cook. Discuss,' he said between tightly gritted teeth. 'I really need some help to get to the bottom of this one, Dorothy. As far as I can see it's turned into a complete and utter bloody disaster. I've already pulled in a crash team to get Nick Lucas out of the safe house – that's if he doesn't do a runner in the meantime.' Coleman blew out his lips thoughtfully. It had been a long day. 'What the fuck is going on here? This TV thing is the last straw –'

Ms Crow, her face an impassive mask, looked up at him. 'Don't worry. It'll be fine, Danny, just leave it with me and I'll see what I can find out.' As she spoke, Ms Crow dropped a cool slim hand onto his in a gesture of almost maternal reassurance, although she was no more than a year or two older than Danny, if that. Dorothy Crow always sounded calm, competent and convincing, her voice and unflappable manner two of the main reasons why Coleman had taken her on in the first place. That and her impeccable service record and security clearance which were on a par with his own. Coleman smiled; she was the only person besides his family who ever called him by his first name.

'I thought he was down to be James Cook?' she said casually, opening up the file.

Coleman shook his head and sighed. 'I don't know any more. That's what the data trail says but it seems as if somewhere along the line Stiltskin threw a shoe and coughed up two names. And looking at all this stuff I can't for the life of me work out whether it's a software error or an operator error, or deliberate sabotage. What makes it all the more peculiar is that this Bernie Fielding appears to have been a real person. How in God's name did that happen?'

Dorothy's expression didn't change. He knew from experience that she was unlikely to venture an opinion until she had read the files and tracked down the necessary information to weigh up any argument. Coleman continued, 'I've just spoken to this Fielding guy's ex-wife who – quite understandably – is a bit pissed off at having a strange man show up on her doorstep with her ex-husband's name, and even more pissed off to have some film crew showing up and broadcasting her details to the nation.'

'Does the woman know who Nick is?'

Coleman shook his head, 'I don't know – probably. I can't see under those circumstances how his cover could have held up. He's not exactly James Bond although God alone knows what he's told her.'

'The truth?'

Coleman sighed. 'The whole truth and nothing but the truth – I don't know. What would you do?'

Ms Crow declined to answer and then pursed her lips. 'The other thing is,' she said slowly, as if her brain was attempting to order facts into neat rows. 'If Nick Lucas has – at the moment – assumed Bernie Fielding's identity, that irons one wrinkle out, but if that *is* the case who is it who is currently pretending to be James Cook?'

'Sorry? I'm not with you,' said Coleman in surprise. 'What do you mean, *who is currently pretending to be James Cook?* No one, as far as I know.'

Dorothy Crow's expression hardened up. 'Well

that is where you're wrong, Danny – *someone* has taken on James Cook's identity, or at least someone is out there drawing money out of his bank account.' She pulled a sheet of paper out of the in-tray on her immaculately tidy desk and handed it to him. It was a photocopy of a request statement for one James Anthony Cook.

'Oh, come on, you're joking?' Coleman protested, shaking his head. He looked at Ms Crow. Humour was not her natural forte. 'Oh for fuck's sake,' he said in exasperation. 'Not another glitch in the bloody system – what the hell is going on here? God alone knows who this is. Put a stop on the account and get somebody in there to see what they can turn up. But before you do any of that get me *Gotcha* Television on line one and then get someone to run a full systems check on Stiltskin. Sodding bloody computers.' He threw the bank statement back onto the desk.

Ms Crow picked up the phone and dialled.

Coleman went back into his office, pulled the shades at the windows to half-mast and, slumping into his seat, pressed his thumbs into his eye sockets, thanking whatever god it was that had sent him Dorothy Crow. The phone on his desk buzzed. He picked it up. '*Gotcha* Productions, how may I help you?' said a cheery female voice.

'Well for a start you can put me through to someone with a bit of clout,' growled Coleman.

* * *

Meanwhile, Bernie Fielding had spent most of the day in Oxford, shopping for new clothes. He'd got himself a zippy new mobile phone that folded up to the size of a tea bag and a very tasty leather jacket – a man in his position needed to create the right impression. Now, back at the caravan, Bernie stuffed the last of the carrier bags and boxes into the bin under the sink, while admiring the way his new shoes looked with the chinos he'd bought. All in all it had been a good day. He'd even taken a test drive in a new BMW; after all his credit record was as white as the driven snow now and there was a limit to how good an impression he could realistically make driving a fifteen-year-old, canary-yellow 2CV, however lovingly maintained.

Easing off his new shoes, Bernie opened the fridge and flicked on the TV. Stella had already said she'd drop by around eight for a drink. He'd bought a couple of bottles of Chablis, glasses, new sheets, a selection of towels and a toothbrush just in case. She had promised to show him the rest of the sights. Bernie grinned and popped the top on a can of ice-cold Pilsner. Stella Ramsey was a girl with a lot of sights worth seeing.

Bernie unbuttoned his shirt and loosened his belt. There was just time for a shower and a shave and a – Something stopped him mid-stride on his way to the bathroom. There on the TV was a woman who looked remarkably like his ex-wife,

Maggie. Weird. He looked again and turned up the sound just in time to catch some guy saying, '. . . finally tracked to ground con man Bernie Fielding.'

Bernie Fielding? Bernie spluttered and inhaled his beer, struggling to breathe as he felt an icy finger track down his spine. Then remembered that he wasn't Bernie Fielding any more. He was James Cook, man about town, man with a healthy bank balance, looking for a new house, with a new woman and a whole shiny, brand-new life to play with. And then, hot on the heels of his sense of relief, was the realisation that it really *was* Maggie on the TV and that – thanks to his interfering – someone else *was* Bernie Fielding. The breath stayed where it was, trapped high up in his throat as he fought to exhale. Someone who he had, in a moment of divine madness, sent to Maggie's home address, someone who at the stroke of a computer keyboard had inherited his whole life. His *whole* life. Lock, stock and litigation.

Bernie shrugged and flicked on the gas to heat the water; it'd be all right, Maggie had always been a smart cookie, she'd sort it out, she was good at . . .

The sound of the gas igniting with a dull spark made Bernie stop dead in his tracks, fingers tightening around the beer can.

He turned to look back at the TV screen, even

though the action had moved on to an advert for Alpen, while something dark and cold slithered down from his brain to his belly.

'Oh my God, no,' he whispered thickly. It was the closest Bernie had said to a prayer in a long, long time. The gasmen.

He had stolen James Cook's identity, an identity that was presumably already earmarked for someone else. Someone who needed to be hidden, someone whose life was at risk, someone who needed to be anonymous. What was it those men had asked him first this morning? Bernie felt the cold thing in his belly slither round and contract into a curled fist.

'Are you James Cook?' That's what they had said. '*Are you James Cook?*' He replayed the words over and over in his mind and, at that moment, Bernie knew without a shadow of a doubt that the two of them had been carrying guns and only by some miracle had he escaped being shot. But worse – much, much worse – was the realisation that because of him the men were probably already on their way to Maggie's cottage looking for the man who really should have been James Cook.

Bernie swallowed hard. Scamming was one thing but this was way out of his league. He might be a thief, a con man and a first-class bloody liar but Bernie Fielding was no killer, and if he didn't do something soon he might as well have pulled the trigger himself.

Galvanised into action, Bernie picked up his new mobile phone, eyes still firmly fixed on the TV screen. He called directory enquiries and then dialled Maggie's number. At first when it rang Bernie felt a great sense of relief, and then as it rang on and on it was replaced by a terrible sense of dread. What if the two men had already found Maggie and the boys?

Bernie shuddered, his heart skipping a beat as a wave of nausea rolled through him. It was too awful to contemplate. Surely someone would have seen the advert and realised their mistake. Someone would help, surely? Mind racing, Bernie hurried into the bedroom and started to collect his things together. He wasn't exactly sure what he was planning to do but he knew that he had to do something and he had to do it fast.

Picking up the keys to the 2CV, Bernie raced out of the caravan. As he got to the car park he was suddenly aware that a police car had pulled up alongside his car and two uniformed officers were busy giving the canary-yellow Citroën the once-over.

'Oh bugger,' hissed Bernie and, head down, hands in pockets, he moved off between the cara-vans, trying hard not to attract attention, and headed for the village.

In West Brayfield Maggie was reversing the Golf out of her driveway. Over the fence Mrs Eliot was smiling and waving them all off with a hankie. The branches of the bay hedge that Maggie had planned to prune scraped past the window and ground noisily over the roof.

'What did you say to her?' asked Nick, fastening his seat belt.

'That we'd got to nip down and sort something out at the beach hut. A minor emergency but nothing that she need worry about. I told her that I'd ring and let her know if we were going to be more than a day or two.'

Nick pulled a face.

'Oh come on,' said Maggie. 'She's my friend as well as my neighbour. I had to tell her. I couldn't just do a moonlight flit without saying something, that really would worry her.' Maggie looked at his face and added. 'Please, Nick, stop panicking. It will be all right, she only knows that the beach hut is somewhere down in Somerset – if I didn't tell her some yarn or other she'd probably ring the police and cause all sorts of fuss. Relax.' Maggie let the clutch out and the car eased across the weedy gravel. 'And besides her memory is terrible these days.'

'So *are* we going back to the beach hut, then?' asked Ben, hanging over the back of the seat.

'No,' said Maggie.

'No?' repeated Ben.

'No,' said Maggie, 'now sit down, put your seat belt on and be quiet. You're going to Grandma's.

I'm taking Nick –' she hesitated, wondering what to tell them.

'Home,' said Nick decisively, without meeting her eyes.

'Home,' Maggie nodded. If only she was half as certain.

'So why did you tell Mrs Eliot that we were going down to the beach hut, then?' said Joe.

Stumped, Maggie glared at the two of them. Joe glared right back. 'You said that you would take us to the zoo tomorrow,' he said. 'You promised.'

Meanwhile, in the hotel room near the airport, Nimrod was waiting for the next part of the puzzle to slot into place; he was waiting for the call that would tell him what happened next. He'd slipped his gun, still in its holster, under a pleat of sheet on the bed so that the butt was no more than a heartbeat away. These days he felt naked and vulnerable if it wasn't close by. Gunmetal is cold in a way no other thing ever is and has a smell that once experienced is never forgotten – a combination of the oil and cordite that settles down deep into the mind, and that if not truly present is always there in the imagination or at least Nimrod's imagination.

Nimrod and Cain were both experts at their craft – cold, accurate, unflinching. They could strip their weapons down and reassemble them blindfolded in a matter of seconds. The weapons the two men carried, manufactured by Heckler and Koch, were familiar, trustworthy tools that fitted as naturally into their hands as the chisel of a master carpenter or the trowel of a brick-layer. Like any other tools, over the years they had become more like an extension of their personalities.

Sitting on the room's only armchair, Nimrod felt a familiar soft glow in the palm of his hand. It was sign – a portent. They couldn't do anything now without further orders but he knew it wouldn't be long before the call came. He had phoned the Invisible Man with what they knew and now they had to wait. Waiting was always the worst part; it made him tetchy, itchy and prone to throwing things. Mostly tantrums.

Across the room, Cain flicked backwards and forwards through the channels. 'So, do you still want to watch *Gotcha* when it comes on, then? It's always a bit of laugh, and maybe we'll get some more information on our man, Nick Lucas, or whatever his name is now. Bloody funny that he showed up on there, eh? Fancy him being a con man, eh? Who would have thought it.' Cain shook his head. 'You'd think he'd be straight as a die. Bloody amazing. Just goes to show you never can tell.'

Nimrod nodded. Across the room the titles for *Gotcha* were already rolling. He had been running through another checklist that began with two pairs of latex gloves and a soft pair of black leather ones to cover them. Without the latex it was possible that the leather would eventually give a print as clear as if he wasn't wearing gloves at all. Besides, Nimrod had always enjoyed the tight, slightly hot and sweaty feel of latex against his skin.

'And tonight, in a change to our advertised programme,' the presenter was saying, 'we bring you a special report on . . .'

'Here we go. Turn it up a bit, will ya?' said Nimrod, moving the chair closer to the screen.

Maggie's mum, who had been watching a wildlife programme about tree frogs on BBC2, peered suspiciously at Nick over the top of her reading glasses and then back at Maggie. The two boys had gone outside to feed the goldfish in Granddad's pond and play in the sandpit, the sound of their voices from the perfectly manicured garden a constant backdrop to the conversation currently going on in the sitting room.

Maggie's mother was sitting in an easy chair near the fireplace. She was a taller, greyer, plumper version of her daughter although somewhere down the line Mrs Morgan senior had ditched the sense of humour and gone for something altogether more practical and hard-wearing. She lived about fifteen minutes drive down the road from Maggie on a neatly clipped and nicely maintained housing estate in a large bungalow on a corner plot, and was currently sipping tea from a bone china cup and saucer.

'So, how long did you say you're going to be away for?' she asked. 'Only I've got W.I. on Monday night and your dad's got bowls on Wednesday. You know that he doesn't like to miss it – not now that they're through to the league.'

Maggie set her cup down on the side table. 'To be perfectly honest I'm not sure yet, that's why I've got to nip down and take a look and see what's what. I had a phone call earlier today –' She tried hard to sound light and bright and matter of fact even though she guessed her mother wouldn't be fooled for an instant. Maggie didn't like lying but couldn't see she had much option and it was almost true; after all they *had* spoken to Coleman on the phone. 'We just need to go to the beach hut and sort a few things out.' Maggie smiled, with a confidence she didn't feel, while trying to be as non-specific as possible.

'We?' Maggie's mother sucked at a stray something in her teeth.

Maggie nodded.

'Down at the beach hut?'

Maggie nodded again.

'In Somerset?'

'That's where the beach hut is Mum,' snapped Maggie.

Her mum looked briefly back at Nick. 'If you

had let us know earlier your dad could have driven down with you and taken a look at whatever it is. He's good with his hands. What is the problem anyway? You know he'll want to know. I've always said that place is a liability, it's like the Forth Road Bridge – I mean I know it's nice to have a bolt hole and all that, but the upkeep, and the petrol to get down there. It isn't the drains again, is it? Your dad said that the whole system was past its best. I know you love that place, Maggie, but sometimes I wonder if it wasn't just a terrible white elephant.'

It was an old song. Maggie made a non-committal noise.

However, her mum didn't intend to be put off that easily. 'So how long do you think you're going to be gone, then?'

'I've already said that I'm not sure,' said Maggie.

'No more than a few days,' Nick added helpfully, 'it shouldn't take us too long to sort it out, should it, Maggie?'

Maggie's mum turned her eyes on him. Her gaze had the same intensity as the spotlight above the chair on *Mastermind*. Maggie sighed; the man really was a fool, cute but a fool nonetheless.

'A few days?' repeated Maggie's mum slowly. It was a technique that had served her well over the years; simple repetition until the accused eventually gave up, broke down sobbing and confessed all. Maggie knew that for a fact – it had worked on her often enough – and like Maggie her mother had sensed that Nick didn't hold up well under pressure. It was time to get him out of there.

Nick nodded. 'Yes, that's right.'

'At the beach hut?' asked Maggie's mother.

Maggie got to her feet with an air of brisk workmanlike endeavour. This was too much like a choral round. It could go on for hours.

'We've been through this already, Mum. If you don't mind having the boys for a day or two I'll give you a ring as soon as I know exactly what's happening and we've had a chance to get things sorted out.'

'And if anybody asks you –' Nick began warily. Maggie swung round and flashed him a warning glance. Instantly, his jaw snapped shut like a mousetrap. He was learning fast. 'I mean, not that anyone is likely to ask you anything,' he concluded lamely. Maggie held his gaze and he smiled with as much sincerity as he could muster.

As they got to the door Maggie's mum caught hold of her arm, eyes alight with barely veiled curiosity. 'So, before you head off into the sunset, are you going to tell me who your new friend is then? Or do I have to interrogate the boys once you've gone?' she asked, nodding towards Nick's retreating back.

'He's just a friend, that's all. No one you need worry about.'

Her mother's expression didn't falter.

Maggie sighed into the pause. 'If I told you, Mum, you wouldn't believe me.'

The older woman sniffed. 'Maybe you're right. With your talent for choosing wrong-uns it's probably better if I don't know anyway,' she said. 'Although I have to say he seems like a nice chap. Just you be careful what the pair of you get up to.' And then she thawed. 'Your dad'll be so chuffed when he hears that the boys are stopping for a few days. Give us a ring when you get yourself organised and if it's a big problem for goodness' sake let us know – your dad'll worry himself sick if we don't hear. And behave yourself,' she added with a sly grin.

Maggie smiled and, leaning forward, kissed her gently on the cheek. 'Thanks, Mum, I'll tell you all about it when I get back. I'm just going to go and say goodbye to the lads.'

As Maggie headed out into the garden Nick said his goodbyes and then went out to wait in the car. Maggie couldn't help feeling sorry for him as she came back; he looked very lonely sitting there all on his own.

8

'And tonight in a change to our advertised programme,' the presenter was saying. 'We bring you a special report on . . .'

'Here we go. Turn it up a bit, will ya –' said Nimrod, moving the chair closer to the screen.

Cain hit the sound button and, scrunching up a couple of pillows, settled himself down on the bed. Cain and Nimrod were both all ears, all eyes, as the *Gotcha* credits rolled up on the screen.

'. . . the rise of street crime in our inner cities. Muggers, pickpockets aggressive begging and unlicensed hawkers are fast becoming the bane of modern urban life.'

Cain grunted and swung round to stare at Nimrod. The female voice continued. 'Some areas of our cities are virtual no go areas – a veritable thieves kitchen for the unwary.' The shot widened out to reveal the *Gotcha* studio where a thin redheaded woman was sitting on a desk, holding a clipboard and looking terribly earnest. 'In Dickensian London we might have expected these things but, as crime figures about to be revealed by the Home Office show, statistically, it appears we are more likely to be mugged or killed on the streets of London than in New York . . .'

The two men looked at each other in bemusement, at which point the telephone rang.

'Yes?' said Nimrod as he snatched up the handset.

At the other end of the line, the cool voice of the Invisible Man said, 'Get yourself a pen and paper – I've got Mr Lucas's new address here for you.'

Nimrod beckoned to Cain. 'Paper, pen, pronto.'

Cain did as he was told.

The man at the end of the phone continued, 'Isaac's Cottage, thirty-four The Row, West Brayfield – it's in Norfolk. You know where that is?' He spoke very slowly and precisely, enunciating every word as if Nimrod might not understand.

'Yeah. I've got it,' snapped Nimrod, scribbling the details down on a menu card.

'Good. In that case it's time to rock and roll – and lads, let's try and get it right this time, shall we?'

Nimrod was about to say something but stopped himself; he was too much of a professional to point out that it was hardly their fault that they hadn't got the right man last time. The Invisible Man should be bloody grateful they hadn't shot the guy in the caravan.

'He was a con man apparently. They pulled the telly programme that I phoned you about, the *Gotcha* thing, you know?' Nimrod complained. He had been quite looking forward to watching it although he didn't like to say so. Nimrod decided not to go into the whole Bernie Fielding versus Nick Lucas thing; in his experience it was the faces not names that counted.

'Well, well well, what can I tell you? Looks like the other side have got some influence after all, probably hoping we wouldn't see the trailers,' his contact said with a grim laugh; it was not an attractive sound. 'Right, so you know where you're going now?'

'Yeah, we're already on our way,' said Nimrod and nodded towards Cain as he hung up.

'What?' mouthed Cain. For a moment he seemed too big, too heavy for the anonymous little hotel room, and it struck Nimrod that, a little like seals or killer whales, the pair of them were only truly at home and at their best in their natural environment.

'Switch the bloody telly off, will you,' snapped Nimrod, pulling a road map out of his briefcase. 'We're on the move.'

'All right, all right, there's no need to shout, I was looking forward to watching that,' Cain growled back. 'I was looking to see if there was anyone on there that we knew. I saw my brother-in-law on a couple of weeks back.'

'Big Tone?' said Nimrod with surprise, before he could stop himself.

Cain nodded. 'Yeah. He looked real well. Put on weight, good tan –'

'What, your Tone was on the box? I didn't know they'd pulled him in for another job.'

Cain pulled a face. 'Well, I assumed it was him. The photo-fit was a dead ringer.'

'What do you mean our date's off, James?' snapped Stella Ramsey, pouting angrily. 'I was just going upstairs to put my face on. I've been looking forward to it all day.' She was standing by the back door of the post office wrapped up in a pale blue dressing gown with a towel around her hair. She smelt warm and womanly and looked all pink and shiny from the bath. 'Pension day is a real pig – I've been on my feet in that bloody shop since eight o'clock and you know how much sleep I had last night.'

Bernie grinned, struggling to keep his mind on track. The combination of memories from the night before and a bathrobe that finished well above Stella's knee, and certainly wasn't generously cut, meant the struggle wasn't a walkover by any means. Where the two sides of the fabric crossed he could see the rise of a generous creamy-white breast. Bernie swallowed hard, reminding himself that this really wasn't the moment.

'I'm really sorry, Stella, but something has come up. I've got to go and – and go –' Bernie hesitated, hastily re-embroidering and bolstering the story he'd been cooking up on the short walk over from the caravan park. He glanced back over his shoulder implying it was vital that no one overheard their conversation and also to check that the police hadn't followed him from the car park.

'The thing is, Stella, what you have to under-stand is that a lot of my work is top secret, all very hush-hush. Government mostly; I can't say too much at the moment, but I've just had a phone call.' Bernie tapped the mobile in his top pocket, then looked up to see how he was doing. He was hoping that if he played his cards right Stella might lend him her car. It didn't look good; she had crossed her arms over that wonderful chest of hers and, pale-faced and silent, appeared to be sucking her teeth. Dark eyes watched his every move.

'I know you're disappointed but I haven't got the time to hang around to explain. Those men this morning, at the caravan?' Bernie continued. 'Let's just say they weren't from the gas board after all. I don't want you to be muddled up in this, Stella, it might get dangerous and messy. But I do want to take you out again – I really did have a lovely time and you truly are an amazing woman. I should be back tomorrow, probably – maybe the day after. I'm really sorry.'

It was almost the truth; certainly the bit about being sorry but perhaps not the bit about coming back. How long would it take the police to find his caravan? Five, ten minutes at most? How much information did they have? From somewhere close by Bernie could hear the sharp, agitated sound of little dogs barking and wondered if one of them was Stella's mother's parrot.

'I see,' Stella said coolly; she didn't sound or look at all convinced. 'Why don't you just say you don't want to see me again, James?' And then she paused and added, 'You know my mother said you looked like trouble.'

Feeling wounded Bernie was about to protest that he hadn't even met Stella's mother when a crisp vision of some wizened old bat watching his progress across the village green sprung into his mind. Bernie could almost see her studying him through a set of high-powered binoculars from an upstairs window.

'I thought we'd had a really nice time,' said Stella.

'We did and it was great,' he protested. 'Honestly – I truly mean it. I've already told you that I'd really like to do it again.' On the walk over it had crossed Bernie's mind to ask her to come along to Norfolk for the ride but then again there were just too many things he would have to explain – like Maggie, for a start.

Maggie. Her name switched on like a neon light in Bernie's head, refocusing his mind and sharpening his resolve.

'It's not like I don't want to see you again, Stella – it isn't that at all. It's just that I can't see you tonight.' Bernie looked down at his feet. Given another half an hour he knew from experience that he could have won her round, but he didn't have half an hour and it didn't look like he was going to get the car, either. 'I have to be going.'

'You could have rung me,' Stella said huffily, pulling her robe tighter. 'You're all the same, you men, take what you want and then bugger off, just like that. I feel used,' she snapped and, turning on her heel, scuttled back into the post office.

Bernie sighed. There was no time to protest his innocence and so he headed out towards the main road. It was early evening and still quite light, although the heat was leeching out of the day. As he passed the front of the shop he pulled a piece of card out of the bin, hoping that Stella's mother had got her spyglass pointed elsewhere, took a felt-tip pen from his jacket pocket and wrote 'Cambridge/A14' in big bold letters. At the next junction he stuck out his thumb and tried hard not to look like an escapee from a lunatic asylum.

'Do you want me to drive for a little while?' asked Nick. 'Give you a bit of a break?'

'No, you're all right,' said Maggie. 'Why? Bored already are you?'

'No, it's just that if I drove for a few miles you could eat that ice cream without having to steer with your knees,' he said, grinning at her.

'I am *not* steering with my knees.'

'You are.'

She made a face. Nick held up his hands in surrender. 'All right, all right, I'm not going to argue with you,' he said, and then, 'How much further is it? Are we nearly there yet?'

Maggie looked across at Nick and laughed. 'Oh come off it – it'll be absolutely ages before we get there. You sound like one of the boys. Just eat your sweets and relax; enjoy the scenery. It's a lovely drive and a beautiful evening. Chill out.'

Nick's expression didn't change. 'I would if I didn't have to keep worrying about what you were going to do next,' he said.

'What do you mean, *what I'm going to do next?* Are you criticising my driving?'

'No, no, not at all. I'm impressed, so far you've tuned in the radio, changed the tape over, rung up the holiday place to let them know we're coming, opened a bottle of water and now you're eating an ice cream. What's next? A crossword puzzle and a bit of light reading?'

Maggie looked at him, eyes alight with mischief. 'Are you serious? Oh for God's sake, Nick, lighten up. Although actually there is a crossword-puzzle book in the back if you fancy doing one. You could read out the clues. I'll even let you write the answers in; I enjoy a good cross-word.'

They had been driving for the best part of two hours. The daylight was slowly fading, the sun dipping down into the western sky, tingeing everything with a delicate golden light. Maggie was right, it was a glorious evening.

Nick folded his arms over his chest. 'Coleman said that he was going to send in a crash team to pick me up.'

Maggie looked across at him. 'Yes, he did, and he also said you would be perfectly safe at my cottage and that there was no such person as Bernie Fielding. Call me cynical if you like but it's not the most impressive track record I've ever come across.'

He shook his head in exasperation. 'I know, but I *need* Coleman. I need him and his bloody relocation squad to keep me safe and help me start over again. I can't do this on my own, Maggie. I'm a chef, not some kind of undercover super-sleuth. Those people will kill me if they can find me. This is not some game. I'm deadly serious. I have to believe that Coleman can make this come right.'

Up until that moment Maggie had almost had a bunking-off-work feeling about the drive, her sense of relief and elation increasing with every mile, but the tension in Nick's voice knocked the feeling right out of her.

'You're not on your own. You can ring Coleman when we get to the beach hut and arrange for him to come and pick you up from there. Surely as far as Stiltskin is concerned one place is much the same as another?'

Nick shook his head. 'God this is such a mess.'

'We had to leave,' Maggie said as gently and persuasively as she could. 'You saw that trailer on TV – we couldn't stay at the cottage. You'll be fine now.'

'If you tell me that this is just a glitch –' Nick said, swinging round to glare at her.

'I wouldn't dream of it,' Maggie said. 'But it will be all right. Cross my heart.' Making the gesture with the hand that she had the ice cream in, Maggie was going to add 'hope to die' but decided under the circumstances it probably wasn't appropriate.

Recovering his composure Nick picked up the map. 'Okay. So where did you say we're going to again?'

Maggie swung round to point out their destination on the road map he was holding. The car swerved with her.

'Just tell me where it is,' Nick growled, hastily shaking the map out straight. 'And keep your bloody eyes on the road, will you? I want there to be something left for Coleman to rescue.'

'You worry too much,' Maggie laughed. 'It's a little cove in the Bristol Channel. Find Minehead first and then come back a little way. It's not far from Watchet, near East Quantoxhead. St Elfreda's Bay.'

Nick looked at her blankly.

'Here, give it to me, let me show you,' she said with a broad grin, making as if to take it away from him.

Nick held the big, badly creased map tight against his chest like a security blanket. Maggie laughed again and licked at her ice cream. 'You are such a big baby.'

'Am not,' he snapped, but she could finally see flicker of humour lighting behind his eyes.

'So tell me again, Robbie, if we filmed the wrong man, why is it that we're going back to West Brayfield?' asked Lesley anxiously, peering out at the passing countryside careering by the car's windows. 'I don't understand. I thought you said we were going to go out for a meal and a drink tonight?'

'You're right, I did say that we would eat out and we will, but not yet. The thing is that they're not answering the phone,' growled Robbie, pulling out from behind some cretin driving a classic Jag at forty-five miles an hour in a flat cap and driving gloves. Old farts reliving their youth, they shouldn't be allowed out on the bloody roads.

Robbie had not been best pleased to find that Madam Upstairs had pulled the plug on his Bernie Fielding special at the last minute. Bitch. No consultation, not so much as a word to him. It was a personal insult – particularly as once he'd finished editing Robbie had spent the rest of the afternoon in the office composing his speech for the Journalist of the Year Award. Sodding bloody woman.

And that stupid bloke from Norfolk had made a complete and utter fool of him, although in his mind Robbie was rapidly transferring the blame squarely onto Bernie Fielding's shoulders. Bernie-fucking-Fielding's prints were all over this one; Robbie could almost hear the smug bastard laughing at him. Well, he'd be laughing on the other side of his face when Robbie Hughes caught up with him. Oh yes he would.

Robbie slapped his hand down hard on the car horn to frighten a woman in a blue Renault out of the middle lane. 'Move out of the way you gormless bitch,' he shouted, powering up behind her and roaring past as she squeaked into the slow lane.

'I thought you said we were going to the Lamb tonight,' said Lesley, in a nervous undertone. She looked a little pale. Robbie put his foot down hard and stormed past the Renault and a dozen others. It felt good. That's what he needed, a bit of speed, a renewed sense of his own power, his own dominance. He was alpha male on a mission.

'What I want to know is why didn't that stupid bugger tell us that he wasn't Bernie Fielding?' Robbie growled.

'I think he tried to,' said Lesley, voice tight. 'Aren't we a bit close to that van?'

'He didn't try very bloody hard, did he?' Robbie snapped back, braking furiously within six feet of the van in front. White vans were all the bloody same; all driven by brainless morons. 'He should have told us – he *could* have told us. Besides, you told me that when you rang the cottage his ex-wife said that Bernie was there.'

'Well, yes, she did,' Lesley protested. 'She said that she could hardly throw him out on the street even though the thought had crossed her mind.'

Robbie, eyes bright, said, 'Exactly. And when we got there she didn't deny he was there, did she? Oh no. She just said that Bernie was out in the garden. *Out in the garden*, that's what she said. We've got it on the bloody videotape.'

Lesley nodded, her expression suggesting that she hadn't got a clue what Robbie was going on about. He sighed in exasperation. Bright girl like Lesley and she just couldn't read the signs when they were there, all laid out in front of her like cue cards.

Robbie had been mulling the conversation he had had with Maggie Morgan over and over in his mind since Madam Upstairs had called him into her office and announced she was pulling the plug on the Bernie Fielding special. Madam had gone on to give him a long expletive-ridden lecture on the importance of a chain of command and how his actions had been a waste of the station's precious resources not to mention the risk of denting their media credibility.

But now that Robbie had had the chance to think, he had been kicking himself for what he was convinced he had missed while they were in West Brayfield. How could he have been so stupid as to have overlooked what was now so glaringly bloody obvious? Bernie Fielding had been there at the cottage all the time and let some other poor sucker take the fall for him.

'*So*,' Robbie said slowly so that Lesley could keep up with him. 'What if Bernie *was* there all along and we missed him? What if he really *was* in the garden but we didn't see him?' Robbie looked at his assistant triumphantly. 'That's what she said, didn't she? "Bernie is in the garden." Surely to God she must know her own husband.'

Lesley's eyes narrowed as comprehension dawned. 'Oh yes, I see what you're saying now – I suppose that it's a possibility.'

'It's more than a possibility, it's bloody obvious. Bernie most probably spotted the cameras and the outside broadcast van and hid in the shed, or went next door. He could have done anything, but she did say he was there. In which case it makes sense to start looking for our Mr Fielding back at the cottage, back where we left off,' Robbie said. 'Now just get the map out and see which junction we have to come off at, will you?'

Lesley pulled the road map out of the glove compartment. 'Robbie, I'm not very good at this sort of thing,' she said nervously. 'Not with maps and stuff. I get into a flap with directions. Under pressure I tend to forget which is right and which is left.'

'Don't be so ridiculous,' snapped Robbie, 'it's very simple. Just look at the big map on the back of the book and find the page we're on – a child could do it. Just look for Cambridge.' He waved a hand towards the road atlas.

'Yes, Robbie,' Lesley said miserably, turning the pages frantically. 'Cambridge you said?'

Robbie sighed. 'Yes, Cambridge.' God save him from women. His wife, the Bitch Upstairs, that stupid woman who was married to Bernie Fielding, and now Lesley. Lesley of all people.

He had been thinking that if it looked as if they were going to be late back they would book into a hotel, but now he wasn't so sure. He could feel his blood pressure rising. Wouldn't do to have a heart attack while on the job, would it? What would it look like in the press? Brush with death for TV anchorman in secret love tryst. Robbie cringed; he could almost see the headlines now, there was bound to be some terrible play on words involving *Gotcha*.

There might be no such thing as bad publicity but Madam Upstairs would go ballistic about what it would do to their serious journalistic credibility. And shagging your PA was so passé, he thought, mimicking his bitch of a boss. And with all the stress Robbie was under it was possible – more than possible – probable – that he'd have a heart attack or worse. And besides, Lesley was beginning to get on his nerves.

'Well, where are we then, woman?' he snapped.

Lesley had turned the atlas upside down and was busy running her finger along what looked suspiciously like the road to Grimsby.

'I told you to look for Cambridge,' he growled.

'I am,' she whimpered miserably.

'It's in East Anglia.'

'I thought Grimsby was in East Anglia,' she said, pushing her glasses up onto the bridge of her nose.

Robbie groaned. Bloody women.

In West Brayfield, Mrs Eliot, Maggie's next door neighbour was enjoying the last of the evening sunlight. She had been busy outside on the terrace watering the hanging baskets while it was cooler but still light. It had been a really nice day so far. Mrs Eliot stretched, pressing her hands into the aching hollow of her back and then walked into the kitchen and plugged in the kettle.

Puffing a little from her exertions the old lady washed her hands. The kettle clicked off the boil and, glancing up at the kitchen clock, Mrs Eliot thought what a shame it was that Maggie wasn't home. They often got together in the evening to talk about the day and the kids over a mug of tea and a slice of cake.

It was a pity Maggie had had to go back to the beach hut. It always sounded like such a long drive. She hoped it wasn't anything too drastic, things always seemed so pricey these days.

As she made the tea, Mrs Eliot glanced at the postcard the boys had sent her. It looked like a lovely place, though. At least this time Maggie had gone with that nice new young man of hers, Mrs Eliot smiled, and not before time either. He looked familiar, she was sure she had seen him around somewhere but couldn't quite place the face. That girl spent far too long on her own with just the boys for company. It would do her good to have a decent man in her life again. Life could be so lonely all on your own.

She pulled out a tray from behind the bread bin. There was just enough time to make a cup of tea and a ham sandwich before *Holby City* started. She enjoyed having Maggie and the kids living next door, not like the rest of the old farts who lived in the Row; they didn't know what living was, most of them. Nothing ever happened down this end of the village and she barely saw another living soul when Maggie wasn't at home. Life hadn't been the same since her Albert passed on, God rest his soul. Mrs Eliot took the tray and settled down in the big armchair by the hearth. It had been Albert's chair when he was alive. She had started sitting in it because she couldn't bear to look at it empty and somehow it had made her feel closer to him; not to mention that she'd discovered it was a lot comfier than hers.

Mrs Eliot settled back and eased off her slippers, slipped her teeth out, put them on the mantelpiece in her hankie and then picked up the remote control. The television screen flickered into life just as the opening credits started to roll; perfect timing. She'd just settle down in the chair and close her eyes for a few minutes, just until the story started.

When Mrs Eliot opened her eyes again it was almost dark in the sitting room. She must have fallen asleep because something had most definitely woken her up. From outside came the sound of voices and tyres on gravel. Surely Maggie couldn't be back already and it was too close to be Mrs Green and that snooty daughter of hers at number twenty-eight. A moment or two later there was a loud rapping at the door. Mrs Eliot slipped in her teeth, fixed the chain on the front door and turned on the outside light before she called out, 'Who is it?'

'Gas,' said a man's voice firmly.

'Oh, right you are,' she said, a little surprised. 'You're out late tonight, is there some sort of problem? I thought you'd finished with the boiler the other day?'

'Emergency call-out,' said the man briskly. 'Someone has reported a suspected leak. Sorry to disturb you, Ma'am.'

Mrs Eliot opened the door up just a fraction and peered out into the gathering gloom.

'Do you want to look at my gas stove? I only had it serviced about three months ago, that and the fire in the sitting room. I've got the receipt somewhere,' she began.

'No you're all right. Actually we're looking for the lady who lives next door,' said the taller of the two men.

Mrs Eliot looked him up and down. They were very well dressed for tradesmen. 'Oh right,' she said. 'Was there some sort of problem with her boiler?'

The man shook his head. 'I've got no idea, Ma'am.'

Probably a different branch, Mrs Eliot thought. Same old story right hand not knowing what the left hand was doing. 'Well, I'm terribly sorry but Maggie – Mrs Morgan – isn't there at the moment, she's gone to down to Somerset to sort out something with her beach hut.'

'Her beach hut? All right for some, eh?' The man nodded and then continued casually, 'Right you are, then. Long way to drive. On her own, was she?' As he spoke he appeared to be looking at a sheet of paper as if it had instructions or something written on it.

'No, she took the boys and she's got a really nice young man with her. Tall, good-looking – I wouldn't have minded going to Somerset with him myself,' said Mrs Eliot flirtatiously.

The man laughed but still didn't look up from the sheet of paper.

'Her husband, is it?' he said, apparently just making conversation as he ticked things off on his sheet.

'Goodness me, no,' said Mrs Eliot. 'No, he's some new chap, I don't know where she met him but he looks very nice, though. Clean. Nice eyes –'

'Right you are – so do you know where we can contact her? I wouldn't press the matter only we really need to know where she is. It's an emergency.'

'A gas emergency,' said the thicker set man who was standing behind the taller one. He didn't seem quite as clever as the one with the sheet of paper but then anyone who wore sunglasses after dark wasn't the brightest bulb in the marquee.

'I'm not all together sure,' said Mrs Eliot, considering. 'You'd better come in for a minute and I'll have a little look. I think I've got her mobile-phone number somewhere. Would that

161

do? Oh hang on – have you got any identification?'

The man smiled and took a card out of his top pocket. Mrs Eliot peered at it. It was hard to make out in the gloom without her glasses, but the photo looked like him.

'You can't be too careful these days,' she said, slipping the chain off the latch, 'You see such terrible things on the telly.'

'Indeed you do.' The man with the sheet of paper smiled and stepped into the hallway. He was smiling; and as he passed, Mrs Eliot thought what lovely sharp white teeth he had.

9

'Where the fuck are we, woman?' roared Robbie, snatching the map from Lesley's trembling hands. 'This is completely ridiculous. We should have been in West Brayfield bloody hours ago.' He didn't add, you stupid, stupid woman, but they both knew that that was what he was thinking.

Outside the night was velvety black. There were no streetlights, no road signs and the only hint of civilisation was a distant row of yellow lights, like fairy lights on what might or might not have been the horizon.

Lesley sniffed miserably. 'I'm sorry. I did tell you –'

Sorry didn't cut it by a long way. Robbie sighed and folded the road atlas back on itself to the page where he hoped – where Lesley had told him – they were.

'If he's gone, if we miss him because of this

bloody fiasco –' Robbie spat. 'Now let me see, where are we – Cambridge, A10. Hold the damned torch steady, will you?'

Lesley whimpered, the beam trembling across the swirl of roads and rivers and mountains. Mountains? Robbie looked again and felt his blood pressure rising. Mountains in Norfolk? He glared at her and then sighed with frustration. 'Would you care to point out exactly where you *think* we are?' he said in a murderous tone.

A great big tear rolled down Lesley's cheek.

'And crying won't help,' he snapped.

'Here,' she said.

'Snowdonia?' he asked.

Lesley nodded.

Robbie threw the map into the back of the car.

'Are we there yet?' said Nick, yawning and stretching as far as the seat would allow.

'Oh for God's sake, you really are a big kid, aren't you? Enjoy your nap?'

'I haven't been asleep,' said Nick defensively.

'Oh really? What, is it just habit then, that makes you snore while you're awake? If it is it's not attractive. Certainly not sexy.'

Nick straightened his clothes and surreptitiously wiped his face. Maggie suspected it was to get rid of the crusty rivulet of drool on his chin but didn't say anything.

'Anyway I wouldn't dare go to sleep while you

were driving –' he said, wide awake now and staring fixedly out at the road.

'Charming. So what were you planning to do, improve my driving by the power of your unconscious mind? If you're that good, open a can of Coke for me, will you? I'm thirsty.'

Nick rummaged around in the footwell, and then in a bag on the back seat, and then said, 'I've found one, but wouldn't it be better to stop and stretch our legs, find a pub or something?'

Maggie sighed. 'Probably, but all I really want to do is get there now – it's not that far and I'm knackered and stiff, and to be perfectly honest if we stop I might not be able to persuade my body to get back into the car.'

Nick shifted his weight. 'Okay, but I've already told you that I don't mind doing some of the driving if you want a break.'

Maggie's expression hardened. 'Kind of you to offer but you're not insured.'

Her hands instinctively tightened on the steering wheel. She'd lost one too many cars to her ex-husband. Bernie Fielding was a man who wasn't adverse to telling her that the family runabout was going off for a service only for her to discover – much later – that he had either sold it or it had been repossessed – and that somewhere between the garage and the trip home it had mysteriously vanished forever.

'Sorry, but nobody is going to drive my car,

especially not anybody called Bernie Fielding. I wouldn't let Bernie Fielding drive any of my cars ever again. Every insurance policy I've had since I left him has got an anti-Bernie Fielding clause written somewhere into the small print.'

'But I'm not really Bernie Fielding, you know that –' Nick protested, popping the lid on the Coke can and handing it to her.

Maggie snatched the drink from his outstretched hand.

'He really pissed you off, didn't he?' said Nick. 'It's amazing after all these years you're still so angry about him. You're so laid back about everything else. He must have really done the dirty on you to make you this wary.'

Maggie snorted and took a long pull on the can of drink. 'Nick, let me explain something to you. Bernie does the dirty on everybody he ever meets. I wasn't singled out for special treatment. He can't help it, it's what Bernie does best. That thing today with the film crew? It brought it all back in glorious Technicolor.

'You have no idea – I used to get little old ladies ringing up all hours of the night and day to remind Bernie about the building work he'd promised to do for them – and they'd paid upfront for, of course. There were deliveries of all sorts of dodgy stuff from China and the Far East. Almost always followed some time later by some guy from the council who would turn up to ban whatever was in the packing cases from going anywhere, least of all on sale, sometimes with the help of a health inspector or the police, or customs and excise. When I was married to Bernie I met them all. And it wasn't just the long line of official bodies that I met – oh no, there were the women he was sleeping with dropping by – sometimes with their enraged husbands for company, sometimes with their fathers or their brothers. They were always a little bit surprised to find me there. Then one day it was Bernie's ex-wife after her maintenance. Oh and then his mother came round one after-noon to pick up the family heirlooms he had promised to have valued by a good friend of his. You'd have thought she would have known better.

And then Bernie would borrow money from all over the place, lots of money, money to finance all sorts of half-baked, crackpot, off-the-bloody-wall ideas. At one point I was on first name terms with the bailiffs.'

Maggie took a deep breath – the first one in a long time and glanced across at the face of her captive audience, he didn't move a muscle or say a single word, so Maggie continued. 'My furniture and household effects travelled more than I did. I must be the only woman in history who divorced her husband for the financial security. Oh yes, life with Bernie was a laugh a minute. Living with Bernie Fielding was like having the circus come to town. So, in answer to your question, yes he really did piss me off, and if I never hear or see him again it will be too soon. Much too soon. Okay? Does that answer your questions?'

'So, you don't want me to drive, then?'

'No, I bloody-well don't,' snapped Maggie, and with that she thrust the can back at him.

'Well, that didn't go too badly at all, did it?' said Nimrod, pulling his jacket sleeves down over his gloves and flicking fluff from his lapels. He eased himself carefully back into the passenger seat of the hire car. 'A job well done.'

Cain grinned. 'Lovely drop of tea as well. What was that you flashed the old biddy?'

Nimrod pulled a little laminated card out of his top pocket. 'My health-club membership. I forgot to take to out of my jacket before I left. I was going to destroy it – I mean it's not what you want to be carrying with you on a job – but then again it just goes to show. Everything in this life happens for a purpose.'

'Is that Zen as well, then?' said Cain, turning the key in the ignition.

Nimrod nodded. 'I should say so,' and with that he turned on the radio scanner to pick up the police channel. In his hand he had the post-card that Maggie's boys had sent to Mrs Eliot while they were away on holiday. Not that she knew he'd taken it. He'd slipped it into his pocket while she was out in the kitchen making them both a nice cup of tea and worrying about not being able to find Maggie's mobile number.

It was an aerial picture of a sun-drenched and very secluded tree-lined cove. Printed on the back were the words, 'St Elfreda's Bay, East Quantoxhead, near Minehead, Somerset,' and on the front in biro someone had kindly ringed a little wooden cabin and written in a scrawling childish hand: 'we are here.'

Nimrod grinned and slid it back into his inside pocket. Bingo.

'So are we going to drive down there tonight?' asked Cain, pulling out of the driveway of Maggie's cottage.

Nimrod shook his head thoughtfully. 'Nah. I reckon the pair of them think that they're home free. I can't see any point busting a gut to get down there tonight – what is it, a five or six hour drive? We'd have heard if the feds had already been in and picked Mr Lucas up. Let's go and get ourselves some kip, there'll be time enough tomorrow. Besides I fancy a beer and we need to let his nibs know what's going on. Let him call the shots – we aren't paid enough to think for ourselves.'

Cain nodded. As they got to the top of the little lane that led down to The Row, a car – its head-lights blazing – roared past them into the village.

'Look at that stupid bastard,' growled Cain. 'He could have killed somebody.'

* * *

'Excuse me but I think you've just missed the turning back there, Robbie,' said Lesley nervously, looking over her shoulder up the narrow and very dark country road.

'What do you mean I've missed the turning?' snapped Robbie. 'An hour ago you didn't know which bloody country we were in.'

'It was back there on the left; I'm sure I saw the street sign.'

'Then why didn't you say something?' One way and another, Robbie had had quite enough.

'You were going too fast and there was a car pulling out of it.'

'Oh yes, that's it, blame me, why don't you? Whose fault is it that we ended up halfway to Whitby?'

Lesley reddened furiously as Robbie did a squealing U-turn in a pub car park. 'We've wasted bloody hours because of you.'

Lesley mumbled something.

'What did you say?' he snapped.

'I said I've never seen you like this. Why are you so angry with me?' she whined. 'I did tell you that I wasn't very good with maps. I'm tired and I've had enough and there's no need to speak to me like that. I've done my best, I want to go home now.'

Robbie snorted, his voice heavy with sarcasm. 'What, when we're almost there? Don't be so ridiculous, and where the hell would you go anyway? What do you want me to do, Lesley, eh? Drop you off at the nearest tube station?' They both looked up and down the narrow, unlit country road.

'I just wanted you to know,' she said miserably, tucking her hands into the sleeves of her cardigan.

'Well thank you for sharing that with me,' said Robbie, swinging the car into the top end of The Row. 'Now if we can just get back to the job in hand.'

The pretty rose-trimmed cottage that they had visited earlier in the day was now in total darkness; although oddly enough Robbie was almost certain that he spotted a figure scurrying away from the car lights as he pulled up in Maggie Morgan's driveway.

'Right – now no nonsense, let me do the talking and keep your eyes peeled. Do you understand?' said Robbie.

Lesley nodded.

'Good.' Robbie took one final look in the rear-view mirror to check his hair and then headed off up the path. The security light flashed on before they were halfway with a beam so bright it felt like being centre stage at the London Palladium. Robbie straightened his tie. 'Do you want to just nip back to the car and get the video camera?' he said, without turning.

Lesley did as she was told.

Robbie must have rung the doorbell for the best

part of ten minutes before finally conceding that there might not be anybody at home. There were lights on in the adjoining house, though, and so he headed round to the next cottage, eyes bright with frustration, and knocked smartly on the door. A moment or two later the door opened just a crack.

'Hello,' said Robbie jovially. 'And what's your name?'

'It's nearly ten o'clock,' said the reedy voice from inside. 'What do you want?'

'I'm so sorry to disturb you so late but this is very important. I need to know if you have seen your neighbours at all recently? Maybe you recognise me – I'm on the television?' said Robbie warmly, laying on an over-abundance of bonhomie to the old lady at number thirty-two, who peered suspiciously at him through the narrow gap between the doorframe and the door, held at bay by six inches of stout chain.

The old woman looked him up and down. 'It's funny you should ask that; she seems to be very popular at the moment. What's going on?'

Robbie stiffened. The old girl sounded as sharp as a tack. 'Sorry?'

The woman screwed up her eyes and looked at him all the harder, and then after a few moments thought, she said, 'Oh, I know who you are – I've seen you on the telly –'

Robbie preened a little. 'Well yes, thank you –

I hoped that you might recognise me. Some people say I've got a very memorable face. Distinguished –' he began, throwing his shoulders back.

The old lady sniffed. 'You're that bloke off the advert for cat food, aren't you? The one that wears the mouse suit. My cat won't touch the stuff – all lungs and lites by the smell of it.'

Behind him Robbie heard Lesley snigger, but decided to ignore her. 'About your neighbour,' he continued, pulling the conversation back on track.

'Well it's odd that you want to talk to her, too – you do know she hasn't got a cat, don't you?'

Wearily, Robbie nodded.

'First of all it was them two men from the gas board and then that ex-husband of hers turned up, bold as brass, nice as you like, and wanted to know where she'd gone. Funny, if you ask me, she never said anything about people coming round.'

Robbie's ears pricked up. 'When you say her ex-husband, do you mean Bernie Fielding?'

The woman nodded. 'Yes I do – I've known him years. He lived in the village.'

'Really,' said Robbie. 'And how long ago was he here?'

But the old lady was already way ahead of him. 'He was no good at all that bloke. Always was a little shite – I told him that Maggie didn't want him running after her. Not now. It's too little too late, I said; she's got herself a nice new fella now.'

Robbie leant forward so that as much of him as possible was squeezed in the space between the door and the frame. 'We are talking about Bernie Fielding, aren't we?' He spoke slowly and very clearly in case the old woman was deafer or dafter than she appeared. And when she didn't answer, he asked again. 'You *are* talking about Bernie Fielding, aren't you?'

The old woman glared at him. 'Well of course I am, I'm not stupid – the slimy little bugger, he told me that she was in trouble, big trouble, and that he had come to warn her about it. Not that I'd believe a word Bernie told me; he'd sell his own granny, he would.' And then she paused and added. 'Actually you've only just missed him.'

Robbie felt his pulse rate lift. 'What, what do mean only just missed him? How long ago was he here?'

She pulled a face and shrugged. 'I dunno, five, ten minutes at the most, I'm surprised that you didn't see him as you drove down the lane –'

Robbie shook his head in frustration. So that was who the shadowy figure had been. He tried hard not to dwell on it. 'And did Bernie say where he was going?'

'He said he's going to go and find Maggie. I did tell him that I didn't know where she was

174

going, only that she and this new chap had gone off to the seaside for a few days to fix something, and he said, "Oh yes, of course." And then he said whereabouts it was only I can't for the life of me remember now.' She screwed up an already well-crumpled face to search for the thought.

'I'm sure you can remember if you try,' encouraged Robbie. 'You have to understand that this is very, very important.'

The old woman stared at him. 'You're not here about the gas leak as well, are you?'

Robbie stared back at her; she was quite obviously senile after all. 'No dear – I'm here about your neighbour, Maggie, and her ex-husband Bernie Fielding, you remember?' he said, enunciating more clearly. 'I just need to know where he – where *she* went.'

The old woman peered at him, eyes as bright as coals. 'Well, to be honest I don't know that I can help you, and I'm not sure I like your tone – I'm a little bit deaf not bloody stupid.'

She made to close the door but before the catch caught Robbie was in there with a flat palm to hold it ajar. 'I'm sorry,' he said. 'But you must remember. I'm sure you do really,' he toadied.

She sighed. 'I don't know – Bernie said she was going to – ooh, it's a funny name –' The old woman pulled a face, as if gurning might help. 'It's on the very tip of my tongue. He said it – but I just don't remember, it's so damned annoying. It'll probably come to me after you've gone. I think it's in Somerset. It's a queer name –'

Robbie pasted over the cracks in his smile. God help him if he didn't strangle the daft old bitch through the gap in the door. He could feel his blood pressure rising and didn't know how much further his patience would stretch.

'Like what?' said Lesley very pleasantly from somewhere behind him. 'What can you remember about it?'

The woman sucked at her top lip and then said, 'It's a religious thing – a saint's name, I think, but unusual –'

'Saint Anne's?' Lesley offered.

'Oh no, much odder than that, sounds foreign.'

'Saint Mary's. Saint B—'

'Saint bloody-Woolwich-ferry,' Robbie snapped. 'She said unusual – foreign – this is getting us nowhere.'

The old lady looked up, ignoring Robbie, her attention fixed on Lesley's face instead. 'I wish I *could* remember. It's really beginning to annoy me now. Saint – Saint –?' She looked for all the world as if she was reaching round inside her head for the answer; it was almost more than Robbie could bear.

'Come on, come on,' he hissed under his breath. 'How hard can it be, you can't have that much to think about at your age – what time's tea and where your teeth are –'

'Somerset, you said?' Lesley was saying conversationally, getting the road map out of her briefcase.

Robbie groaned. Some help that was likely to be. Beside him Lesley flicked on the torch.

'Have you any idea whereabouts it is, roughly?'

'In Somerset –'

Robbie's temper was almost at boiling point. They would be lucky if Lesley could find England. Beside him she poured over the map book running her finger down the Saints' names listed in the index.

'Do you know where it is near to?' she said.

'Minehead, I think –' said the old woman. 'I did have her mobile-phone number here somewhere as well but I can't remember where I put that either – I only had it here a minute ago.'

Lesley smiled. 'Don't worry –' and with that she began to read the Saints' names aloud.

Robbie wanted to throttle her. It would take forever and there was no guarantee Mrs-bloody-Whatever-her-name-was would recognise the name even if she heard it, but framed in the wedge of light the old lady nodded and listened and then all of a sudden, as if a button had been pressed in her head, she said, 'That's it, that's it – St Elfreda's Bay. St Elfreda's Bay, East Quantoxhead, near Minehead, Somerset. Oh I'm glad I remembered, it was really beginning to craze me.'

Robbie stared at Lesley in total amazement. 'I

might not be good with maps but I'm very good with lists,' she said triumphantly.

Bernie took a short cut across the fields at the back of The Row where Maggie lived and then on through the playing field at the back of West Brayfield village hall until he had finally made his way back out onto the main road.

He looked at his watch. It was getting late and chilly and he was tired. Although at least Bernie knew that Maggie was safe for the moment. The news that the gasmen had already been to the cottage didn't bear thinking about, but the only good thing was that Mrs Eliot couldn't tell them any more than she had told Bernie – except that every instinct told him that they wouldn't be long in finding out what they wanted. Whoever they were, they weren't acting alone. That was for certain. Bernie knew that it wasn't a question of *if* they found Maggie but *when*.

He pulled the new mobile out of his jacket pocket and tapped in the number of Maggie's mobile that he had pinched from under a magnet on Mrs Eliot's fridge. He wasn't altogether surprised when after ringing twice he got her voicemail service. It had been a while since Bernie had heard her voice and it made him smile; good girl was Maggie. He had never quite understood exactly why she left him, but then again she'd been young, maybe she just needed to find her feet, see a bit of the world.

'Maggie, this is Bernie here. I know I must be the last person on earth you expected to hear from but I want you to listen to me. You have to get away from St Elfreda's as soon as you possibly can. This is not bullshit, Maggie. You have to understand, there are two guys coming after the man that you're with. The thing is, babe, the pair of you are in real danger and for once it's got nothing to do with me.' It wasn't exactly true, Bernie thought, and was about to try and explain some more when his calling credit ran out.

He looked back at the football field. Tendrils of mist were rising up out of the drainage dykes on the far side of the road and were rolling towards him across the tarmac like avenging wraiths. The cool of the evening made him shiver. Bernie shoved his hands deep in his pockets and looked up the road. The pub was still open, the only welcoming sight for miles in any direction.

He'd done what he could, hadn't he? Maggie was bound to pick her messages up sooner or later. Wasn't she? And what could he do against two professional gasmen anyway? Now that he'd sorted things out Bernie decided to grab a couple of pints and a pie. Maybe he'd ring Stella to let her know that he was with her in spirit if not in body; keep his options open. He just needed a little change for the call box.

Hands in pockets, and head down, Bernie headed towards the lights trying to remember

179

what the state of play was between him and the landlady and whether he had ever paid off his tab. Fortunately there was a large sign in the car park that read 'Under New Management'.

Bernie made his way into the snug bar. The first pint didn't touch the sides, nor the second. He had a pie and a pickled egg and by the time he was halfway down the third pint Bernie began to feel the kinks easing out of his soul. Maybe it would be all right after all. He'd have another pint or two and then get on his way back to – Bernie hesitated, trying to focus on his destination – back to where exactly? Where could he go?

The caravan site behind the Old Dairy? Stella Conker-Eyes? Hardly. Maybe the crappy little bedsit he'd been shacked up in before the job in Colmore Road? It had to be said that life had been pinching Bernie pretty tight over the last few months.

But then again what if Maggie didn't switch on her mobile? What if she didn't get his message after all? Bernie sighed as the last pint vanished down to the suds. There was no escaping it, he still had to go down to Somerset to make sure that she was okay – but before he went anywhere he really had to have a kip and he knew just the place.

Bernie set the glass down on the counter and ambled out of the warmth of the pub back across the playing field. Glancing left and right to make sure that he wasn't being watched, he popped the back window on the sports pavilion and slithered in over the sill like a black cat. The interior smelt of damp netting, mould and sweat but at least it was dry and free. Taking off his nice new leather jacket Bernie curled up on one of the benches, pulled the coat up over his shoulders and, belying the old saying about the sleep of the just, was asleep in minutes.

10

'Oh, this is really quite nice, isn't it?' said Nick, looking round the spacious kitchen of the little beach hut. He sounded surprised, more than surprised, he sounded astounded. It was embarrassing.

'What were you expecting?' growled Maggie, following close behind him up the steps carrying a holdall and the box of groceries she'd brought with her from the cottage.

Nick reddened. 'I don't know, actually. Something a bit more Spartan, I suppose,' he said, lifting a hand to encapsulate the bright, cosy interior. 'You know, those little gas lights and pull-out beds made from tables and –'

'And a bucket in the corner?' she said grimly, sliding the food onto one of the kitchen counters before filling up the kettle and plugging it in. It had turned out to be a long, long drive. Nick might be deeply attractive but he could also be extremely annoying. Over the last twenty-five miles he must have asked her at least ten times how much longer and how much further it was. Even her youngest son Joe wasn't that bloody aggravating, nor did he criticise her driving.

Nick looked around again, with an expression on his face that wouldn't have been out of place on a tourist in the Sistine Chapel. 'I only stayed in a beach hut once before. I was about ten, I think – we went with my cousins to Skegness for a week. The flush toilets and the showers were in a wooden shed full of spiders on the other side of the site. We used to go in twos with a torch and a rolled-up newspaper in case they jumped out and attacked us. It rained the whole week. Put me off for life. But this is more like a bungalow, though, isn't it? Great kitchen. Is it yours? How far is it down to the beach? I should have brought my shorts.'

Maggie, face and mind grey with tiredness, stared at Nick in total astonishment and then burst out laughing. All this from a man who was supposed to be on the run.

'You're mad,' she said. 'I'll give you the Cook's tour first thing tomorrow morning, Nick. Just go and fetch the rest of the stuff out of the car, will you? I'm completely shattered. All I want to do at the moment is to have a cup of tea, get the beds made up and go to sleep.'

Nick walked towards the door and then hesitated. 'Do you think I should ring Coleman before we get settled in?'

Maggie shook her head. 'How the hell do I know? The only thing I know for certain is that I want today to be over and done with.' He didn't move, so Maggie continued. 'No one knows where we are. There'll be time enough tomorrow, and besides Coleman was hard enough to track down during office hours, God alone knows where he'll be on the wrong side of midnight.' She paused and, looking at Nick's anxious face, shrugged. 'But then what do I know?'

Nick sighed. 'I just wanted a second opinion from you, that's all – that and to say thank you.' As he spoke Nick stepped closer and hugged her, brushing a funny little self-conscious kiss across Maggie's cheek. 'I'm really grateful – actually, that doesn't cover it at all, but it's the best I can come up with at the moment.'

He was warm and smelt wonderful. 'It's all right,' Maggie stammered, 'don't mention it.' Instinctively she pulled away. God it was so tempting just to melt into him. 'It's nothing. Honestly.' It sounded as if she was being dismissive, which was stupid – obviously hiding fugitives wasn't something Maggie did every day of the week.

Nick grinned. 'I just wanted you to know. I don't know what I would have done without you –' he said, and then turned away.

With her pulse still cracking out a samba rhythm, Maggie watched him stroll back across the damp grass in the light from the kitchen window.

Okay, so maybe Nick Lucas was bloody annoying, but he also made her feel that zingy little something that was impossible to define, and he was gorgeous in a lived-in, slightly crinkled round the edges way. Not hard-faced at all, nothing like the face of a man you would imagine to be on the run. Nick Lucas just looked rumpled and crumpled and easy on the eye, like a good-natured hairy mongrel.

Damn. Maggie struggled furiously to whip her brain – not to mention her body – back into line, firmly reminding herself that Nick Lucas was also a walking time bomb, tick-tick-ticking away. One false move, one wrong step and it could all go horribly wrong, for both of them. In amongst the low-level lust she kept catching glimpses of just how dangerous things might get if they were caught.

Maggie sighed. Why was it she never seemed to be attracted to straight up-and-down men? Men who managed shops and wore suits and came home at half past five with a carrier full of yoghurts for the boys.

'Is this what you meant?' Nick said, reappearing with her duvet and a great pile of sheets and pillows as Maggie was just squeezing the teabags with a spoon.

'Yes thanks, that's great – you can just dump them on the sofa if you like. I'll take them through in a minute. You'd better go and get yours in, too – it can get really nippy in here if that wind picks up.'

Nick looked at her blankly. 'Mine?'

Maggie, taking a pull on the tea, nodded. 'Yes, yours – your bedclothes – I told you before we left to get your things, when we were back at the cottage. Duvet? Teddy and toothbrush?'

'Oh damn,' he paused and then pulled a face. 'Sorry, I didn't realise that you meant me to bring bedclothes as well.'

Maggie sighed. Of course not. He wouldn't, would he? Nick hadn't been in a beach hut since he was ten; what did he know? Maybe some hairy mongrels were not as bright as they looked. Maybe he had planned it all along, who knows . . . Maggie was way too tired to try and fathom the answer.

'Don't worry – there are some spare blankets in the – Oh shit,' she slapped her forehead and groaned. 'No, no there aren't. I took them home with me to wash. Bugger, bugger, bugger.'

Nick looked sheepish. 'Is that my tea?'

Maggie sat down. 'Yes – here –' she said. At least she knew they had teabags and milk.

'Are there any biscuits?' he said.

In a motel, not far from Swindon, Cain slipped his trousers out of the Corby trouser press and hung them very carefully over a wooden hanger, flicking away a minute fleck of something or other, all the while being watched by Nimrod, who was already in bed with a book. As Nimrod observed him, Cain looked round the room with a thoughtful sweeping gaze.

'If you turn that fucking TV on I'll break your fingers,' growled Nimrod.

'Don't be like that. I was going to turn the sound down. Wouldn't disturb you. I was just going to see how the darts was coming on –'

'It's not just the noise. I hate the light – all that flickering and stuff. Drives me nuts.'

Cain slipped into bed looking sullen and hard-done-by. 'I don't moan when you keep the light on so that you can read, do I?'

'That's only because you've got the bloody TV on all the time.'

The two men glared at each other and then looked away. Cain sniffed. Waiting didn't do either of them any favours. Seconds ticked past. Nimrod turned the page, aware of Cain's eyes boring into the back of his head.

'What?' he snapped. 'What is it now?' There was another pause and then he threw the book down. 'All right, all right, switch the bloody thing on, just don't have it up too loud.'

Cain picked up the remote. 'It'll all be over tomorrow,' he said calmly, as the screen crackled into life.

Nimrod nodded, the tension easing out of his shoulders. 'Yeah, I know. You're right. What is that, anyway?'

'Looks like late-night reruns of *Water Colour Challenge*. I love that Hannah Gordon –'

Nimrod sighed. Waiting was always the worst part.

At a nice little country five-star hotel a few miles down the road, Robbie Hughes was having problems of his own.

'What do you mean you're not in the mood? For Christ's sake, you're always saying if only we had more time alone together, Lesley. Come on, let me in. Why don't you just come out of there so that we can talk and have a little drink? I'll pour you something out of the mini-bar if you like, how about a Tia Maria? Or a Baileys, you like Baileys. Or we can have room service if you like – or we can go out. Are you hungry? Lesley, this is getting beyond a joke. Lesley!' he snapped finally. 'Let me in.'

Robbie was standing outside the bathroom door, his mouth pressed to the crack between the door and the frame. He had had to book the two of them into separate rooms, obviously – surely Lesley ought to understand that. What would people say back at the office if he'd just booked a double? His reputation as a clean-cut family man was very important to him and to the company.

He and his wife had been in a double-page spread in one of the Sunday magazines at Christmas: TV's avenger at home with the family. It had gone down very well with *Gotcha*'s target audience.

And all right, so Lesley's room wasn't *quite* as nice as his, but surely she must understand that it was all about rank and position and prestige, and besides Robbie hadn't planned that Lesley should spend much of the night in her room anyway.

'I've got some Anadin in my briefcase if you'd like some?' he said more gently.

The wood muffled Lesley's reply.

'I was just thinking it might help, you know, if you've got a headache or something.' He was beginning to lose patience and thumped on the door with the butt end of his clenched fist. 'If you'd just let me in, Lesley, we can talk about this. I'm a very reasonable man but I draw the line at conducting our relationship through a closed bloody door. Open up, will you? This is totally and utterly ridiculous.' Particularly, Robbie thought, as this was his bloody room anyway and there was no way he was going to go and sleep in that broom cupboard over the kitchens that they'd given her. Bloody women.

'Lesley!' he barked.

Caught in a jaundiced arena of lamplight Coleman had in front of him the complete data trail that traced Nick Lucas's life to date. He almost knew it by heart he'd read it so often. He could even see where the data had branched and the point at which everything had gone tits up. Up until now one of the great givens in Coleman's life was Stiltskin's infallibility. Witnesses may come and witnesses may go but Stiltskin lived forever. Under normal circumstances Coleman took on the new relocations until they were settled in, had calmed down and relaxed, and then he handed them onto someone lower down the food chain. If Stiltskin was compromised the repercussions were almost unthinkable. How many people would get caught in the fallout?

Despite interviewing the whole Stiltskin team one by one Coleman still didn't know and couldn't fathom was how this had happened and if it was likely to happen again. Or, come to that, where the fuck Nick Lucas was now.

He rubbed his eyes and tried hard to suppress a yawn. The crash team had gone in to pick Nick up from West Brayfield. They'd given the cottage the once over and come up empty. Coleman stared at the phone, willing it to ring, and for the first time in years wished that he had a cigarette. He pulled the nasal spray out of his top pocket and took a chug, relishing the little chemical hit it gave him as it cleared his sinuses.

The door to his office cracked open an inch or two. Coleman looked up in surprise. 'What are you still doing here?' he asked as a familiar face appeared around the door jamb.

Ms Crow tipped her head on one side. 'Funnily enough I was just going to ask you the very same question, Danny. I've been to the theatre this evening but I can't get this Nick Lucas thing out of my mind so I thought I'd just pop back and –' She looked down at the file of computer paper spread out across Coleman's desk and raised an eyebrow. 'Two minds with but a single thought?' she observed.

He nodded. 'And still no answers.'

'Well I'm sure you'll be relieved to know that I've found the source of one glitch. I've just come up from talking to the night shift and one of the girls downstairs owned up to having dumped James Cook from the data base in favour of Bernie Fielding.'

Coleman pulled a face and then threw his pen across the desk. 'Oh for fuck's sake. And her excuse was what exactly? PMS? A bad day? What was she hoping, that nothing would come of it? That it wouldn't show up somewhere? That it was her little secret? Jesus – there are error protocols that need to be followed. Has she got no idea that we are dealing with people's lives here, or what we've been frantically trying to sort out for the last two days?' he roared furiously, livid with frustration.

'Of course she knows – just calm down, Danny.

She said it was an accident. She'll be formally reprimanded; and she certainly won't do it again. I just don't think she had considered the possible repercussions. You look like you could use some coffee.' Dorothy Crow turned towards the percolator and added casually, 'Has our man rung in yet?'

Coleman shook his head. 'No. Looks like he ran away and to be perfectly honest I can't say I blame him. In his shoes, and given our recent track record, I'd have done exactly the same thing. We just need to find out where he's gone – simple.' Danny held up his hands in frustration.

Ms Crow took two mugs down off a shelf and swilled the thick slurry of coffee round the bottom of the pot on the machine.

'Don't worry, he'll ring in – they all do. You want to drink this or shall I make fresh?'

Coleman shrugged; he'd drunk far too much already. If they opened him up now his gut would be lined with a skin of coffee as black as tar and probably two inches thick.

'We'll track him down and bring him in, don't you worry. It's what we do best. We're like the Mounties; we always get our man. I'll just go and fetch some fresh water.'

Coleman snorted as Ms Crow headed off to the staff kitchen. He hoped that she was right and that they got it sorted out quickly before anything else went wrong. He looked down at the files again. He already knew from the notes made by the original investigating and assessment teams that Lucas's case was a Code Red; the two women and the organisations they were working for wouldn't stop until Nick Lucas was a stain on the carpet.

In the beach hut in Somerset, Nick was huddled up on one of the boy's bunk beds under a tartan picnic rug, two beach towels and a sheet. He was shivering. Or at least that was what Maggie had convinced herself. He had kissed her goodnight, and now he was in bed, shivering. All on his own. Two totally unrelated events that she was replaying over and over in her mind.

Outside, a raucous summer squall had rolled up off the Bristol Channel, and was currently backcombing the trees, bringing with it great sheets of driving rain. Maggie, snuggled up under her king-size duvet, was way beyond tired, with only her guilty conscience holding her eyelids open. Wide open.

She had been in bed ten, maybe fifteen minutes now.

'Go,' Nick had said, waving her away after she'd finished her tea. 'I'll be just fine. Really. It was my own stupid fault. Go on, go to bed, you look all in. I'm a big boy and after all it's only for tonight. I can always buy a sleeping bag tomorrow if Coleman doesn't come and get me –'

Outside, the wind ran round the bins, tipping the lids. Rain lashed against the windows, Mother

Nature cheerfully doing Hammer House of Horror movie impressions. Maggie's conscience poked her again; that poor man lying there in the dark, all alone, cold, probably freezing by now. She surrendered, sighed, got out of bed and, pulling on a shapeless tee shirt and dressing gown, headed out into the hallway.

She tapped on the door to the boys' room. 'Nick?' she whispered. 'Are you still awake?'

It was dark now, with just the light of a watery moon sneaking in through rain-crazed windows.

'Uh huh, what is it?' he said thickly, although Maggie couldn't work out exactly how awake or asleep he was.

'Nick, I don't want you to take this the wrong way but would you like to come and sleep with me. In my bed, I mean – I mean, that's not an offer – you know, I don't mean, er –' Maggie reddened, while struggling to find the right words. Any words. 'And it's raining outside.' She sounded pretty pathetic, she thought grimly.

'Come in,' Nick said, and as Maggie opened the door wider he switched on the bedside lamp. He looked ridiculous. He was curled up on the bottom bunk covered in sections by the plaid picnic rug and two beach towels with dolphins on them. He was bare-chested, with one long, slimmish but nevertheless muscular leg peeking out from under Flipper's artful beak. His feet hung over the end of the bed.

'So, do you want to come and sleep with me, then?' Bugger; that wasn't how she'd meant to say it. Maggie reddened up to a nice shade of rose the instant the words were out.

'I thought you'd never ask,' he said, with a slow sleepy grin.

'Don't push your luck,' Maggie muttered as he followed her back into the main bedroom. 'I'm not in the mood.'

Under his amused gaze Maggie very carefully arranged a wall of pillows down the middle of the bed.

'I can take a hint, you know,' Nick said as he clambered in alongside her and pulled up the duvet. He was dressed in black cotton boxer shorts – she tried not to think too much about that – and en route from his room he had pulled on a tee shirt, too. Ummmm, yes, nice bum and very nice legs purred the salacious part of her brain as she switched off the light.

As soon as she was horizontal Maggie closed her eyes and willed her mind to let go. After all, Nick was warm and comfy now. Her body was still hanging on tight to consciousness by its fingernails. If it would just let go and jump, Maggie knew that sleep would catch her on one of those big rubbery mats that fire crews always had in American films. She closed her eyes tighter and tried hard to block Nick out.

He smelt nice. Nice in a warm, musky, male

way that made her mouth water. It had been so long since she had slept with a man. Maggie stiffened as the thought gelled and then Nick moved, snuggling down, settling, rolling into a comfy space.

Damn. She lay in the dark for what seemed like an eternity, eyes resolutely closed, worrying that he might move closer, worried that he might not. For God's sake this was even more ridiculous than leaving him freezing in the spare room, complained one side of her brain, while the other side whined and struggled away from sleep's hold like a badly behaved child. What exactly did Maggie know about Nick Lucas anyway? He could wait until she was sound asleep and then do God knows what to her. Why hadn't she left him in the spare room? Eh? Could she explain her reasoning? A peck on the cheek and a hug was neither a promissory note nor a guarantee of good behaviour.

Alongside her, Nick let out a long sigh and then rolled over. If he started to snore now she would murder him herself.

'Maggie?'

His voice sounded odd and overly loud in the darkness.

'Yes? What do you want?' she hissed.

'This isn't going to work out, is it? I appreciate the gesture but it's like trying to sleep next to an ironing board. I can feel how tense you are from here. Why don't I just go back in the spare room,

I don't mind. Honestly.'

'No, you're okay, I'm fine,' she lied.

'No you're not. I'm not going to jump you. Honestly – I promise – it's just that I haven't slept with anyone since my wife left. It feels odd sleeping with someone I don't know.'

Maggie snorted. 'We're not exactly sleeping now.'

'What I meant to say was –' Nick began, but Maggie was way too quick for him.

'And at least you've got a good excuse for feeling a bit odd. I haven't slept with anyone since, since the last ice age. Or maybe even the one before that.' She was annoyed by the sound of her voice; it came out brittle and sharp and needy despite the veneer of humour.

There was a long, pregnant pause and then Nick said, 'Do you want a cuddle?' He spoke quietly into the stillness.

Maggie sighed. 'God, yes.'

Nick made as if to move closer.

'But I'm not going to have one,' she snapped, thrusting a pillow into his chest.

Nick laughed. 'You really are completely and utterly crazy.'

The affection in his voice made something tighten low down in her belly. Maggie groaned. God, this was all she needed.

'Go to sleep,' she snapped and with that rolled over, taking most of the duvet with her.

11

It was barely light when the alarm clock beside Nimrod's bed went off. The rolling, roaring beep was raw and insistent and inescapable. He groaned and stretched, slamming the button down, collecting his thoughts – an instant later Nimrod's eyes snapped open and he smiled, his expression cold and lizard-like. Today was the day, he could feel it; the waiting was finally over.

'Wakey, wakey campers,' he called to Cain, as, naked, he rolled out of bed and headed for the bathroom. His companion grunted and turned over, pulling the bedclothes up over his head. In the corner of the room the TV was still on, sound down, picture flickering like manic candlelight.

Nimrod savoured the sensations of the cool shiny tiles under his bare feet and admired his body in the full-length mirror beside the hand basin. He had an all-over tan, a belly like the underside of a turtle, and the rest of his frame was nicely muscled up without being too obvious or too heavy. Nimrod struck a Mr Universe pose and smiled wolfishly at his reflection. From the other room he heard the sounds of Cain stirring and climbing out of bed. Not long and it would all be over and done with.

He stepped into the shower and switched it onto full blast, letting the needle points of hot steamy water drive away any last remnants of sleep. He soaped his body with the tender caress of a lover. When he had washed, Nimrod turned the dial to cold. A long, long time ago, one of his instructors, a man who professed to be a psychic and who had taught him martial arts, had explained to him that a cold shower first thing in the morning cleansed and sealed the aura, the electrical field that encased every living thing. Cold water made a warrior stronger, more alert; he was less likely to be caught out if his aura was crystal clear.

Nimrod gasped as the water hit him. It was like a body blow driving the breath from his lungs. He hoped the psychic was right because whatever it did to his aura it always gave him a blinding headache.

Curled up on a damp wooden bench in the West Brayfield Memorial Jubilee Pavilion, Bernie Fielding dreamt that he was stretched out on the village green just outside the post office in

Renham. It was raining hard and he was stark naked, and so it appeared was Stella Conker-eyes – although it had to be said she didn't look best pleased with the situation. Funny things, women. Bernie thought she looked bloody gorgeous. In the dream he was cold, partially covered in damp leaves, and the grass was wet and some old lady kept poking him in the back with her umbrella, telling him that he really ought to get himself covered up – he should be ashamed of himself. It wasn't decent. Hadn't he got a home to go to? Bernie was just explaining to her that in fact he hadn't, when it struck him he was asleep, dreaming, and on his way back to the surface.

Very slowly, Bernie headed up towards consciousness, opened one crusty eye and took a look around. The sports pavilion was filling with pre-dawn light, tentative fingers of vapid yellow picking their way through the piles of damp netting and stacks of metal-framed chairs.

It was unnaturally early for Bernie to be awake and his mouth tasted as if something had died in it overnight. Bernie stretched and instantly regretted it. There was still something jabbing into his spine – which on closer inspection turned out to be an old football boot – and every bone in his body ached as if he had been kicked. For a few befuddled seconds he couldn't quite work out what the hell he was doing in the pavilion but then, very slowly, it all came back to him in glorious detail. Maggie, James Cook, *Gotcha*, the gasmen, and what felt disturbingly like a guilty conscience.

Moaning, Bernie pulled himself up onto one elbow and looked out of the dusty, cobweb-decked windows at the new day. The prospect of heading off into the grey, drizzling misty morning didn't cheer Bernie up one iota. But the sooner he started the journey to Somerset the sooner it would over, and there would be lots of lorry drivers on the road at this time of the morning who wouldn't give a shit how rough he looked.

Bernie tidied himself up as best he could, combed his hair, and then clambered unsteadily back through the pavilion window. Banging his elbow on the way out, Bernie stopped long enough to pull on his jacket and have a pee up against the bike shed. The steam rose up from the damp grass as if he had uncovered a vent straight to hell. Shivering, Bernie made his way back towards the village and the main road.

Nothing stirred, not even the birds were awake yet. It felt as if he was walking into a ghost town, and for a few seconds Bernie wondered if he might still be asleep. He looked up and down the deserted main street; there wasn't a car in sight. He shivered again as the cold nipped at his bones. It had to be at least a mile walk down to the nearest worthwhile road. Bernie sniffed, stuck his hands in his pockets and set off towards the new day. It struck him that being good really wasn't all it was cracked up to be.

Danny Coleman woke up with a peculiar sense of pleasure. Somewhere in the disconnected bliss of sleeping and dreaming he had had an idea on just how to fix the whole Nick Lucas problem once and for all. One that would suit everyone, including the women currently banged up on both sides of the Atlantic. Danny let the idea run through his head frame by frame and wondered why nobody had thought of it before. If you can't beat them, join them. He smiled wolfishly; although the smile still didn't warm anything above his mouth.

A few miles further south, Robbie Hughes was up as well. He couldn't bring himself to speak to Lesley as he got into the car, or maybe it was the other way round. He wasn't sure. He had seriously considered leaving her behind at the hotel to teach her a lesson. He would have, too, until it had occurred to him, as he tried to sleep despite the clank and groan and wheeze of the hotel's central-heating system below the room that he had booked for her, that he had left his bloody car keys on the bedside table in his suite.

Not that he had planned to spend the night in the little room over the kitchen. He had been trying to make a point. After a lot of fruitless banging on the bathroom door and pleading, Robbie had announced that he'd had quite enough of her behaviour and that she was being unreasonable and childish and that he was fed up and hungry. He was going to go and eat and by the time he came back she had damned well better have calmed down. Oh yes. All right, so maybe he had shouted at her, but that had been in the heat of the moment. He was creative, passionate, in tune with his emotions – isn't that what she had said about him once? Well, it was a double-edged sword. She had annoyed him but he wasn't cross with her now, quite the reverse. He wanted nothing more than to spend a nice quiet evening in her company. Just the two of them – all alone together. *Now* would be good. Lesley?

When it was obvious that he wasn't making any headway at all, Robbie had snatched up a swipe-key card from the bedside table and stalked out of the bedroom, slamming the door angrily behind him, which had immediately locked. Locking him out.

Robbie had glanced down at the card in his hand, knowing even before his focus sharpened that he had picked Lesley's key-card up by mistake. Standing out in the corridor, incandescent with fury, he had considered fetching the night porter to let him back in, but then again he didn't want to draw attention to his sleeping arrangements. The red tops would have a field day if they found out he was shafting Miss Goodie-Two-Shoes. There was nothing they liked better than the chance to expose a public figure's feet of clay, or any other part of his anatomy come to that. And Lesley wasn't the first – God alone knows what would happen if the story ever ran. It would probably open the flood gates.

'I had Robbie Hughes's love-child. I *was* Robbie Hughes's love-child. Three-in-a-bed romp for TV's Mr Clean.' God, Robbie groaned, he could just see the headlines now. No, he would go and sleep in Lesley's room and hope she felt terrible about it. Bitch. He'd remember next time and take someone else instead. Oh yes. Lesley should realise by now that Robbie Hughes was not a man to be trifled with.

The early-morning call in his cupboard had been fifteen minutes late. Robbie couldn't remember booking one for Lesley's room – mainly because he had assumed it would be empty – so he had come to the conclusion that Lesley must have rung the night porter when he didn't show up to meet her at the arranged time. There didn't appear to be any hot water in his room and the selection of towels that hung limply over the bathroom rail smelt as if they had been there since D-day.

So by the time Robbie got down to the hotel car park – still wearing the shirt, pants and socks that he had worn the previous day – he was absolutely fuming, while Lesley was sitting triumphantly in the front seat, all clean and smug. She certainly looked as if she had had a good night's sleep, and was clutching an empty carton of fresh coffee. His coffee – standing on the driver's seat – was stone-cold and scummy. Oh, she would pay for this.

As Robbie got into the car he held out his hand. Lesley dropped the keys into them and in stony silence they drove out of the hotel yard.

He noticed as they pulled out into the street that sellotaped to the dashboard was a large sheet of paper on which was written, in thick marker pen, the road numbers and junctions that would take them down to St Elfreda's Bay.

He sniffed. It would take a lot more than that to appease his wrath. Lesley looked at him and tried out a little smile. Robbie's face remained impassive; she was going to have to try an awful lot harder than that if she wanted to make up for last night.

Maggie Morgan drifted slowly back towards consciousness, eyes still closed. She sighed and then eased her bum back into the lap that was snuggled up around her, relishing the comfortable weight of the arm casually draped across her waist. Bliss. It felt so good that she almost purred with the sheer pleasure of it.

She loved the warm, cosy feeling of early

morning spooning almost more than anything else. As the thought formed, Maggie froze. Purring? Spooning? Hang on a minute. That wasn't right.

Full consciousness splashed over her like a bucket of cold water. Maggie opened her eyes while her mind did a complete recce of the current situation. It appeared that she was spooning with Nick Lucas, the man in black cotton boxers who she barely knew, and who sometime during the night had obviously illegally crossed the piled pillow checkpoint and was currently indulging in a spot of unscheduled snuggling. The bastard.

Struggling to ignore how good it felt, Maggie let the indignation roll through her. She was about to say something but before she opened her mouth she looked again at the far side of the bedroom and hastily recalculated her position in relation to the wall – and reddened. Unfortunately it seemed to have been her who, overnight, had climbed, unconscious, into enemy territory. The pillows were all on what had formally been her side of the bed – most of them on the floor. Her rogue body had been very busy while she was asleep.

Apprehensively, Maggie shuffled through the card index of her memory to see if there was anything else that she ought to be ashamed of, and was relieved when the search came up empty.

If she could just slither out from under Nick's

arm. Maggie, holding her breath to make her body even thinner – who was she kidding, just slightly thinner – squashed herself down into the mattress.

He was sound asleep, his arm almost a dead weight. He'd never know if the movement was really quick and smooth. She'd just have to wriggle her bum a bit, move away from his . . . Maggie reddened furiously. It didn't bear thinking about where her bum was currently snuggled. Maybe she could slip out without him noticing; pretend to be sound asleep, groan a little and then just roll over. How hard could it be? Except that it felt quite nice – no, not quite nice, very nice. Very nice indeed. Damn.

Nick, still sound asleep, moaned softly and pulled her closer. Closer? Maggie stiffened, her eyes wide open now. What the hell was he playing at? His lips and face settled close to her shoulders as if he was breathing her in. Maggie groaned quietly. If only she hadn't woken up and had just left their bodies to get on with it. Nick snuffled, then his hand slid artfully up from her waist over her ribs and under her tee shirt.

Under her tee shirt? Good God, she barely knew the man. Her stomach did that funny nippy flippy thing as the sensation roared through her, at which point Maggie squeaked, some kind of moral fail-safe cut in, and she was out of bed like a whippet out of a butcher's shop.

Back in the bed, Nick yawned and blinked and

then focused on her. 'Morning,' he said sleepily, rubbing his eyes. 'You all right? You sleep okay?'

'Who, me? Yes, fine, I'm just fine. You want a cup of tea?' she said, far too brightly and far too quickly, but at least got it all in before Nick had a chance to recall any purring or snuggling or spooning.

'That would be great,' he said thickly. 'What time is it anyway?'

'Um, I don't know – seven, maybe half past? It's early yet, there's no need to get up –'

Nick stretched, while Maggie made a conscientious effort not to look at just how broad his shoulders were or stare at the nice flat area of hairy belly exposed between the bottom of his tee shirt and the top of the duvet. Damn, if only she could have just pretended to be asleep.

'I have to ring Coleman and let him know where I am, and that I'm safe.'

'Do you want to use my mobile?'

'Thanks,' said Nick. 'You know, I had the strangest dream this morning.'

Maggie nodded, not trusting herself to speak. She just hoped that Nick had enough sense to wait until she left the room before getting out of bed or recalling his dream.

'Tell me again, why exactly are you doing this? Why don't we just ring the AA and be done with it?' growled Robbie. 'This is what I pay my annual subscription for. Roadside rescue, roadside recovery –' He stamped his feet and flapped his arms angrily. The day hadn't quite had the chance to warm yet, and there was a nippy little wind blowing across the motorway that took his breath away now that they were out of the warmth of the car.

They had been on the road for less than an hour.

Lesley pulled the wheel brace and the jack out from the boot. 'What? For a puncture?' She sounded incredulous, heaving out the spare tyre and dropping it onto the tarmac with a confidence that belied her size. 'But we can have it fixed by the time they get here; the only problem we might have is with the wheel nuts.'

Robbie glared at her – what was all this 'we' stuff?

'They'll probably be a bit tight,' she was saying, 'if they've been put on with one of those pneumatic guns. I might need something to give me a bit of extra leverage.' As she spoke, Lesley looked around expectantly.

'Leverage?' growled Robbie.

Lesley, rolling up her sleeves, nodded. 'Yes, leverage. "Give me a lever long enough and a fulcrum strong enough and I will move the world,"' she said confidently, prising the hub cap off with a screwdriver.

'Who's that? Rocky? Popeye? George W. Bush?'

'No actually, it was a paraphrase of something that Archimedes said. Do you know where the jacking point is on your car?'

Robbie shook his head. What was the bloody woman talking about? Jacking point-schmacking point, Robbie took his car to the garage where some pimply youth drove it away so that whatever they did to it could be done by whoever it was that did it, and then they'd send him the bill. His idea of car maintenance involved signing cheques and putting in the petrol.

On the hard shoulder, Lesley walked round the car, bent almost double so that she could see underneath the sills, past the trims and the go-fast faring, and then she grinned and said, 'Eureka.'

Robbie groaned. Presumably that was something else said by bloody Archimedes. He buttoned his coat up to the chin and sat down on the grass verge, opened his briefcase and pulled out his notes on Bernie Fielding.

'We're not supposed to be in Bristol, are we?' said Nimrod, watching the signs to the city centre whizz past the hire car. 'I thought we were supposed to have gone round it?'

Cain nodded. 'I know, I know – I dunno where I went wrong to be honest. But don't worry, we'll turn off up here somewhere.' He looked across at

Nimrod. 'You all right?' he asked casually, tucking in behind a lorry. 'Not too tense or anything?'

Nimrod shook his head. They were getting closer to the moment, he could feel it in his bones. If Nimrod was honest he'd nearly had enough. The high-octane burn that propelled him through a hit only lasted so long and he could feel himself running low. He wanted the job over now, no more cock ups, no more close shaves or near misses. Of all the things that Nimrod Brewster hated, mess was right up near the top of the list. Not that you would guess from his demeanour. But he wanted the job done and for him and Cain to be back in Marbella, to be out on the terrace tending to his cacti and pruning his bourganvillea.

He popped another Minto into his mouth, jaw snapping shut like a guillotine. 'Nah, you're all right – I'm fine – and let's face it, it's easy enough done. If I was driving we'd probably be in bleeding Glasgow by now.' And then he added, 'Up there,' waving a hand. 'You can get off up there on the left.'

'Right you are,' said Cain, and he indicated and changed lanes.

Nick took Maggie's mobile outside, switched it on, and – pulling a piece of paper out of the wallet in his back pocket – tapped Coleman's phone number in. As he did a little symbol flashed up on the screen; missed call, new voicemail. Nick made a mental note to tell Maggie when he got back.

While waiting to be connected, Nick stared out into the bright new morning. St Elfreda's was a good place to be. Mature trees were alive with rooks calling the odds. Someone close by was frying bacon. He could hear a baby crying and children chittering. Across the broad strip of grass that divided Maggie's hut from the next fenced garden plot, a row of sandals and buckets and spades stood guard outside the back door by the steps. Red sandals, yellow buckets, a bright blue spade. Primary-coloured fun that made his heart ache.

For a moment Nick felt the pain in his chest as he caught a glimpse of normal lives; kids and holidays and sand and other people just doing ordinary things. It seemed a lifetime ago since things had been that simple.

'Good morning,' said a polite female voice at the far end of the phone line. At least he wasn't held in a queue. 'How can I help you?'

'Oh hello, I know it's early but I wondered if Mr Coleman is in yet – or maybe you could get a message to him for me?'

There was a pause and then the woman said, 'Is that Bernie Fielding?'

Nick reddened furiously as if he had been caught out, and instinctively looked over his shoulder to check who else might be listening in to their conversation. 'Yes, it is –' he said in surprise and then continued in a lower voice, barely more than a whisper, 'How did you know that it was me?'

'We've been expecting you to ring in. Just stay on the line and I'll try and connect you. I'm transferring your call through now.'

Finally, thought Nick.

'Well, hello there stranger,' Coleman said in a warm, almost chummy tone. 'What the hell happened to you?'

It wasn't quite the reception that Nick had expected. 'I'm sorry –' he began, even though it wasn't really true. 'Maggie thought it would be better if we left West Brayfield straight away. After the TV thing and the trailers – you know.' What else was there to say? Surely Nick didn't have to justify running for his life to a man who was supposed to protect it?

'Umm,' said Coleman thoughtfully, without committing himself. 'Maybe she was right. So where are you now?'

Nick hesitated, realising that he was reluctant to tell him. 'In Somerset,' he said cagily.

'Okay – Somerset – nice place. Care to be a little more specific?'

Nick looked back towards the beach hut. What he wanted was to be safe and to begin again more than anything else in the world. Through the open door he could see Maggie in the kitchen, all wrapped up in a big woolly dressing gown, making them tea and toast. As he watched she tucked a stray strand of hair behind her ears and for an instant he relished the peculiar feeling of tenderness that it gave him inside.

Realistically the ache was not purely for Maggie, although there was no denying that she had whatever it was that attracted him to a woman. More than that, though, her being there, waiting for him to come back, was like a warm echo from another life. For an instant he had a laser sharp-image of another, imaginary Somerset time, when everything was all right, when he and Maggie would have been here with the kids on holiday, where they would all be looking forward to a day out or a day down on the beach. As if Maggie was aware of his thoughts, she looked up at him and smiled. Nick winced; the smile was way too close to the happy families that he was dreaming of to be comfortable.

'You want the truth, Coleman? To be perfectly honest; I don't trust you any more. You told me that I'd be safe and I'm not, am I?' Nick said flatly. 'One cock-up and my face is all over nation-wide TV. I don't call that safe, do you?'

Coleman sighed but Nick noted that he didn't argue with him.

'I can't say that I blame you, Nick, but what other choice do you have? Seriously? We both know that you can't keep running forever. You haven't got the resources or, come to that, the nature for living outside the law. There is nowhere for you to hide that you can't be found, at least not unless *we* hide you again. You will be safe –'

'That's what you told me last time.'

Maggie – out of earshot – grinned and waved the buttered toast in his direction. The warm expression on her face fed the feelings of loss and longing in Nick's heart.

'Don't be a fool,' Coleman was saying. 'I need to know where you are, Nick. For God's sake – I can help you, but only if you let me. We can have a team down there to pick you up in a couple of hours, wherever you are. Do you understand? *Wherever you are.* We are all on the same side –'

Nick sighed and as Maggie walked towards him bearing toast, said, 'Okay, maybe you're right but I just want to be free for a little bit longer. I'll ring you back later today and arrange a pick-up point.'

And before Coleman had time to answer or argue or protest, Nick pressed 'End call' and then switched the phone off, every instinct telling him that while it was on, the guys at Stiltskin could probably track him down.

'Did you get through?' Maggie said, handing him a mug of tea.

Nick nodded. She smelt good; of sleep and woman and warm buttered toast. This was hardly a good time to think about falling for someone, but then for an instant he remembered how good it felt to wake up with her in his arms and how very still he had lain for fear of frightening her away.

'And what did they say?' she said, taking a big bite out of the toast.

'That they want to come down to Somerset and rescue me – apparently I'm screwing their success rate up while I'm on the loose.' Maggie's expression hardened in reaction to his flippant tone. 'Keep you hair on,' he said gently. 'It's going to be all right. I told Coleman that I'd ring him back later and that he could come and get me once we had arranged a pick-up point. Meanwhile, how do you fancy a walk on the beach?'

She stared at him. 'Are you serious?'

Nick stared right back and nodded. 'Never more so.'

12

Bernie unfolded himself from the lorry cab, dropped down onto the unforgiving tarmac and lifted a hand in salute to the driver. He stretched. It was still misty but with the promise that before too long the sun would burn away the haze to reveal a perfect summer's day – and it was getting warmer with every passing moment.

'Cheers, mate.'

The driver nodded. 'Not a problem. You won't forget me, will you, you know, about the villa?'

Bernie shook his head. 'Not a chance,' he said, and with an open palm tapped the sheet of paper that was folded and tucked into the breast pocket of his jacket. The man had given Bernie his name and address, just in case Bernie ever got anything concrete on another time-share property like the totally imaginary one he had pretended to have sold for a song and had just spent three hours or so talking about.

Oh how Bernie missed that beautifully appointed three bedroomed, ground floor apartment that would sleep eight without any difficulty whatsoever. Bernie grinned – and it got better. It looked like things had turned the corner. He hadn't lost his touch after all. He'd told the driver all about his fictitious friend, presently going through a very nasty and very messy divorce. They had had adjoining villas in an imaginary but very quiet little family-run resort in Tenerife, and had spent the same fortnight there for the last ten years. As Bernie let the lie catch light, the driver had nodded, his eyes bright with avarice as he sniffed the odour of a genuine copper-bottomed bargain. 'And you reckon he's up for selling his, too, do you?'

'Oh yes,' said Bernie, although careful not to sound too eager. It was always best to let the victim do as much of the running as possible. 'We've already said it won't be the same any more anyway, not without both families being there. The years go by so quick.

'Now my kids are grown up, me and the missus decided it was time to look around for somewhere a bit more upmarket. You know how it is – this place is great for kids but you get past all that, don't you, really? These days I see meself more as a cocktail-by-the-pool man rather than a sandcastle and red-pop bloke. Anyway, I'm more or less a hundred per cent certain his place'll be coming up within the next couple of months. His wife wants a quick settlement, you know how it is. My mate loves that villa; it's right next to the pool, lovely views out over the bay, everything. Best spot on the whole development, I've always reckoned – and that's why she wants him to get shot of it – you know what women can be like. Bloody spiteful if the mind takes them.'

The lorry driver nodded ruefully. 'Yeah. My first missus was like that, but not Cindy – she's a lot younger than me, nice girl, used to work in the office. Since we've had the kiddies it's calmed her down a lot. We like it down here, don't get me wrong, but she misses going up West with the girls – and the shopping, you know. She likes her shopping and her holidays does our Cindy – and a place that size would be ideal.'

Bernie nodded. 'Course it would. Nice shopping centre just down the road, good food, nightlife – and the beauty of having yer own villa is that you can rent it out the rest of the year. You can make your money back in no time at all. We go through a letting agency to handle all the paperwork. The villas are all serviced, you just pay an annual ground rent – it ain't that much. Me and the missus have done very nicely out of it over the years.'

The driver totted up the maths in his head as Bernie casually plucked a whole string of fictitious numbers out of his head.

'Sounds like a really good investment on top of everything else. I could take my older lads as well – they live with me first missus, although knowing Cin' she'd want to take her mum and her sister an' all. How many bedrooms did you say it's got?'

'Three nice-sized doubles and a bed settee in the lounge, but it's a big lounge –' Bernie could almost see it in his mind's eye; French windows opening up onto a marble-paved terrace looking over an azure-blue sea. God he would have bought it himself if he'd had the chance. You wouldn't feel tucked up or anything. And with this agency that I'm signed up with you have first pick of the dates you want each year.'

The driver had nodded and narrowed his eyes. Bernie could track the man's mind moving off into the middle distance, working out all the possible permutations of sleeping arrangements. 'What sort of money do you reckon your mate's going to want for it?'

Bernie smiled and shrugged, not wanting to appear too eager, not sure of how much he could squeeze from his companion.

It seemed that the journey wasn't wasted after all. The warm glow of a nice new scam washed over him. 'Let me ring my mate and then I'll give you a buzz – sort you out a few photos to show to your Cindy.'

The man grinned. 'Thanks mate. Good luck,

and I hope they can fix your motor, it's a bastard when they let you down like that. You reckon that the garage will have come out and picked it up by now, do you?'

'I hope so. The amount of money they quoted to do it I'd have expected them to fly and pick it up by helicopter.'

The man laughed. 'Yeah I reckon we're in the wrong game, don't you?'

Bernie nodded. He'd had to come up with some sort of explanation why a man of means like himself was hitch-hiking.

The lorry driver gave another wave as he drove off towards Minehead.

Head down, Bernie walked up the hill towards the entrance to St Elfreda's Bay, grinning. He most definitely hadn't lost the old magical Bernie Fielding touch, although on a better day he would have had a cheque out of the bloke as well. Selling time-share on the hoof – selling anything – was for Bernie, like a concert pianist doing scales. Maybe this good deed was just what he needed to bring about a little luck, a change of fortune. He could certainly use one; things had been a bit lean of late. But then he'd always had his ups and downs, life was like that. Bernie picked up the pace and started to whistle. He was about due an up.

St Elfreda's holiday park was a mile or so off the main road, at the bottom of a steep roadway cut through mature woodland. It had once all been farmland and, realistically, despite tarmac and passing places the road was still more suited to tractors and four-wheel-drives than most family saloons. Even so, it was an idyllic setting for a holiday. Around a sharp right-hand corner at the bottom of the hill lay the caravans, cabins, tents, and old-fashioned beach huts tucked up amongst old trees with proper gardens. There was a shop and stables, and outbuildings that had been converted into a cosy little bar and café. Away to the left down a cobbled track, where once men had brought coal ashore from Wales on a whole string of mules, lay a private cove and a secluded sandy beach. Nearly there, thought Bernie, whistling a medley from *Les Miserables*.

At this time of the morning the beach was bright, blustery, and almost deserted. The little sandy cove was one of the main reasons Maggie had always loved holidays at St Elfreda's. The bay was like a nibbled bite out of the coastline, sheltered on two sides by sweeping cliffs, and was totally private, used only by the people on the campsite and intrepid walkers who ambled up from Watchet or down the coast from Kilve.

It was an astonishing landscape. The cliffs were made up of layered, waved and slanted rock formations, some in varying shades of red, some cream, some grey and some further round the bay tinged with green, so that it looked as if the cliff face was made of great folds of chocolate-chip ice cream. Across the beach great rills of rock, which had survived time and tide and winter storms, cut through the sand at odd angles like spines, making sheltered spots to sit under or flat surfaces to bask on. On one edge of the cliffs that embraced St Elfreda's Bay a waterfall tumbled down over the raw edge, fuelled by an upland freshwater stream.

'It's a great place to wash the sand off. The boys love it – although it's always cold,' Maggie said, nodding towards the column of water, hands stuffed in the pockets of her fleece as she and Nick ambled along, heads tucked down against the breeze. The wind cut the water into a fine mist that clung and hung in the air, sunlight slicing it into rainbows.

Nick – who had taken his shoes off almost as soon as they hit the beach – grinned, paddling bare feet into the fresh water where it cut through the broad delta to the sea.

Maggie laughed. It was the most relaxed she had seen him since they'd met, with his trousers rolled up, shoes in hand, big chunky sweater tied around his broad shoulders. Maggie peeled strands of hair off her face as the wind wrapped it tight over her eyes and mouth, watching Nick as he picked his way gingerly through sun-warmed run-offs.

It felt so easy and so very, very right for him to be there with her.

'I wish this could go on forever,' he said, as if reading her mind. Maggie turned away so that he couldn't see her face, struggling to stop her thoughts from running away to the warm and tender place that they were heading. This wasn't real, or even possible, it was just a hiatus – a break in real life for her. And for Nick? Well, for Nick it was a moment of relief before the madness began all over again.

He looked across at her as they scrambled over the rocks, jumping down and waiting to help her, the touch of his hand making her shiver. There were just so many things that Maggie wanted to ask him but she had no idea – worse still, not enough courage – to know where or if to start. So they had walked and talked about her and the boys, and the school where she taught. Nick was easy to be with. They talked about how she had been left the beach hut by an elderly family friend and how she had struggled to keep it for years, long before they became trendy.

It was a notch or two up from polite conversation, but not much more, except that all the while Maggie could sense that odd little tingle that only comes when you fancy someone and it is reciprocated, and she didn't know whether to be relieved or worried and so swung uneasily between the two.

'So, how about we go back to the caravan?' Nick said softly as they reached the path. Their eyes met. There was a loaded silence; Maggie felt her colour rising while she waited for his next words. 'I'll cook you eggs and bacon,' Nick said.

Maggie looked across at him, not sure if she was relieved or disappointed. 'Aren't you forgetting something?'

'What?' He pulled a face. 'Tomatoes, hot buttered toast? Good coffee –'

'Coleman.'

He sighed. 'You know, for just a moment there I genuinely had forgotten all about him.'

'Sorry.'

Nick waved the comment away. 'Hardly your fault, is it? I'll ring him after we've had breakfast.'

Maggie laughed. 'You have got a very peculiar set of priorities.'

Nick mimed an enormous pantomime shrug. 'What can I say? It's a gift – besides, I've decided I'm going to enjoy this moment while I can. After all, no one knows where we are, so what difference is another hour or two going to make. And it's ages since I've been to the seaside.'

Good luck – wasn't that what the driver had wished him? Bernie hoped it would hold. Once he got to the bottom of the steep road he stood for a few moments to catch his breath, wondering what he would do if Maggie wasn't there after all. Walking down through the trees a peculiar sense of dread began building up in his belly.

Maggie's beach hut was situated on the oldest part of the site, tucked away between a row of horse chestnuts in a proper little garden, boarded all around with pebbles and driftwood brought home from countless beach walks. Her plot was tucked back off the track that meandered around the site. Maggie loved it because it was so secluded.

Secluded. It crossed Bernie's mind that the gasmen might already have been there, or worse still were there now. Who would know if she was in danger? Maggie's plot wasn't overlooked by anyone.

Everything else forgotten, Bernie picked his way nervously along the track between the huts, part of him terrified of what he might find. Maggie's car was there, drawn up under the lee of the hedge which was cut through with a great swathe of wild honeysuckle. The curtains in the bedroom were closed.

Bernie climbed the steps and knocked, once, twice and then he waited. Nothing. The knot in his belly tightened. Cupping his hands around his face, Bernie peered inside. There were definite signs of life – a box of teabags and an open milk carton stood on the worktop, bags and boxes on the table. She had most definitely been there. A jacket was casually slung over a chair. He wasn't sure whether it was a good sign or a bad one. What if this bloke – the one that they were relocating – was violent, too? After all, there was no telling what sort of a rogue he was. He could easily be a criminal turning his mates in, some sort of supergrass. What if he had forced Maggie to help hide him? What if the danger wasn't just from the gasmen?

Bernie swallowed hard to try and still the butterflies in his stomach and was just looking around for something to help him pop the lock when he heard a familiar giggle behind him and turned towards the sound.

Maggie and a tall, good-looking man were walking back up along the path from the beach. They were both carrying their shoes, but very artfully so that the hand closest to each other was empty, and they were walking just fractionally too close together for comfort.

Bernie stared. He knew exactly what he was seeing but was still surprised. As he watched, the man's hand brushed Maggie's and almost instantly they both stopped dead in their tracks, and then, right in front of his eyes, the man turned to Maggie and very gently tipped her face up towards his and kissed her.

Unable to look away, Bernie felt his jaw drop open. Maggie didn't move; she didn't shriek or slap his face or run away. Quite the opposite in fact, she moved a little closer and kissed him right back.

Bernie groaned. Bloody hell. That was all he needed. Maggie didn't need rescuing, what she needed was a bucket of cold water and a bloody good talking to. Had she got any idea what she was getting herself into? How long had she known this bloody clown? After all Bernie had gone through to get himself down to Somerset to warm her – to warn them. Bloody women.

'Maggie?'

She swung round violently, almost as if Bernie had slapped her.

'What the hell are you doing here?' she said. Bernie could hear the astonishment in her voice. He held up a hand to silence her but should have guessed that it would be nowhere near enough.

'Spying on me, were you?' She was blushing furiously and had leapt away from pretty boy as if he was on fire. 'You've got a nerve showing your face round here –'

'Shush,' said Bernie gently. 'Don't get so wound up, Maggie. Calm down; it's all right. I haven't come to cause any trouble – I've come about him.' He waved towards the tall man.

'Him?' Maggie said suspiciously. 'What do you mean, *him*, Bernie? How come you know anything about *him*?' Her voice was heavy with sarcasm and her eyes darkened as she looked him up and down. Bernie flinched. He didn't know how much

Maggie knew about what was going on but he sensed that she could detect his fingerprints all over this job.

Bernie nodded towards her companion. 'I don't know much at all, if I'm honest.' He heard Maggie snort but apparently she decided not to pass comment on the state of his honesty as he turned to face the man. 'I don't know who you are or what you did, but two men came to visit me yesterday. They thought I was you and they had guns. Ring any bells?'

There was a dark and nasty silence. The man paled.

Maggie looked first at the man and then at Bernie. 'And?' she said, not dropping her gaze.

Bernie sighed. Maggie knew him too well – with Bernie there was always an and or a but.

'And I think they're on their way down here to find you – to find him. In fact, I'm surprised they aren't here already.'

'How do you know that they're coming here?' said Maggie, eyes narrowing.

Bernie sighed. 'Because Mrs Eliot told me that she had told them –'

'What? She told them that I was here? I don't believe she'd tell anyone unless –' and then Maggie blanched as the realisation hit her. 'Is she all right? Did they – they didn't hurt her, did they?' She looked at the her ex-husband who shuffled nervously from foot to foot.

'No, no, she's absolutely fine. Fit as a fur coat full of fleas when I left her,' said Bernie quickly. 'She thought they were from the gas board.'

Maggie rolled her eyes. 'I'm going to have to have a word with her about that.'

The man pulled out a mobile from his jacket pocket. 'I ought to ring in now,' he said. 'Now that we know they're on the way.'

'Okay – but can we arrange to meet the cavalry somewhere else? I don't want them turning up here.'

'I'm not sure that you should be there at all,' the man said. Maggie sighed. Bernie looked at him. Despite appearances he obviously didn't know Maggie very well.

'Can we talk about that later?' she asked. The man nodded, giving Bernie a sharp look, and then moved away to make his call.

Bernie shifted uncomfortably under Maggie's icy stare. 'I did try to ring and warn you, Maggie.'

She lifted an eyebrow. 'Did you? And I wonder why that was, Bernie? Guilty conscience, was it? I get the distinct impression that you have had more to do with all this than meets the eye.'

Bernie stared at her. 'Well that's gratitude for you, I bloody-well hitched down here as well, and that's all the thanks I get. I'm sorry I bothered you.'

Maggie held his gaze without flinching. 'And

don't do that face on me, Bernie – or that "who – me" expression. I know you from way back, don't forget that.'

Bernie shrugged the tension away. 'What about pretty boy over there? Do you know him, too?'

'Nick, his name is Nick. Although for a while he was called Bernie Fielding. Odd that, isn't it?'

Bernie decided not to take the bait. 'Nick, eh? What on earth were you thinking about, Mags? You should know better than to go around rescuing strays at your age. You don't want to get mixed up with someone like him – you know, on the run. A criminal. He could have done anything, you know.'

Maggie laughed. 'Who, Nick? Don't be daft, Bernie, you only have to look at him to know that that's not true. Nick's not a criminal, he's innocent.'

'Oh right, well of course, that makes it all right then, doesn't it?' said Bernie, turning up the sarcasm to sear. 'First rule of being a criminal is to say that you're innocent. What did he tell you? That he was framed? That it was all a terrible mistake? That he took the rap for his mate? Honour amongst thieves? They all say that, you know. Don't you ever learn, Maggie?'

Maggie beaded him with hurt and angry eyes. 'When you say "don't I ever learn", I presume you are talking about yourself?'

Bernie shook his head and groaned. 'Oh come on, Mags, give me a break. You have to admit that you've got crap taste in men, look at that other tosser you married.' Maggie opened her mouth to speak but before she could strike, Bernie said, 'So are you two an item, then? You and the lovely, innocent Nick.'

'And what exactly has that got to do with you, Bernie?'

'Just curious; he doesn't look like your type.'

'What do you mean? That he looks normal and he hasn't got a dodgy past that he needs to lie about?'

Bernie winced. 'Ouch, that was a bit below the belt, Mags.'

Maggie didn't look amused.

'I thought that you might at least have had the good grace to thank me. I came down here to warn you, I've most probably saved your life.'

'Not yet you haven't,' she said indignantly, and then – after a few seconds – more kindly, 'Thank you, now bugger off.'

At which point Bernie's stomach rumbled. 'Any chance of a cup of tea and a slice of toast, only I'm totally famished.'

Maggie didn't move.

Nick arrived back, cradling the phone. 'He said we ought to be going as soon as we can – that we'll be safer in a crowd. They're already well on their way.'

Maggie nodded. 'Okay I'll go and get the car keys.'

'Any chance of a lift?' asked Bernie brightly, with feigned innocence.

Maggie put her hand in the pocket of her jeans and pulling out a crumpled fiver pressed it into his hand. 'Don't push your luck, Bernie. Go and get yourself a cab.'

'But you're going into town,' he protested.

Maggie rounded on him. 'Don't give me all this crap. I *know* that you have had a hand in this somewhere, Bernie – I don't know how and I don't know why, but I know without a shadow of a doubt that somehow all this is your fault. I don't want you in my car; I don't want you in my life. Just the thought of you makes me furious – beyond furious – way out beyond furious. Do you understand?'

'But I came to warn you,' he protested.

'For which we are very grateful,' said Maggie, shooing Nick towards the car. 'But every bone in my body tells me that the reason that we're in this mess in the first place is most probably down to you. Go on, tell me I'm not right?'

Bernie flinched. 'You've gotten so hard, Maggie, so very hard. I never thought I'd see you like this. Hard and bitter – it doesn't suit you, you know. You were never like this when we were married.'

She laughed. 'No, because I was too bloody

naïve back then. I believed every word you told me and just look where it got me. Thank you for coming, thank you for warning us – now just bugger off home, will you?'

'But I'm hungry,' Bernie whined. 'I've been on the road for hours to get down here; I could murder a cup of tea.'

Maggie sighed but he could see that she was relenting. 'Oh for God's sake, Bernie. All right. Help yourself. There's milk and cereals and bread in the fridge. Eat, drink, and then drop the latch when you leave. And if I find that you've nicked anything or sold the bloody beach hut to some gormless American I will personally hunt you down and rip your throat out. Don't say that you haven't been warned.'

Nick looked on at her in amazement. Bernie grinned and, turning on his heel, followed Maggie back to the hut. He had no real intention of having tea or anything else come to that. He just wanted a nose around.

Maggie got the keys and headed back to the car with a goodbye and another warning about theft.

It was nice to feel that he had won on points over pretty boy, maybe even shown Nick a side of Maggie that he didn't know existed, and besides there was a little bit of Bernie that wanted to see if they had slept together. As they drove away Bernie waved from the steps and then pulled the door too behind him.

His plan was to hang around for a few minutes and then head off into Watchet. He was bound to be able to get a lift with someone. Bernie pocketed the fiver and then thought that maybe a cup of tea wasn't such a bad idea after all. He lit a cigarette and plugged in the kettle and while he waited for it to boil he set about a little light exploration. First port of call – the master-bedroom.

Bernie smiled to himself as he opened the door; there was a tee shirt slung over the chair, pillows all over the floor. So they were an item after all.

At the entrance to the site, Maggie hesitated. 'Where to?'

'Coleman said we were to meet him in Minehead.'

Maggie nodded and turned right along the coast road. As she did so she noticed a car in the distance, creeping up the hill. 'How long did Coleman say it would be before he got there?'

Nick laughed without humour. 'They patched him through by some sort of satellite link; he's already well on his way here.'

'That's good, isn't it?' said Maggie, with what she hoped was a reassuring smile.

'Depends on how you look at it, I suppose. So,' said Nick thoughtfully, 'that was the infamous

Bernie Fielding. It was good of him to come and warn us.'

Maggie cocked an eyebrow; at least her instinct hadn't been that far out of kilter. Bernie had had a hand in what was going on, although try as she might Maggie couldn't work out exactly what. But then again, Bernie had always managed to surprise her. She was still trying to fathom out what exactly Bernie's angle was; she found it very hard to believe he'd warned them out of a sense of philanthropy.

'He seems like a good man to me.'

Maggie snorted. 'Well there we have it, Nick, with intuition like that it's no wonder you're on the run.'

He smiled. 'You've always got a smart answer, haven't you?'

Maggie reddened, sensing that it wasn't meant as a compliment. 'Meaning what, exactly?'

'Meaning that it's a great defence – a nice verbal sleight of hand – and that to be that defensive Bernie must have hurt you very much,' Nick continued.

Maggie's heart softened.

'And about kissing you? You know, when we got back from the beach –' he said experimentally.

Maggie glanced at him out of the corner of her eye. If Nick pulled back now and apologised, if he said he was wrong or sorry or that he really didn't mean it, she would be devastated. She knew that they had both felt that insistent little buzz since they met, felt it so much on the beach that it was like walking with a generator for company. Kissing him hadn't been so much a turn on as a relief – as if the energy had finally earthed itself before it exhausted the pair of them.

'I just wanted you to know that, whatever happens, I'm glad that we met, Maggie. I just wish that it hadn't been under these circumstances. I keep thinking that if Coleman whips me away today there is a good chance I may never see you again –' She could hear the pain in his voice '– and I probably won't be able to contact you once I've been relocated.'

Of course, he was right. Maggie sighed, wishing with all her heart that she had had the courage to creep across the pillow barrier when she was awake. What harm would it have done?

'I'm so sorry,' he said.

'Me, too,' replied Maggie softly, as she felt her heart sink.

Meanwhile, back at the beach hut, Bernie, hands cradled round a mug of Yorkshire's finest, looked longingly at the sofa. He hadn't realised until now just how tired he was. First off he'd had a long hard night with Stella Conker-eyes, followed by a night on a damp bench in the pavilion. He stretched experimentally – no wonder he was so knackered, after all he was no spring chicken.

Bernie considered his options. The sofa looked very comfortable – then again, why trifle with the sofa when he could just as easily slip into Maggie's double bed? After all, she could hardly object – she'd never know. He wouldn't get in it, obviously, just lie on the top. Okay, so perhaps pull the duvet up over his shoulder just to get comfortable. It would be so nice to close his eyes for half an hour or so and then he would be on his way. He padded through into Maggie's bedroom, set the mug down on the bedside table and then slipped off his boots. Half an hour; what harm would it do?

Bernie yawned. Maybe the gasmen had got lost, maybe they weren't going to show up after all. Whatever the case, Bernie knew that if he didn't lie down soon he would fall down.

'So here we go again. Photos, gloves, guns, Mintoes.' Nimrod ran though his mental checklist.

He slipped the envelope of photos out of the glove compartment of the discreet silver-grey hire car and took a final long hard look at the images of Nick Lucas before tapping the number of the campsite into his mobile. What followed was a masterful piece of bullshit.

'Hi –' Nimrod's voice warmed to almost jovial, 'My name is Jonathan Smith – I'm sorry to disturb you so early but we're on our way down to see Maggie Morgan. God, I feel so stupid – I can't remember the number of her beach hut and I've left the piece of paper on the kitchen table. I'm just glad I could remember the name of your site – we're supposed to be meeting her this morning. I've tried ringing her mobile but she must have switched it off, and then I panicked in case we'd got the wrong week. Do you know if she's arrived yet?' He managed to sound cheery and respectable and helpless in that warm, puppyish way that women in particular respond well to.

The woman at the far end of the line giggled. 'Don't worry, I'm just the same. Maggie's most definitely here, although I haven't seen her yet this morning, she rang to say she was on her way last night. It's number twenty-six. As you come into the site, carry on straight ahead when you get to the bottom of the hill – it's down a little track – and then bear right at the first turning you come to. Would you like me to send someone down to tell her you're on your way?'

Nimrod snorted. 'What, and let her know I'd forgotten, God no – she'd never let me live it down.'

The woman laughed, too. 'All right. Well in that case maybe I'll see you later in the bar.'

239

It was Nimrod's turn to laugh. 'Maybe you will.' He could almost hear the woman in the office purr. He hung up. 'Number twenty-six and Ms Morgan is most definitely there.'

Beside him Cain grunted to acknowledge that he had heard. He indicated right and swung into the narrow roadway that led down to the camp-site.

'So,' Nimrod said as they parked under a stand of trees close to the beach huts at St Elfreda's Bay. 'Number twenty-six. In, out, over and home in time for tea and buns.'

Cain pulled a face. 'What, buns, for breakfast?'

'I told you last time it's just a turn of phrase.'

Cain thought for a few seconds and then said, 'Bloody daft one if you ask me. And you still haven't said if I can have the window seat?'

Nimrod pulled a face. 'No. What the hell brought that up? It isn't a done deal yet.' He nodded towards the regimented row of huts and took a deep breath. Déjà vu. Photos, gloves, guns, Mintoes. Today's mantra.

They were out of the car now and walking without apparent hurry through the crisp early morning light of a brand new summer's day, every sense alive, sniffing the air like feral dogs.

'But you promised,' said Cain petulantly.

'I did not,' said Nimrod, all the while his eyes working over the little numbered plaques stuck into the verge beside each of the plots.

Just before they got to number twenty-six the two men fell silent. It was time.

As they stepped into the neat little garden of plot twenty-six, Nimrod took a deep cleansing breath; in and out, in and out, each breath rising in his chest seemed to take a week to run its course.

The two of them took up positions either side of the door. Pressing himself tight up against the bodywork, Nimrod gave an almost imperceptable nod and an instant later Cain slipped a jemmy bar down his sleeve and prised the flimsy door open. There was barely any noise, certainly no fuss, just a faint, satisfying thunk as the lock popped under the pressure. As it did there was the sensation of time rushing forward to meet them, catching them like elastic snapping back.

Silent as cats, despite their bulk, the two men sprung inside, covering each other's backs.

Scanning left and right Nimrod's senses burnt white hot; it was pure Zen.

The kitchen was clear; corridor, second bedroom, bathroom, too. The whole place smelt of toast and air freshener.

Cain pressed his ear to what had to be the master-bedroom door and with a quick glance at his partner kicked it open, covered by Nimrod, who then strode inside, his gun ahead of him like some dark divining rod.

'What the fuck,' grunted a sleepy voice from under a duvet.

Later, Nimrod would say it was prescience that stopped him from opening fire there and then, although actually it was an unnerving and continuing sense of déjà vu.

Cain whipped back the bedclothes.

There was a long thin hairy man in the bed, fully dressed except for his boots, which stood on the floor beside him.

'What the fuck are you doing here?' Nimrod barked furiously.

'I was only having a kip,' the man spluttered after a second or two, 'Oh bloody hell,' he said as his focus sharpened. He looked anxiously from face to face and swallowed hard.

Cain looked at Nimrod and sniffed, 'It's not him, is it?'

Nimrod shook his head. 'No it's not,' he snapped, bitterly angry in a cold, icy way. 'But I get the distinct impression that our friend here knows exactly what's going on. What's your name?'

The man was wide awake now. 'Bernie Fielding,' he said quickly.

'Really, so it was you they thought they'd caught on *Gotcha* last night?' said Nimrod, pulling a photo out of his inside pocket. 'Well, Bernie, you had better come up with a bloody good reason why I shouldn't shoot you like a dog.

You can begin by telling me what you know about this man and where the fuck he is.'

Bernie, taking the photo, sniffed. 'So you're not really from the gas board then?' he muttered.

13

'So whereabouts did Coleman say we were supposed to meet him?' said Maggie, driving round the roundabout that would take them down into Minehead town centre.

'Somewhere called Blenheim Gardens? It's a park. Do you know it? There's meant to be a café there or something?'

Maggie nodded. 'Oh yes, I know exactly where that is. It's beautiful. We shouldn't be too much longer. I reckon about another ten minutes or so by the time I've found somewhere to to leave the car.'

Nick stared at the passing lamp posts, every single one of which was decked with great festoons of summer flowers and tumbles of greenery cascading from enormous hanging baskets. Then he looked at Maggie and for an instant she saw his gaze darken and deepen again like it had when they were at St Elfreda's. 'I want you to know that I really wish we could have met each other some other way, Maggie,' he said, and then after a second or two continued, 'I know that it's crazy but –'

Afraid of what he might say, Maggie held up a hand to silence him. 'Please don't. You freaked me out when we came up from the beach – I thought you were going to say you were sorry you'd kissed me and that you really didn't mean it. I don't want you to do the "but" thing, Nick. Whichever way you look at it, it's crazy – can we leave it at that while we're ahead on points. Is that okay?'

He laughed. 'No, I wasn't going to say sorry, I'm not sorry I kissed you. What I was going to say was I know it's crazy but can we drive down along the front? You know, along the prom? I've always loved the seaside.'

Maggie shook her head, laughing, too, now – he was right, it was crazy. They headed off towards the Esplanade, although it did feel a little like giving the condemned man one last cigarette.

'It's a really nice place, isn't it? I've never been here before –' Nick said, with his face pressed to the window like an over-excited eight-year-old. 'Oh look, they've got a railway station – oh and there are steam trains. God, I've always loved trains.' He sounded so happy it was ridiculous.

Even so, Maggie got caught up in the spirit of it. 'There's a much older part to the town, too –

up there – it's lovely, all whitewash and narrow steps, and little streets running down to the harbour –' she said, pointing towards the tree-covered slopes of North Hill that rose sharply to shelter the bay.

'I only wish we had a bit more time,' Nick murmured.

With her eyes firmly fixed on the road Maggie cursed whatever obscure deity it was who thought it was a good joke to dangle the best man she had met in years under her nose with such a short sell-by date. Not fair didn't even come close to how she felt about it.

'I wish –' Nick began again, turning to look at her, and then just when he had Maggie's full and undivided attention thought better of it and fell silent, but that look, that brief glance, told Maggie everything she needed to know. Nick Lucas wanted her in all the ways that she wanted him. Turning her attention back to the road Maggie felt a weird little kick in the bottom of her belly and found herself struggling not to fill up with tears. Fate could be such a bloody cow at times.

Hovering somewhere over the Bristol Channel, Danny Coleman could barely hear his thoughts above the ungodly roar of the helicopter's engine and rotor blades. He pulled his coat tight around him. Stiltskin didn't normally run to helicopter rescues but he had pressurised the people at the top, pointing out that it didn't look very good for other would-be prosecution witnesses if their system fell down at the first hurdle. That and an oblique reference to the fact that Minehead and St Elfreda's were very close to Hinkley Point – the nuclear-power station just a few miles up the coastline – had clinched it. Coleman had just dropped the information into the sentence while they were discussing transport; that and the fact that the people chasing Nick Lucas had used a rocket launcher to blow his car up.

Coleman slipped his mobile back into his pocket and then glanced down at the screen on his lap-top. He'd had to get some sort of special gizmo fitted to both so that he didn't press Send and accidentally plunge the whirly-bird and its occupants screaming into the sea.

Lucas's two calls into the office had already been logged into the computer, that and the place where they were due to meet. Normally Coleman wouldn't accompany the crash team, just send the lads in and let them do their job, but this time it was different. Nick Lucas had evaded pick up – he was careful not to use the word capture – once before. It wouldn't do for them to let Lucas give them the slip again.

And – wherever the leak was – maybe, just maybe, bringing Nick Lucas in was the very thing that would flush the system through – maybe. That's what his bosses thought anyway and if that was the case they wanted Coleman there; in at the kill, as it were. He smiled; it was an interesting choice of words. That was something he really didn't want to miss. The chopper swung in low over the sea, the down-draft from the blades cutting the grey water into mare's tails of foam.

'How long before we get there?' Coleman shouted and mimed, stabbing one finger furiously at his watch. 'ETA?'

A man on the far side of the cabin, dressed in combat khakis and with a helmet and headset on, held up his hands, palms flat forward, fingers outstretched, and mouthed ten minutes, then shrugged, implying a minute or two either way. The rest of team, six square-shouldered, clean-shaven young men dressed in neat and unremarkable suits, looked calm and cool and as if dropping out of helicopters was something they did on a daily basis. Two of them were wearing headsets, which implied they knew what they were doing.

Coleman glanced down at his watch, willing them to arrive soon. He hated flying and always felt air sick in helicopters however many little white tablets the doctor prescribed for him. The fleeting thought was enough to remind him. He swallowed back a great wave of nausea. He tried running through the plans he had discussed with his superiors as a way of stopping him from throwing up.

Dorothy Crow had taken the file from his hand as soon as he had walked back into the office from the Nick Lucas emergency meeting.

'It's a go,' was all he had said to her.

Dorothy had nodded and with a smile not unlike his own, added, 'I know. The helicopter is already on its way.' As she spoke she had handed him a glass of water and two Quells.

Hunched and trapped now in the uncomfortable helicopter seat, Coleman nipped the bridge of his nose and closed his eyes. It wasn't meant to be like this; he was supposed to be a desk jockey these days not hurtling round the country like some stupid bugger out of *Mission Impossible*. Across the cabin two of the crash team appeared to be talking in sign language, hands a blur, the flash little gits. He was about to curse under his breath until it occurred to him that they could probably lip-read as well – he wondered if they did ESP.

Coleman settled back, trying to find some way to stretch his legs, struggling to ignore the headache cradled deep in his forehead and avoid vomiting. Only a handful of people had access to the information about Nick Lucas's whereabouts and they were being watched and monitored. Most of them were the same people who knew about the error that Stiltskin had thrown up – but only Coleman knew what connected them together and what was planned.

Today was rather like the children's game of Mastermind, played out with people. The solution might well show itself; the players in their various positions finally revealing their true colours. Maybe. And if he was lucky today everything would be sorted out once and for all. If he was lucky. Across the cabin one of the sign-language guys was laughing at something his companion was spelling out. Coleman sighed and closed his eyes. Bloody kids.

Bernie Fielding, his arms and ankles tied tight to one of the chairs in Maggie's beach hut with a length of guy rope, was busy explaining to Nimrod exactly how very, very well he and Maggie got on, still friends after all these years. Amazing, really. How she would do anything for him, anything at all. No question. Maybe if he rang her, maybe he could persuade her to tell him where she and Nick were, maybe even persuade her to give him up. It was worth a try, surely. Wasn't it? He whimpered.

Nimrod considered the prospect for a few moments. He had certain standards; even though he was angry and frustrated it didn't do to pop too many civilians when you were on a job. He was, after all, a paid assassin not some amateur thug. Despite some of his baser instincts he didn't do freebies these days, unless it was very special circumstances – and he didn't like mess.

He was just about to suggest Bernie improved the strength of his argument when there was a short series of beeps announcing the arrival of a text message for one of them.

All three men looked from face to face.

Bernie shrugged. 'Not me, mate,' he said, eyebrows raised in a gesture of surrender. Slowly, Nimrod pulled a mobile phone out of his pocket, flicked through the screens and then smiled as the message appeared.

'Well, well, well. Seems we haven't lost our friend Mr Lucas after all,' he said to Cain. 'Which means that we won't be needing you, Mr Fielding. Pity about that but there we are.'

Bernie blanched to the colour of skimmed milk, fear strangling his breath in a rasping, ragged, gasping sob.

'Blenheim Gardens, Minehead, it says here,' said Nimrod glancing down at his watch. 'There we are, then. I think we need to be gone, Cain. Apparently the crash team are already on their way to pick Lucas up. So —' he turned his attention back to Bernie, wondering what was the best course of action. Leave him tied here or dump him in the middle of nowhere and hope he didn't blow the whistle before it was too late? It was painfully obvious that Bernie thought that they had a more permanent solution in mind. Nimrod sighed and shook his head; hit men always got such a bad press.

Still tied to the chair, Bernie wriggled frantically. 'But you need me, I know where the gardens are,' he stammered. 'Please, I can show you the way. I can lead you straight to them. Let me help you,' he implored. It was quite touching really.

'We've got a map in the car,' said Cain laconically.

Bernie swallowed hard; Nimrod could almost see his mind working, like the fingers of a drowning man desperately grabbing hold of something, anything that might keep him afloat. 'Yes, but what if Maggie is hiding him somewhere – you have to admit she's a smart cookie, is Maggie,' Bernie said. 'She gave you the slip before. I wouldn't put it past her to do it again – you'll need me to point her out.'

Nimrod considered for a moment or two; there was a certain kind of warped logic to Bernie's suggestion and the woman was certainly sharp enough to come up with something out of left field. And maybe, if she was as fond of Bernie as he said, they could use him as a bargaining chip.

It also struck Nimrod that Bernie Fielding was the kind of greasy little low life mammal that it was best to keep an eye on. Instinct told him that Bernie Fielding would sell his granny for chops and dog mince if he thought it would save his own hide. It made sense for Nimrod to keep Bernie where he could see him, at least until they caught up with Mr Lucas and then he would have to reconsider the position.

Nimrod nodded to Cain. 'Okay, untie him. We'll take him with us.'

'You sure?' said Cain.

Bernie whimpered and tried hard to make himself smaller and more appealing.

Nimrod slipped on his shades. 'And you'd better know where this frigging park is, Bernie, or you might find yourself in deep trouble.'

Bernie Fielding's expression implied that he thought he was in quite deep-enough trouble already.

'Robbie, if you are so unhappy about my directions why don't you let me drive for a while and then you can navigate?' said Lesley coolly. She still had the road atlas balanced on her lap, currently unopened.

Robbie Hughes didn't even bother gracing her words with a reply. This was not how he had imagined the last couple of days going at all. Not at all. His big moment bringing Bernie Fielding to book had turned into a complete fiasco and overnight Lesley had transmogrified into an ice queen from hell. He would seriously have to reconsider her position as his PA once they got back to the studio. There was a nice little brunette in reception who always blushed when he arrived at work and who looked as if she might be just ripe for promotion. Besides, on top of everything else, thanks to Lesley he had missed breakfast. Robbie was hungry and when he was hungry he was bad-tempered.

What he wanted was a mug of tea and a decent fry-up, but Lesley had refused to go into a transport café with him. Robbie had always loved rubbing shoulders with the hairy-arsed hoi polloi, it reminded him vividly of his roots when his dad had a bread van and did the rounds at the back of the gasworks and down by the railway station. Robbie often imagined how it would look with a sepia-coloured tint if they ever showed the footage on *This is Your Life*. Since his first big break in TV, Robbie had kept a Dinky car – a battered red Montego glued onto a mahogany plinth – in front of him on his desk to remind him of what he would be driving now if he had stayed at home and taken over the family bread round.

Even so, those good working-class roots were there, buried deep in his bones, and he felt it was important to go back, to remind himself once in a while of how life might have been. And Robbie always enjoyed the big mugs of tea, and the plate of egg, bacon, beans, black pudding and a fried slice, and the surreptitious glances from the drivers as they worked out whether or not he really was that bloke off the telly. Every so often one of them, some big bluff chap in overalls smelling of diesel oil and cheap aftershave, would amble over and ask for his autograph – almost always for the wife or the girlfriend – and pat Robbie on the back or shake his hand to say what a good job he was doing, fighting crime and righting wrongs, leaping tall buildings in a single bound.

But oh no, the bloody ice queen wanted to come off the motorway and look for a decent restaurant, complaining that she hated the way men in transport cafés always leered at her, and so as a result they had reached a bad-tempered impasse and were now both hungry. He knew that because Lesley's stomach kept rumbling furiously and he was glad, it served her right.

She'd relent eventually; she looked a bit pasty. Robbie had brought a video camera in the car with them so that Lesley would be able to capture the denouement of the Bernie Fielding story, but he was beginning to think now that without the *Gotcha* film crew behind him he might well have to do it as a reconstruction later. After all, he wasn't exactly sure what Lesley was capable of in the point-and-zoom department and given her present state of mind he didn't like to ask.

In quieter moments he was mentally framing the shot where he had had a blow-out in the fast lane of the M6 and had wrestled the car fearlessly onto the hard shoulder. Battling his way across three streams of motorway traffic before leaping out and single-handedly mending the flat with just a Swiss-army penknife and . . .

'It's just up there on the right.' Lesley's voice cut through his thoughts like a blowtorch.

'What is?' snapped Robbie.

She was waving with her hands about. 'The holiday camp.'

'Is that my right,' he growled, 'or some obscure alternative female right that can only be divined psychically?'

Lesley lifted an eyebrow and peered at him. It was such an aggressive little gesture; he was almost certain that that little girl in reception wouldn't do that.

Lesley had changed the tyre fairly quickly – but what she hadn't pointed out when they got going again was that, under the stress of it all, Robbie had taken a wrong turn at the next big junction and thanks to her they had almost ended up in Wales. Wales for God's sake, why hadn't she said something? Lesley had refused to admit to doing it on purpose.

'Right.' She pointed with one chubby little finger.

Robbie sniffed, an instant before clocking the sign to St Elfreda's Bay Holiday Centre. Okay, maybe Lesley was right this time, there had to be a first time for everything. They were about to swing into the entrance when a large silver-grey car pulled out in a hail of loose chippings and stopped. Robbie waved them on. Beside him Lesley made a peculiar noise in the back of her throat.

'What is it now?' Robbie snapped.

'That's him,' she said, ventriloquist fashion.

'What's him?' growled Robbie. He had just about had enough of Lesley.

'That man in the back of that car, there. Don't look now but it's Bernie Fielding.'

Robbie snorted. 'Oh really, and how would you know that, eh, Lesley? We haven't got a decent picture of him.'

'I know it's him,' said Lesley firmly. 'Remember the wedding photograph we've got on file from when he got married to Maggie Morgan? It looks just like him. His hair's shorter and thinner now but I'd know that face anywhere.'

Robbie glared at her. He had spent hours staring at the thin grainy paper-clipping until all he could see were the bloody dots. The freebie newspaper that had published the original had long since closed down so they hadn't been able to track down a decent copy or a print. There was no way he could conjure a face out of the grey tones, however hard he tried, but it seemed that, miracle of miracles, Lesley had.

'Are you sure?' Robbie couldn't quite keep the scepticism out of his voice.

Lesley nodded vigorously. 'Oh yes, that other man, the one at West Brayfield? I knew that he wasn't Bernie.'

Robbie stared at her. 'What? What do you mean you *knew* he wasn't Bernie? Why the hell didn't you say something before I started filming the bloody interview, then?'

Lesley paled. 'Because you seemed so certain, Robbie,' she said nervously. 'I was worried in case you got angry with me. I thought I must have made a mistake.'

Robbie felt his blood pressure rising. 'So thanks to you, Lesley, I fell flat on my arse and made a complete and utter tit of myself?' he growled.

She stared at him. 'What do you mean, *thanks to me*?'

'What I said. You should have said something. You're my PA, that's your job.'

Lesley glared at him; it certainly seemed that she wasn't worried about him getting angry any more. 'Oh is it?' she snapped. 'And what exactly could I have said, Robbie, that would have shut you up? Let's be frank. What was it that you would have listened to?'

'You still should have tried,' grumbled Robbie petulantly. 'I am the first one to admit that I'm not infallible.'

Lesley looked heavenwards as if waiting for a sign from God; the truth was that they both knew that when Robbie was hell-bent on something, with his beach-storming hat on, he was almost impossible to stop, and infallible didn't come close to what he thought he was.

'So what are you suggesting that I should do now, then?' said Robbie. 'Given that Mr Fielding

is, according to you, heading off down the hill?'
Their car was now sitting slap-bang in the middle
of the road. Behind them a minibus full of what
looked like boy scouts pipped hopefully.

'Follow that car,' Lesley said, waving her hand
like a wagon-train master cracking a whip, and
then added as an afterthought, 'Would you like
me to drive?'

Maggie drove up the Avenue – one of Minehead's
main tourist and shopping streets – found the
turning that would take her up to Blenheim
Gardens and a place to park on the first attempt.
Easy. She sighed with relief as she backed into the
space – although almost as soon as the thought
formed the easy feeling faded. Making contact with
Coleman would mean there was a good chance
that Nick Lucas would vanish from her life forever.

The main road had been busy with cars, holidaymakers wandering up the broad paths and
straggling into the road, slowing the traffic to a
snail's pace. By contrast, Blenheim Gardens was
a haven of tranquillity.

'I wish –' Nick began as they headed towards
the gates and then he stopped himself again.

'I wish you'd stop saying "I wish",' said Maggie
grumpily.

Catching hold of her hand Nick pulled her up
against him. 'Maggie, you are the most amazing
person I've ever met.'

Maggie groaned. 'Oh for God's sake, Nick – that is such a corny thing to say.' Not that it stopped her from turning in his arms or tipping her face up towards him so that he could kiss her.

'But I mean it,' he said, looking hurt as a moment or two later she pulled away. 'Seriously. Of all the women who could have found me semi-naked in their hall, I'm –'

She kissed him quiet and then said firmly, 'Coleman. Come on, we have to go –' as he made to kiss her again.

Nick's face fell. 'I know, I was just hanging on, relishing the last few minutes.'

'But you have to go.'

Once they were through the gates there was a signpost indicating the way to the café, amongst other places. For all her encouraging, Maggie was in the same state of mind as Nick, torn between wanting to linger and getting him to Coleman and safety.

Without another word Nick caught hold of her hand and they made their way towards the café. It was the most perfect day to be wandering through the park with a new lover. Maggie felt tears catch in her throat – it was as wonderful as it was ridiculous to be walking hand in hand in the sunshine.

Ahead of them the gardens looked stunning – great beds full of riotous hot summer colours, interspersed with palms and shrubs and trees. The perfume of the flowers was a heady counterpoint to the rich aroma of coffee that carried towards them on the light breeze.

As they walked Maggie was aware that her eyes were working left and right across the faces of the people around them; the sunbathers and the strollers, the courting couples and the old ladies clutching their ice creams. Maggie wasn't altogether sure what she was looking for but knew for certain that she'd recognise it the instant she saw it.

'We have them both in our sights, Sir. They have just entered the park,' said a hissing metallic voice in Coleman's ear. 'They're currently heading towards the café and should be with you in a matter of minutes –' There was a crackle and then Coleman smiled. Not long now, he thought. 'We have a vehicle on standby. Would you like us to close in?'

'No, stay exactly where you are, don't move –' barked Coleman. 'I don't want him scared off.' And then with enforced nonchalance Coleman began to scan the faces of the approaching holidaymakers, looking for Nick Lucas amongst the happy throng.

As they rounded a neatly clipped hedge, Maggie saw a young guy in a suit talking into his lapel and knew, without a shadow of a doubt, that he was what she was looking for.

'We've been spotted,' she said under her breath.

Nick glanced across the grass, following her gaze and then quickly looked away. She could almost see the tension easing out of his shoulders and face. For him this was the home run; she couldn't help but wonder exactly where that left her, although there was no way Maggie planned to go all limp and girlie on him now.

'Don't worry, not long now,' she said in a small, quiet voice. Nick squeezed her hand, although Maggie wasn't entirely sure whether it was meant to reassure him or her.

'There,' said Nick as they rounded another corner, unable to keep the relief out of his voice. 'Over there. Look, that's Coleman, standing by the ice-cream stall –'

Maggie looked up and saw a man dressed in a long dark coat hanging around outside the café. He was quite obviously loitering with intent and had made no attempt to blend in in any way. The heavy overcoat looked odd and slightly sinister in the heat. Coleman certainly wasn't the best-looking guardian angel she had ever clapped eyes on but he would have to do.

Nick started to walk faster, and as he did Maggie saw something else – something that took her breath away.

'Oh my God,' she hissed in astonishment.

Slightly ahead of her Nick was making his way to safety; he didn't slow his pace; unaware that she had stopped.

On the far side of the park, Bernie Fielding and two men were walking across the grass, two men wearing sharp suits and shades. Two dangerous-looking men, men who made Maggie's blood ice up, and then something else occurred to her, something much more sinister.

'Nick?'

He turned to look at her.

'Don't look so worried – just a few more minutes and it will all be over,' he said with a smile.

That was the last thing she wanted to hear. Maggie swallowed hard as the rest of the world slowed to a snail's pace. She stepped forward, grabbed tight hold of Nick's arm and turning away from Coleman, turning away from the men in the sharp suits, Maggie hissed, 'We have to get out of here. Now –'

'What on earth are you on about?' protested Nick as they wheeled round. It appeared that he was too surprised to resist her.

'Trust me, please,' she said, trying hard not to panic, trying hard not to break into a run, willing Bernie not to look around, not to spot her, or if he did to have the good sense to keep his big mouth shut. Maggie knew if it came to it there was no way they could outrun the two hyenas either side of Bernie and any change of pace might catch their eye.

With her arm through Nick's she executed a perfect 180-degree turn taking him back along the path, back the way they came, zigzagging in and out of young mothers with buggies, old men with walking sticks and a jogger sweating hard. Maggie hardly dared breathe; the exit that had seemed so close moments earlier now seemed a million miles away.

Maggie could see the young man who had been talking into his jacket, saw him look at them, saw the surprise register on his face and kept on walking as he wheeled round to follow them.

And then they were at the gate. Heart in her mouth, Maggie pulled out her car keys and – sheltered by the hedge now – barked, 'Quickly, quickly, Nick – run!'

Nick, although totally bemused, did as he was told, and began to hurry after her, back towards the car.

'I don't know what the hell's going on. Our man and the woman are heading back out of the park,' said the voice in Coleman's ear.

'What?' snapped Coleman furiously. 'What the fuck do you mean they're heading out of the park – why – never mind – just get after them – get after them now and bring me Lucas and that mad bitch he's got with him. Go!'

* * *

264

'Get in the car,' Maggie yelled, leaping into the driver's seat, followed more slowly by a bemused Nick.

'What's going on? Are you mad? He was there, you saw him. Coleman was waiting to take me in,' said Nick. 'What the fuck are you playing at, Maggie?'

Maggie gunned the engine and pulled out into the road.

'Steady,' said Nick nervously, as the car leapt forward into the stream of traffic. 'Do you want to tell me what the hell is going on here?'

'I just saw Bernie,' said Maggie, peering anxiously into her rear-view mirror to see if they were being followed.

'Bernie? What do you mean, Bernie? *Bernie Fielding*? In the park? Are you sure? I don't understand – why did we have to run away from Bernie of all people?' Nick looked back over his shoulder towards what had been his salvation.

'Because he wasn't alone, Nick – he was there with two men, two men in shades who looked – well, just how you would imagine hit men to look.'

Nick stared at her. 'Oh come on, that's crazy, Maggie. Are you certain? Coleman was there waiting for me. Another couple of hundred yards and I would have been home and dry.'

'Would you?' asked Maggie quietly, almost to herself, thinking about the stray thought that had hit her as they had crossed the Gardens. 'How did those two men know where we were?' she asked slowly.

Nick Lucas stared at her. 'I'm not with you. What do you mean?'

Maggie's brain tried to rationalise what some deeper instinct understood only too well. 'What I mean is how did those men know that we would be in Minehead – in Blenheim Gardens – at that moment? Who else knew where we were going?'

'Bernie?'

Maggie shook her head. 'No. We didn't tell him where we were going. Even I didn't know until we drove out of St Elfreda's and I asked you.'

Nick's expression registered confusion for a few minutes and then cleared as some ghastly comprehension dawned. 'Oh my God –' his colour drained. 'Coleman? Is that what you're trying to say? It can't be Coleman who told them – he's one of the good guys. It has to be a coincidence.'

Maggie snorted. 'Some coincidence. Who else knew? Can you really afford to take the chance?' she said, accelerating down towards the seafront. The pedestrians scattered like confetti in front of the Golf.

'What the hell are you doing?' gasped Nick.

'Putting as many miles between you and Blenheim Gardens as I can.'

Nick sighed. 'Maggie, for God's sake, slow down. This is crazy – I want you to stop the car and to drop me off here.' He pointed towards the next junction.

'What?'

He turned round to look at her. 'You heard me, Maggie; those people want me dead. It's not some joke, it's real – and they are not going to stop until I am dead. And I don't want you involved in this. It's way too dangerous – now drop me off. Over there on the corner.'

'But what are you going to do?' she whispered.

'It doesn't matter, just let me out.'

'Don't be so stupid,' Maggie shouted, unable to hide her frustration. 'There has to be some way out of this. What about if I take you to a bigger town, you could hide out there. There must be someone who would help you, someone you could ring?'

Nick shook his head. 'Maggie, look, you don't understand. That isn't how it works. I'm not the sort of person who can go on the run, and even if I was it's too dangerous to get any of my family or old friends involved. Coleman knows that. I just need a bit of time to think.'

Maggie turned the car and headed back towards the seafront. 'What is there to think about. There has to be something you can do. You can't just hand yourself over to those killers – that's crazy. What if Coleman is working with them, too?'

Nick slumped forward cradling his head in his

hands. 'I don't know any more. I can't take any more of this, I just want it to be over.'

Maggie looked at him. 'But not by giving up, Nick?' she said expectantly. 'Not by handing yourself in to Coleman?'

He sighed. 'I don't really see what other choice I have.'

'So you think I'm wrong about him betraying you?'

Nick shook his head. 'I don't know any more.'

Coleman stalked backwards and forwards across the front of the café, his coat – far too heavy for the day – blowing out behind him like a cloak. He looked like a disgruntled bat.

'So where the hell has he got to?' he barked into the little microphone on his lapel.

One of the young, broad-shouldered six said, 'Don't worry, Sir. We've got men at strategic points; all the exits are covered. He can't get very far.'

Coleman snorted. 'What do you mean he can't get far?' He didn't doubt for a moment that his rescue squad were the business. What worried Coleman was not how his team might acquit themselves but why Nick Lucas had bolted again. The man was too highly strung for his own good and that bloody woman was a nuisance. What the two of them failed to realise was that it didn't matter how far Nick ran. All alone, without police protection or Stiltskin to hide him, Nick Lucas was as good as dead. There were people in high places – people who had taken out a contract on him – who wouldn't stop until Nick was six-feet-under. Coleman sighed. Lucas had been a fool not to come quietly.

Unconsciously Coleman brushed a hand down over his shoulders, his fingertips just brushing the butt of the gun he was carrying in a shoulder holster. Maybe Lucas would be better off dead after all, at least then all the running and the fear would be over and done with.

'Stand by.' His ear piece crackled. Coleman waited.

14

While Coleman prowled backwards and forwards waiting for news, on the other side of the park Robbie Hughes had been watching, Lesley, who had looked left and right, all the while bobbing up and down behind the hedges that lined the paths, trying to spot where the two heavies had taken Bernie Fielding. She looked for all the world like a meerkat in a pale pink cardigan.

They had only just missed Bernie and his dodgy-looking friends, pulling up in the car no more than a moment or two behind the three of them – although fortunately not close enough to catch Bernie's eye, so with a bit of luck their prey hadn't bolted; at least not yet.

It had to be said that Robbie was beginning to lose patience with the whole bloody scenario. They had been so close and yet were still so far from any decent filmable conclusion, and Lesley really wasn't helping at all. Behind the hedge she had been going through another cycle of bobbing, poking and peering.

'Well?' he had snapped, waiting for her expert opinion. 'Did you see where they went?'

But before Lesley had been able to reply, two people, a man and a woman, had hurtled past them as if they were running out of a burning building, and this time even Robbie recognised that it was the man he had interviewed at West Brayfield and Bernie Fielding's ex-wife, Maggie Morgan.

Robbie had stared at them as they ran towards the car park. What in God's name was that about? Were they were all in cahoots? Did it imply that there was something else going on that he didn't know about? Had Bernie and his ex-wife got some cosy little *ménage à trois* going on in a beach hut somewhere? A sex romp might be just the thing he needed to weigh the scales with the Madam Upstairs at *Gotcha*. Or was it a conspiracy? People always enjoyed a good conspiracy theory.

Robbie looked at Lesley; maybe she had some idea.

'Was that who I think it was?' she said, pushing her glasses back up onto the bridge of her nose.

Robbie nodded.

'What on earth do you think is going on?' asked Lesley.

On another path, not too far away from the café,

Nimrod scanned left and right. He had already spotted the heavily set guy in the unseasonal black coat waiting around outside the coffee shop, snorting on a nasal spray. He knew instinctively that even if this was not Lucas's contact then he had an important role in picking him up.

Walking beside Nimrod, Cain said very little, while Bernie shambled along between them looking decidedly hangdog and very, very uneasy. Nimrod had already decided that if Bernie made a break for it they wouldn't expend too much energy bringing him back. He was probably more trouble than he was worth.

Over by the café, Nimrod saw the coat man's face twitch into life and watched as he pressed a finger to his ear, talking into his lapel. Nimrod scanned backwards and forwards amongst the walkers and the sunbathers, trying to pick up the other members of this guy's team, all the while willing Nick Lucas to come into view. It surely wouldn't be long now; time had begun to slow down to a crystal-clear syrupy flow. Nimrod smiled as every face, every flower, every detail of the day became sharp as glass, while the adrenaline pumped through his body as warm and welcome as good whisky.

A public, daylight execution was far from ideal, but from this distance it would all be over in an instant and they would be away before Nick Lucas had hit the neatly clipped grass. It would be like the grassy knoll all over again.

Nimrod grinned, letting the idea roll through his mind. Every sense was alive as he imagined the instant when he picked his shot – felt his finger squeeze the trigger, the motion as smooth as silk – and as his mind cleared, Nimrod let out a long slow breath and with it the tension rolled out of his body like fog.

Soon, crooned the dark voice deep in his mind. A heartbeat away, Cain caught his eye and grinned back; he could feel it, too.

An instant later, the coat man in front of the café started off across the park towards the far gate, walking smartly, his head down, a finger pressed into his ear. Nimrod tracked his progress like a laser. Another man hurried across to join him – by his dress easily identifiable as another of the pick-up squad. If they were breaking positions then something had gone badly wrong. Damn. Where the hell had Nick Lucas got to?

'After them,' Nimrod snapped to Cain, and began to stride out after the man in the black coat and his sidekick. He didn't doubt for an instant that Cain would know exactly who he meant. Cain wouldn't consider questioning Nimrod's instructions and instantly did as he was told. Bernie came too, mainly – Nimrod reasoned, as he headed off after their prey –

273

because he was too scared and far too stupid to do otherwise.

'Our man just got into the woman's car and they've pulled away, and appear to be heading back towards the town centre,' said a voice in Coleman's ear.

'What? What do you mean *pulling away*? Why didn't you stop him, you dozy pillock?' roared a furious Coleman.

This wasn't how operational procedure said it should be done; debriefing and explanations should come later, when a mission was over. In the moment all energies, all attention and resources needed, should be concentrated on what *was happening*, not what should or might have happened, but Coleman was so angry he couldn't stop himself.

'But I was under the impression that this was supposed to be a walk in,' whined the man. 'Our mark was supposed to come over and just give himself up, not turn round and bugger off again,' he continued in the same high-pitched whinny, and then recovering himself, added, 'and I didn't have orders to detain him, Sir, and besides we don't want an incident, do we.'

'An incident?' barked Coleman, glowing white-hot with frustration. 'He's a chef for God's sake – what did you think he was going to do, break out a palette knife, beat you senseless with a fucking éclair? Give me strength – bring the car round. I'm already on my way. I assume someone saw which way they went?'

'Maybe Maggie Morgan and that chap are just here on holiday. It could be a coincidence,' Lesley said to Robbie Hughes.

Robbie stared at her. 'What? Bernie, Maggie and the other bloke are all here together, in Minehead, and that they were all at the holiday park together earlier? What are the odds on that, then, Lesley, eh?' He couldn't keep the derision out of his voice.

'I was only thinking aloud,' Lesley said, her mouth narrowing down into an angry, tough little line that made Robbie feel very uneasy indeed. 'I was just saying –'

Two more men hurried past them. One was middle-aged and thickset, with a thick black wool coat on. He looked important and hot, while the other one, younger in a navy-blue suit, was scurrying behind him trying to keep pace. The older man did not look at all pleased – they both had the appearance of policemen in plain clothes and they were making for the car park.

Lesley looked at Robbie. 'Something very strange is going on here,' she said, stealing the thought clean out of his head. 'What do you want to do?'

So now, fresh out of ideas of her own, Lesley

wanted to play the willing little assistant, thought Robbie grimly.

But the decision and any possible retort was whipped away as not more than thirty seconds later two other smartly dressed men, flanking a third, hurried out of the gardens too. This time Lesley visibly brightened.

'That's him,' she said, waving furiously. 'There. Look. It's Bernie Fielding.'

The man in the middle looked up briefly, blanched milk-white, and at that moment even Robbie could see that the face now staring at them with a mixture of horror and total astonishment resembled the wedding picture in the newspaper.

'Oh my God. Bernie Fielding,' Robbie snorted in disbelief. Finally, here he was, face to face with his arch enemy at long last. God, Robbie wished that he'd brought the whole bloody crew with him now. Whether the segment got shown or not, Robbie wanted this moment recorded for posterity. 'Have you got the video camera?' Robbie hissed from the corner of his mouth, expectantly holding out a hand.

'No, I thought you'd got it,' said Lesley. 'It must still be in the car.'

Robbie groaned. Bloody woman.

'Oh fucking hell,' said Bernie, turning at the sound of his name.

Nimrod looked down quizzically at him. 'What's the matter with you?'

'Over there. It's that bloke off the telly,' Bernie said, pointing towards the hedge.

'Robbie Hughes. He's the presenter of *Gotcha*. He's very good –' Cain offered helpfully.

Christ, that was all they needed. Nimrod looked round in horror and caught a fleeting glimpse of what had startled Bernie. If they had a film crew with them then he and Cain were screwed, but no, it was just a small plump man and a skinny blonde woman who at present were standing with their mouths wide open, staring at Bernie, although Nimrod knew from experience that it wouldn't take long for them to defrost.

Before they had the chance Nimrod caught hold of Bernie's arm and frogmarched him to the car park. The last thing they needed right now was for Bernie Fielding to tell some investigative reporter all about their search for Nick Lucas in an attempt to save his own skinny little arse. And Nimrod didn't doubt for a moment that that was exactly what Bernie would do if he got half a chance.

'Get in the bleeding car. Now!' Nimrod growled to Bernie, and Bernie did exactly as he was told, as meekly as a little lamb.

Maggie drove Nick straight out of town, up along the coast road to the little village of Selworthy without so much as a backward glance. All right, perhaps a look or two but once she was clear of the town she was almost certain that they weren't being followed.

The irony was that it was the most beautiful day on Exmoor. The sky was cornflower-blue without a single cloud muscling in to dilute the colour, the light sharpening the edges and warming the curves of the rich green landscape. In the tiny village, sunshine reflected off the glorious white-painted cottages nestling up under their thickly thatched roofs. As Maggie eased her way into a parking space the village looked as serene and as unruffled as any place could possibly be.

But serene or not, Maggie guessed that she and Nick were sheltering in the eye of the storm and that they had to get away, but exactly how and where and for how long was totally beyond anything Maggie could get her head around. It seemed impossible to find a way out of their current predicament, and even more impossible to think straight.

Maggie couldn't go anywhere with Nick – even if she was tempted to. She already had a life, the cottage, the boys – and part of her brain was demanding that Maggie put Nick out on the side of the road and drive away as far and as fast as she could. Good God, just how much deeper did she need to get entangled with him before she saw sense? The voice sounded a lot like her mother –

which was another thing. She couldn't leave the boys with her mum and dad indefinitely and she hadn't rung them since she had arrived in Somerset.

It was Nick that the hit men were after, not her. Maggie hadn't done anything, but if she continued to help him how much longer would it be before she was at risk, too? But on the other hand, how could she possibly just abandon him to the wolves? The thought of it made her heart hurt and the dilemma made her head ache.

'Maggie?'

Maggie jumped; for a moment or two she had almost forgotten Nick was still there. Painting on a cheery smile she looked across at him.

In the passenger seat Nick looked pale and tired, and Maggie sighed. She had had only a couple of days of being hunted down, God alone knew what the effects on her would be if, like him, she had lived with the threat of discovery and death for months on end. It was amazing that he wasn't stark-staring mad by now.

'What is it?' she asked gently.

He pulled her close and kissed her, clinging to her for a second. The sensation of his lips on hers made Maggie shiver. 'You want the truth?'

She nodded while her stomach flipped over and over with desire. 'I most certainly do.'

When Nick spoke it was as if he had been reading her mind. 'I've had enough, Maggie. I'm so tired of running. I just want to go home. And I've had an idea; I don't know if it'll work but it's got to be worth a shot.' He grinned. 'Maybe that wasn't a very good choice of words.' Pulling away he took her mobile out of his jacket pocket. 'I'm going to ring the police and give myself up –'

She looked at him. 'What? But I don't understand, Nick – surely Coleman *is* the police?'

He shook his head, 'No, I don't think so, at least not directly. Coleman is part of some other government organisation but if anyone looks at my files they'll be able to find plenty of evidence that I've been harassed and threatened and that I've been placed under protection. All of that is on the record. If I can talk to someone high enough up – even if I can't – surely to God I'll be safer in police custody than I am out here on the run? Someone, somewhere has to know that Coleman's precious relocation system is leaking like a sieve – how else would those guys have found me? And if it is Coleman – well –' He shrugged. 'I still have to make the call, I don't know what else to do. I haven't got what it takes to fight them all.'

He looked across at her, his blue eyes dark with a pain that she didn't dare fathom.

'But what if the police don't believe you – what if they think you're mad?'

He laughed. 'It's a chance I have to take. But

if I can persuade them to look at my record, even if I'm banged up in a cell for a few hours until they pull my case notes, it has got to be safer than being out here in the open.'

Maggie wasn't so sure. 'How about if I come in with you and tell them what I've seen?'

Nick shook his head. 'I'd rather you didn't – I don't want you involved any more than you already are, Maggie. It's time to let go now.' He sounded warm but determined.

'But – but –' she protested, feeling her eyes fill up with tears. 'I don't know if I can just let you go, Nick. I am already involved. And I care. How will I know what's happened to you? How will I be able to find you –' Any further words stuck in her throat and one big tear rolled down over her cheek despite her best efforts to keep it back.

Nick stroked her face. 'Please don't cry, and don't worry. I'll try and find a way to let you know that I'm all right, I promise, but in return you must promise not to come looking for me or to try and contact me. Do you understand? Is it a deal?'

Maggie stared at him. 'But –' she began.

He shook his head. 'But nothing –'

Maggie stared at him, unable to say the words, although it appeared Nick took her silence as agreement. Picking up the phone he rang directory enquiries and a few minutes later tapped in the number of Minehead police station.

'Hello? Can I speak to the Duty Sergeant, please?' he said, sounding remarkably calm.

Maggie heard the low rumble of a reply at the far end of the line and then Nick said, 'Yes, of course. My name is Nick Lucas; please could you tell him that it's urgent.'

Maggie couldn't bear to hear Nick trying to explain what was going on. Where on earth do you start to try and tell a stranger how your life has been torn apart, and how the very people meant to help appeared to be the ones who were out to get you? Said out loud it sounded mad and paranoid and beyond the realms of reason, so while Nick waited to be connected Maggie got out of the car and made her way slowly up into the village, eyes still full of tears. How the hell had she got herself into a mess like this?

The cottages of Selworthy with their deep thatched roofs, eyebrow dormers and tall chimneys were almost too picturesque. It looked as if nothing ever ruffled Selworthy. It was a place Maggie had been to time and time again over the years, exquisitely beautiful, with gardens basking in full bloom in the summer sunlight.

The peace of the place made Maggie ache with a pain she had no name for. It was still quite early in the day but even so the village had a few walkers and tourists exploring and enjoying the views.

Waiting was hard. Maggie sat on a low wall and watched the world go by for a while, her mind clouded by random thoughts, fears and ideas, until at last she saw Nick making his way slowly up the hill towards her. He smiled and lifted a hand in greeting. As Maggie's mind focused on him she realised with a terrible sense of certainty that she could really love this man given half a chance. Really, truly love him. How cruel was that?

'And how did it go?' she said, making an attempt to sound cheerful.

'Well, it took a while to get through – but the long and short of it is that they want me to come in to the police station as soon as possible.'

'That's got a familiar ring to it,' she said with a wry smile.

Nick sighed. 'Don't. I don't know what else to do, Maggie. The guy was sceptical at first but then they transferred the call through to someone higher up the food chain. It took a while to make them fully understand what was going on, and then the penny seemed to drop at their end – and I don't know –' Nick held up his hands in surrender. 'I don't see that I have that many other choices.'

'Okay,' Maggie said as gently as she could. She could hear the uneasy, nervous edge in his voice. What was the point in torturing him over an already impossible situation? 'In that case we had better get you back to town then. Is there anywhere you want to go or anything you'd like to do before you give yourself up?' she asked.

Nick's face broadened out into a grin. 'Actually I can think of lots of things I'd like to do, but I'd prefer it if we had the chance to do them somewhere a little less public.' Maggie blushed crimson and then he blushed, too. 'Sorry, maybe I shouldn't have said that – it's a bit presumptuous, and there is also the little matter of time. It just seems so unfair –'

'Tell me about it,' said Maggie.

'The other thing is I've already told the police that I'd come in straight away.' She looked up at him expectantly and he continued, 'Actually it was their suggestion; they said the sooner I was under police protection, the better for everyone concerned.'

Maggie looked away. Easy for them to say.

'So, tell me, Sherlock – did you get the number of Ms Morgan's car?' said Coleman in disgust when it became quite obvious that the away team had lost Nick Lucas and Maggie when they left the park.

'I most certainly did, Sir,' the man growled indignantly, and pulled out his notebook.

'Good, well in that case,' said Coleman, producing his mobile and tapping in a number. 'Let me have it.' And then into the phone he said, 'I'd like to report a stolen vehicle please.' Coleman spoke briskly into the handset. 'Yes, about five minutes ago from the public car park outside

Blenheim Gardens, Minehead, Somerset. It's a navy-blue Golf – registered I presume to one Ms Margaret Morgan. I want the occupants stopped and detained, my clearance codes are –'

At the far end of the line Dorothy Crow said very calmly, 'You don't need clearance codes with me, Danny. Not going well down there?'

Coleman snorted as he took the notebook from the boy's hands. 'You could say that. Hang on – he flipped through the pages past a doodle of a small cartoon dog that appeared to be winking. Bloody kids. 'Have you got a pen there, Dorothy?'

'I most certainly do – and I'll have her car up and on the wire as soon as you put the phone down.'

Coleman sighed and read out the registration number.

'Can you still see Bernie's car?' said Lesley, stretching up in her seat and peering myopically into the distance as they headed slowly through the centre of town.

'I most certainly can,' said Robbie confidently, his mood lifting considerably now that their prey was in plain sight. 'And I plan to stick to that car like shit to a blanket until they pull over. You have got the video camera all ready, haven't you?'

'Oh yes,' said Lesley, tapping the machine cradled in her lap. 'I've been thinking, do you think we should phone in to the studio and let them know where we are? Make sure they're ready for any footage we pick up?'

Robbie shook his head. The last thing he wanted was to be pulled off the chase by that bloody harridan upstairs. 'No, not yet. We'll ring when we've got the whole thing on tape. I hope we can get enough for a half-decent segment – Bernie looks very uneasy at the moment, which could very well be to our advantage. Maybe we should corner him if the opportunity presents itself and push for an interview, after all his ex-wife did say he was very keen to talk to someone. You know what they say, confession is good for the soul, and those guys he's with do look very dodgy – they can't be up to any good.'

'Who, the two men or Bernie?'

'All of them by the looks of it,' Robbie said confidently. 'Although the two heavies he's with look a cut above your average villain. I just wonder if Bernie has finally got himself in too deep – finally got in out of his depth. I'd like to be a fly on the wall in that car and hear what's going down.'

Lesley pulled a face. She still wasn't totally au fait with all the patois that went with the territory.

'Going down – going on,' he translated, 'you know, what it is that they're up to.'

Lesley nodded, 'Oh right, yes, I'm with you. Me, too.'

*   *   *

In the silver-grey hire car Nimrod handed Bernie a Minto as they drove slowly up the main street and along the esplanade.

'I could murder a hot dog,' said Cain, looking out onto the busy seaside frontage. 'Smell them onions.'

'. . . a dark blue VW Golf, registration number Lema Foxtrot . . .' the measured voice of the police controller on the radio scanner was busy saying, fading in and out and interspersed with regular beeps and crackles as the signal fluctuated, '. . . driven by a white female, medium height, mid-thirties, with dark hair; and male passenger, dark hair mid-thirties, approx six foot. All units are requested . . .' Crackle, hiss, pop '. . . the occupants are to be stopped and detained . . . it is unlikely they will put up any resistance . . .'

'Hang on, hang on,' said Nimrod triumphantly, turning up the volume. 'That's them, we've got them. The control room are talking about Nick Lucas and –' he jerked a thumb towards Bernie in the back seat, '– his ex-missus. They've come up on the police frequency – APB –'

Bernie grunted. 'What the hell does that mean?'

'Come on, Bernie, some kind of bad guy you turned out to be. All points bulletin. Coat man at the park must have some bloody clout to pull that off. In that case your missus and Lucas can't have got too far away if they're calling the local plod out to pick them up – and that heap your old lady's driving probably won't go more than fifty. We just need to hang tight and wait to see who calls them in.'

The radio crackled furiously.

'You're going to take Lucas out with the law on the job?' asked Cain in surprise.

Nimrod sighed. 'Come on, who's going to stop us? A couple of country coppers? The chances are if we can pick the call up early enough we'll be there before them anyway – we'll be in and out –'

'– And home in time for tea and buns,' concluded Cain.

Nimrod nodded. 'Yeah, right – I couldn't have put it better myself. We'll play it by ear. All we have to do now is park up somewhere, wait and listen. Look over there – there's a space.'

Robbie eased into another parking space, no more than a hundred yards away from Bernie and his companions. Within seconds Lesley had got the men in the sight of her telephoto lens and was clicking away.

'So what are they doing?' Robbie asked, frustrated, trying to persuade her to part with the camera by beckoning towards her.

Lesley, face screwed up in a mask of concentration, sighed. 'It's very difficult to tell from here but it looks to me as if they are listening to the radio.'

Robbie groaned. 'The radio, what do you mean listening to the radio? Are you sure? What do you think they're doing, taking part in a phone-in pop quiz?'

Lesley turned to stare at him. 'You asked me what they were doing and I just told you.' Her tone was icy.

Robbie sniffed. 'There's no need to get shirty with me, Lesley. I was only asking.'

Undeterred, Lesley held the camera back up to her eye. 'Do you think, now that they're parked up we should go over and confront him? I mean he's a sitting duck over there –'

Robbie shook his head. 'No, it would be far too easy for them to drive away; besides in my experience there is no such thing as a sitting duck. Who knows what we'll catch them doing if we bide our time for a while longer. No, we'll sit tight. I'd really like to see what they're up to –'

'But how are we going to know?'

Robbie grimaced; the woman really had no imagination at all. 'We're going to sit and we're going to watch and meanwhile give me the camera and turn on the radio.'

'What do you want to listen to?'

Robbie sighed. 'I don't *want* to listen to anything, I want you to go through all the stations until you find something that sounds as if those lot over there might want to listen to it.'

'Right – only there is something on Woman's

Hour I'd like to listen to later on if you don't mind. I've been following the serial.'

Robbie glared at her and without another word Lesley pressed the buttons that would scan through the radio channels.

15

Maggie drove slowly away from Selworthy back towards Minehead town centre. The sea still reflected the unbroken cloudless blue above. The sun shone, the coastal strand edging the sweeping coastline looking for all the world like a golden collar, the rolling feminine lines of the Somerset landscape oddly accentuated by the white, tented skyline of the all-weather holiday resort down on the seafront. It was the most perfect summer's day.

Below them Minehead was on holiday. Surrounded by great swathes of woodland, the seaside town basked in the morning sunlight and it was hard not to contrast Nick's nightmarish-situation with the simple pleasures of families busy on an old-fashioned beach holiday.

Maggie slowed the car, wanting to delay the moment when it all finally ended. Alongside her Nick sat in total silence, his gaze apparently unfocused while his mind was who knows where.

'Are you all right?' she said. All in all it was a pretty stupid question but the best she could come up with under pressure.

Nick smiled, but it looked more like an instinctive reflex reaction rather than anything particularly positive. 'Just thinking. You know –', he mumbled.

Maggie knew only too well. 'What happened with you and your wife?' she said, as the traffic ahead of them slowed to a disgruntled crawl. 'You said that you were married –'

Nick looked round as if trying to gather his thoughts back together. 'Sorry?'

'Your wife? There are so many things I don't know about you, Nick, and I was just thinking –'

'Do you ever do anything else?'

'Occasionally,' Maggie laughed.

'So what is it you want to know?'

She smiled, trying to make light of the way she was feeling. 'Everything I suppose.'

He lifted his shoulders in a gesture of resignation. 'She left. Her name was, is, Anna – she's a great person, small and blonde, very pretty in a pixie-ish, elfin way. Good family; likes to drive fast –' He smiled as his mind flooded with images of his ex-wife.

Maggie waited. Maybe now wasn't the right moment – but then again, if not now then when? 'We met when we were working in the same restaurant. She was a student and I was – well, a general dogsbody, I suppose. I'd just finished college.' He stopped.

'And?'

'You are relentless, aren't you?' he said, wearily.

'I prefer to think of myself as thorough. In a few minutes you are going to vanish out of my life forever. I need to put you into some sort of context. I have to try to make some kind of sense of what's happened, what I feel –'

'What possible sense can you make of it? It doesn't make any sense,' he protested. 'I thought we'd already agreed on that?'

Maggie shrugged. 'I know – which makes it all the more important that I try, so you fit somewhere in my head. I don't know anything about you, Nick. I don't know where you lived, where you grew up. Where you came from, what your restaurant was called – if you've got any brothers and sisters – nothing. And then,' Maggie slowed down, aware that she was gabbling '– I was thinking how bad it must have been to lose everything and how it would have been easier if there were two of you, to share it.' She paused; it wasn't the most sensitive way to say what she meant and Maggie looked up at Nick to try and read the expression on his face, before adding very quietly, 'I keep thinking how lonely it must be.'

'You know what I think, Maggie? I think that you think too much –' Moving closer, Nick gently stroked her face with an open palm. 'It's a real shame that we didn't meet years ago –'

Maggie shivered; his skin was warm and soft and almost too much to bear.

'I'm sorry,' she said. 'But we have so little time – and I want to know, I want to understand.'

'It feels as if being married to Anna was part of a totally different life now – like I watched it, not lived it. I've been moved from safe house to safe house over a dozen times in the last eighteen months – a couple of times in the middle of the night because there had been some sort of tip-off.' Nick smiled reflectively. 'Anna couldn't have hacked it – don't get me wrong, she is truly gorgeous and a good woman, and I loved her very much when we were married, but there was no slack with her. Things are either right or they're wrong. On or off, up or down. No grey, no middle ground, no room for manoeuvre. When I first talked to her about the police bugging the restaurant, she thought I was totally and utterly mad. She warned me that it was a mistake – said that she didn't want to get involved.

'Then when things started to go wrong, she hated it – not that I blamed her for that, I hated it, too – but in the end she hated me for not listening to her and bringing our nice, bright, successful life crashing down around our ears. Maybe she was right – I don't know, maybe if I'd just kept my head down and my mouth shut I'd have saved myself a hell of a lot of trouble. I'm sure they would have found another way to nail the women.

'Anna stuck it as long as she could, but in the end she left and I let her go. It felt as if I owed her that much; she was right – it was my fault that we were in the mess we were in.' Nick's last few words rattled out, like machine-gun bullets.

Maggie looked at him. 'I'm so sorry. Weren't you afraid that they'd target her?'

'Up until the trial she was under police protection, too, but once I'd testified, or at least that is how it seemed – it was me they wanted. I don't know, to be honest –' Nick reddened as if she had caught him out. 'It wasn't that I didn't care about what was happening to her, it was that everything was a blur. They moved me from place to place and her family shut me out, as if it had been me who was the criminal. I wasn't able to contact her again and she didn't try to contact me.'

'Maybe she was frightened.'

'Maybe.'

'Do you miss her?' Out loud it sounded crass but there was no way to take the words back.

Nick stared at her. 'We'd been married for nine years – but I don't blame her for running out on me if that's what you mean. She was no good in a crisis. She was kind of deliciously ditzy – it was one of the things I loved her for and one of the things that used to drive me mad about her. There is no way Anna could have coped with all this.' Nick lifted his hands to encompass the muddle and fear of it all.

'But you *were* happy? Before the bugging, I mean?'

'I suppose so, we were okay. I know now that I wasn't good at balancing things. I was building for the future, our future – but I suppose that at the same time I was excluding her from the present. I felt she ought to have understood that. So, no, it was already shaky, we'd both kind of lost sight of what we set out to do, maybe even why we were together. We were very different kinds of people. Anna liked things. How many things we had defined how successful, how happy we were. Looking back I don't think I was supplying her with all the things she needed. But I felt that it was nothing that I couldn't have put right – given the time.'

Nick sounded cool and distant; the wound may have scabbed over but the hurt certainly hadn't gone. 'So –' he turned to Maggie, eyes bright with emotion. 'Is that enough for the Maggie Morgan archive?'

'I'm sorry. But part of me wants to know everything about you – and there isn't any way to do that, is there? We're out of time and there are so many things I'd like to know.'

He laughed, the atmosphere between them lightened by her candour. 'Why am I not surprised? Do you actually know where this police station is?'

'More or less – it's not far now. Why, do you want to get away from me?'

'What do you think?'

Maggie looked at him and shrugged. The trouble was that she couldn't work out what Nick Lucas was thinking. She would need to know a whole lot more about him before she could say with any certainty what was going through his head, and now it looked like she wouldn't ever get the chance.

'. . . Golf saloon is currently travelling northbound on the A39, towards Minehead. It appears to be heading for the town centre –'

'There we are. Bingo –' said Nimrod, jabbing his finger towards the radio scanner. 'That's them. Which street did he say?'

Cain grinned. 'Don't worry, I'm already on the case.'

The car pulled quickly away from the kerb. In the back Bernie nearly choked on his Minto.

'Here we go,' said Nimrod, fastening his seat-belt.

'What's the plan?' asked Cain, nosing his way back out into the stream of traffic.

'Watch and wait, don't you worry, we'll have

our moment,' said Nimrod. 'I can feel it in my bones. Every dog has his day.' He pulled the mobile out of his pocket and looked at the screen in case he had missed a text or a call from the Invisible Man.

For once Cain didn't look so confident.

'You feeling all right? What is it?' asked Nimrod.

'You want my honest opinion?'

Nimrod nodded.

'It's all getting too sticky for my liking. Too messy – what with him –' Cain nodded over his shoulder, '– and the woman and the bloody fuzz and that bloke with the coat.'

Nimrod paused for a moment and then nodded. 'Yeah, but I don't really see what choice we have. We haven't been stood down yet.'

'Yeah, but – I dunno, it just doesn't feel right. We're sticking our necks out a long way with this one. Do you think it might be a trap?'

Nimrod stared at Cain in amazement; the idea hadn't even crossed his mind. 'No – I would have an inkling by now – no, I think it's just bloody messy.'

Cain nodded, but the conversation had rattled Nimrod. It was the first time in their long and very profitable association that Cain had ever voiced any doubts about a hit. Nimrod sucked his teeth; it didn't strike him as a good omen.

'Tell you what,' he said after a moment or two's

consideration. 'I could check in to see if there are any new orders.'

Cain shrugged. 'Nah, you're all right – they would have rung if there was a problem. All I'm saying is we need to watch our backs with this one. It don't feel right.'

Nimrod unpeeled another sweet from its wrapper. 'You know me well enough by now to know that I won't see you wrong, don't you?'

Cain nodded. 'Yeah, I know, mate. I was just saying.'

'We'll find the pair of them and play it by ear.'

'Sounds like a plan.'

'But if there's a clear shot . . .' Nimrod began.

'Goes without saying,' said Cain, lifting a hand to thank the car behind him for letting him change lanes.

'Look, Robbie. They're moving off,' said Lesley anxiously. 'Quick. They're pulling away.'

'What?' said Robbie, who had taken over playing with the radio when it became patently obvious that Lesley was getting nowhere fast.

'Bernie and those two men. They're pulling away from the kerb –'

'Damn,' said Robbie. The automatic selector on the radio had just slipped past something that sounded quite promising onto some foreign station playing salsa. Robbie turned the key in the ignition and the engine kicked into life.

'Try jiggling the knob backwards and forwards around where it is at the moment,' he said, pulling out without looking.

The driver in the car behind beeped furiously; only to be rewarded by Robbie flipping him the middle finger. Bloody country drivers; couldn't the man see that there was plenty of time for Robbie to pull out. If they'd been in London no one would have turned a hair. The man gesticulated back. Robbie pointedly ignored him, even when he drove right up to Robbie's car and beeped again. After all, Robbie didn't want to give the game away and let Bernie know that they were behind him. He glowered at the man in his rear-view mirror.

'We've got them, Sir,' said a voice in Coleman's earpiece. 'They're coming back down into town even as we speak. Do you want us to get the uniformed mob to pull them over?'

Coleman considered for a few moments. He'd already been contacted by his office to let him know that Nick planned to come into the police station, should be simple enough. But then again he reminded himself that Nick Lucas had also planned a walk in Blenheim Gardens. God alone knew what was going through his mind. Coleman still hadn't quite worked out why Nick had done a runner in the park; something had to have spooked him, but what? Add to that his vanishing act from the cottage at West Brayfield and, to say the least, Coleman's patience was wearing a little thin.

Coleman considered for a few seconds – maybe it had been the feds who had spooked Lucas, all done up in their nice Sunday suits. Who knows, maybe Nick would feel safer if his rescuers arrived in familiar uniforms.

'Sounds like a good idea to me. Nothing rough – just blue lights, a little assistance, and this time if he tries to scarper for God's sake get someone to bloody-well stop him.'

'Right you are, Sir. Do you want us to bring the woman in as well?'

Coleman considered the possibilities. His first instinct was to say no. The fewer people involved in this the better. Although he hadn't any idea what Nick had told Ms Morgan, surely she would keep quiet to keep him safe? After all, she had risked her neck to save him more than once already. He deliberated for a few seconds and then said, 'No, but if she kicks up a fuss, tell her . . .' Tell her what? 'Tell her to ring in to the station later on.'

It was a sop; by the time she rang in Nick Lucas would be long gone. It was thanks to Maggie Morgan that Nick had run before and although Coleman could see the wisdom in what she'd done he wasn't too keen on civilians who thought for themselves. Every instinct told him that Maggie was fierce and protective and when it came to doing his job, more trouble than she was worth. Coleman doubted that she would go quietly, but he could live in hope.

'Where would you like Mr Lucas taken to, Sir?'

Coleman stretched. 'Minehead police station will do very nicely – that's where he expects to go, and it's not too busy – we can arrange to have his nibs picked up from there without attracting too much attention.'

'Right you are, Sir,' he said, and with that signed off.

Coleman pulled his mobile out of his pocket and tapped in his office number. 'We've got him,' he said.

He could hear the amusement in Dorothy Crow's voice. 'Are we talking in the hand or in the bush now, Danny?'

'All right, all right,' Coleman snapped peevishly. 'It won't be long now, though.'

'You said that about the pick-up in the park.'

'You are such a bloody cynic, Dorothy.'

'I like to think of myself as one of life's realists,' said Dorothy Crow, darkly. 'Besides, the guys upstairs in the big offices are getting very annoyed about the way this thing is going down –'

'That's just what we bloody need. Tell them if they think they can do any better to get their arses down here,' he grumbled. 'Anything has got to be better than the space cadets they've sent me. You know these kids use sign language to talk to each other? They can't carry out a decent surveillance but they can draw a very nice cartoon dog – and then they do all this bloody stuff with their hands. I'm getting fed up with it; they're taking the piss.'

'You're just getting to be a grumpy, paranoid old fart, Danny,' said Ms Crow.

Coleman laughed and then hung up. She might well be right. As he moved he felt the shoulder holster he was wearing slide, warm and shiny, over his shirt. The day was way too hot for a coat. He sniffed; with a bit of luck it would soon be over and done with and they could all go home. All except for Nick Lucas, that was.

Maggie could see the blue light flashing in her rear-view mirror and pulled off the road to let the police car pass. She was completely taken aback when instead of hurtling by her, sirens blaring, it pulled up in front of her car and, lights still flashing, a policeman got out and made his way back towards her side of the car.

She looked across at Nick. 'I wasn't speeding or anything,' she spluttered nervously.

He shrugged, looking as bemused as she did.

Maggie opened the window as the policeman approached.

'Good morning, Madam.'

'Hello, Officer – can I help you?' she said, unable to keep the surprise out of her voice.

The man nodded towards Nick. 'Actually, Madam, I have been instructed to ask your passenger to accompany me to Minehead police station. You are Mr Bernard Fielding, aren't you?'

'You're not arresting him, are you?' she hissed.

The policeman shook his head. 'No, my goodness me, no, not at all, Ma'am.'

Maggie beaded him. 'But we were already on our way to the police station – he phoned in –' and then turning towards Nick continued, 'Tell him, you did, didn't you?'

'In that case. Madam, I'll be saving you the trip, won't I?' The man smiled pleasantly, although Maggie couldn't quite shake the sensation that any headway she hoped to make was being blocked by a polite but unmoving weight.

'Mr Fielding?' It was an invitation for Nick to join him.

Maggie peered up into the man's face to see if there was any trace of subterfuge, any hint of a lie or a trick or a plot. There was nothing there but firm, good-mannered, impassive features that met her gaze with no hesitation whatsoever.

Nick sighed, 'Okay,' and unfastening his seatbelt made as if to get out of the car. 'Maybe it would be a better idea for me to go with him anyway.'

'Hang on a minute,' said Maggie, catching hold of Nick's arm. 'What about me?'

The policeman shrugged. 'My orders are to ask

Mr Fielding to accompany me to the station, Madam.'

'Is that all you can say?' protested Maggie.

'I was instructed to suggest that you ring the police station later, Madam.'

Maggie squared her shoulders. 'Later?' she began. 'But why?'

'Sshh, don't fight it,' Nick said, and leaning over kissed her gently. 'It will be all right.'

'No –' she hissed, resisting the temptation to be pacified by him. 'No, it won't be all right. I don't want it to end like this, Nick. Is this the end? I mean is this good bye – where you ride off into the sunset?' She swallowed back a great prickle of tears.

Nick pulled her mobile out of his jacket pocket and handed it back to her. 'No, it isn't – and it will be fine. I know your number. I'll be in touch as soon as I can, I promise, but you have to let go now. It will be safer for both of us this way.'

'But what about all your things? At the beach hut and back at the cottage?'

He smiled. 'I'm sure somebody will come and pick them up.'

Maggie felt her eyes filling up with tears, that wasn't what she meant at all. She wanted them to represent a connection: that he would be back to collect them; that he would want to come back.

'But you can't go like this, Nick. It's not fair –'
It sounded petulant and childish but Maggie was

past caring. His fingertips pulled through hers as he climbed out of the car and walked away with the policeman. As he got into the back of the other car Nick turned and smiled.

Maggie shivered; it felt like something had been ripped away from her leaving a great, gaping hole in its place, but what could she do other than watch in stunned silence as the panda car pulled slowly away from the kerb.

'Bugger,' she snorted, banging her clenched fist on the steering wheel as the police car moved off. 'Bugger, bugger, bugger. How could he just leave me like that? It's not bloody fair. The bastard – bastard –' Great, hot, wet tears of frustration rolled down her face.

Now what was she supposed to do? Go home to West Brayfield and get on with her life? Pretend that none of this had ever happened? Just as Maggie was getting really angry something caught her eye in the rear-view mirror. A car was coming up behind hers. Some survival instinct made her drop down low in the seat, instinct and the fact that she recognised the silhouette of Bernie Fielding picked out against the back window.

Maggie lay very, very still across the seat as the car slowed down to a crawl as it passed her, and then sighed with relief as she heard it accelerate away. Maggie hadn't been spotted but guessed that the two hit men were following the police car into town – the last time she had seen Bernie was on his way to her beach hut. Was that where they had found him? She shivered – a little earlier and it would have been her and Nick they had found, instead.

Did the police have an idea about the danger Nick was in? Would Nick be all right? Where was Coleman, and had it been him who had betrayed Nick in Blenheim Gardens?

Maggie sat for a few minutes trying to calm her anxious mind while the assassins' car drove out of sight, and then she turned the key in the ignition. Maggie had made up her mind. It didn't matter what Nick thought she had promised; there was no way Maggie was going to leave him to deal with all this on his own. Checking her mirror she pulled out and headed into town.

As she drove it occurred to Maggie that someone had to have tipped the police off about her car. She couldn't imagine that Nick had told them what she was driving. Which brought her suspicions squarely back to Coleman.

'Can you still see them?' asked Lesley. She had had no luck at all finding anything even vaguely suspicious-sounding on the car radio.

Robbie nodded, 'Yes, they're four cars ahead.'

Bernie and the thugs were heading back into town. Robbie was tucked in behind a delivery van and try as he might he couldn't get past it.

'Get the little map book out,' he said. 'There

is one in the glove compartment with town centres in it –' He wasn't holding his breath that she would be any help at all, but at least it would give Lesley something to do other than criticise his driving.

Lesley flicked through the pages and then peered round like an owl to find a road sign. 'We're heading down towards the police station,' said Lesley, pushing the glasses back up onto her nose.

Robbie smiled indulgently. 'Really? Are you sure you've got the right continent?'

The mobile in Nimrod's pocket peeped, once, twice. Hastily he pulled it out and opened up the text message. 'Hang fire,' it read.

'Stand down. That's our call. We're out of here,' said Nimrod, pointing towards the next junction.

'Home?' said Cain expectantly. Nimrod couldn't quite miss the relief in his voice. Behind them Bernie sighed.

Nimrod shook his head, 'No, not yet, old son, just a little respite until we get fresh orders. We need to park up and keep an eye on what's going on. Take a left up here.' His instructions made Bernie groan – this time Nimrod suspected it was with despair.

'I think we may have found out what spooked your man in Blenheim Gardens,' said the tinny

308

voice in Coleman's ear. 'We've picked up the CCTV footage from the park, and it seems that we had two old friends taking a little stroll – a little constitutional – while you were waiting for your man to show up.'

'Uh-uh,' said Coleman. 'Cut to the chase, who exactly are we talking about?' He was sitting in the car a street or two away from the police station waiting for Nick to be brought in.

'The names Nimrod Brewster and Cain Vale ring any bells?'

Coleman laughed without a trace of humour and pulled out the nasal spray that went everywhere with him. He squeezed and inhaled, relishing the cold wet chemical droplets as they delivered their hit, waiting for his nose to clear. 'Well, now there's a surprise, and how come no one spotted the pair of them before? What are bloody security doing at the airports? No one thought to mention that those clowns were in the country until now?'

'Apparently not, Sir.'

'Okay, well no point dwelling on it; get photos out to everyone and keep an eye out for them. Oh, and do make sure that the whole team knows who they are and what they're up to – and be careful. Those guys play for keeps.'

'Just one more thing, Sir; it looks like they've got company.'

'Company? Who?' asked Coleman. He had

never known Nimrod or Cain to carry a spare before.

'We're not sure at the moment, Sir, but don't worry – we're on the case.'

'Okay,' said Coleman grimly, but then before he could say anything else the line went dead. Bloody technology. Coleman looked at his mobile phone – at least they hadn't used sign language. What was next; morse? He wondered whether to ring Dorothy but then what was the point? There was nothing she could do about Messrs Brewster and Vale, and without the CCTV footage she would be none the wiser about who the third man was.

Coleman wondered what it was *exactly* that had made Nick run in the park, some uncanny sixth sense that had told him when he saw Nimrod and Cain that these men meant trouble. Or was it Maggie Morgan who had pulled him out? If Coleman were a betting man his money would have been on Maggie.

As Robbie Hughes was about to pull out to overtake the delivery van his mobile phone rang; plugged into the hands-free frame it played the theme from Dambusters very loudly. Robbie jumped in surprise and missed his moment, nearly hitting a red Datsun as he swung back in.

'Who the hell is that?' he snorted furiously, stabbing at the handset with one pudgy finger.

Lesley was already leaning across and in front of him and plucked the phone out of the frame before he had time to stop her.

'It's the studio,' she said, peering at the caller display window. 'Upstairs.'

'Oh for God's sake,' growled Robbie. 'That woman certainly knows how to pick her bloody moments.'

'Do you want me to answer it?' asked Lesley helpfully.

'No, no, give me it here. Madam won't take kindly to being fobbed off with a minion,' said Robbie, and then, pressing the button to open the line said, in a warm and cheery tone, 'Hi, and how are you this morning?'

'Don't give me all that crap, Robbie, where the fuck are you?' she shouted.

Robbie sniffed; maybe letting Lesley answer the phone would have been a better idea after all. 'I'm out on a story at the moment,' he began, but Madam had other ideas.

'Really? I suppose it slipped your mind that we had an editorial meeting at ten, Robbie – remember? And then you were supposed to be out with Crew Two on that market trader's story. It's taken weeks for us to set things up with that dodgy video guy.'

'Right,' said Robbie, treading water, 'well – the thing is, I –'

'The thing is, Robbie, you're an arrogant stuck-up little arsehole who –' He held the phone away from his ear to avoid the tirade of abuse. It didn't sound as if his boss actually drew in a single breath, which was quite some trick. After a few minutes the volume settled to an angry rumble and then she said, her voice still tight with anger, 'Is Lesley there with you?'

'She is.'

'In that case put her on; I might get some sense out of her.'

The line into Coleman's ear crackled again. 'Yes?' he snapped irritably. No matter how well-fitting the earpiece it always gave him a headache.

'We're still no wiser who the guy with Nimrod and Cain is, Sir, but HQ thought you might like to know that he was picked up on security cameras going into the Colmore Road offices early last week – and guess where he ended up?'

Coleman was in no mood for games. 'Go on. Surprise me,' he said.

'One of the offices with a direct access terminal to Stiltskin.'

Coleman felt his stomach tighten; so there was their link. 'Well, well, well – there we are, then,' he said dryly. 'Now all you have to work out is who the hell he is and who he's working for and what he's up to and we're home and dry.'

As he spoke he saw the police car bearing Nick Lucas turn the corner and pull into the car park.

'Yes, Sir, but the thing is –' said the disembodied voice.

'Not now,' snapped Coleman, 'I've got another problem to solve.' He screwed up his face and turned the key in the ignition, wondering which was the best way to play this. Act now or wait until all the other players were in place? The sounds in his earpiece crackled and died.

In Robbie's car the mobile phone rang again.

'Oh bloody, hell, now what?' snapped Robbie, throwing a furious glance at Lesley. 'Answer it, will you?' And then after a few seconds, once Lesley had worked her way through the social pleasantries, Robbie said, 'Come on, then, what does the old bag want now?'

Lesley blanched and put her hand over the phone. 'Actually, Robbie, it's your wife; she said she rang the studio to talk to you and they said that they had got no idea where you were.'

Robbie felt his heart shudder messily before it kick-started back into a regular rhythm. Bloody women; they'd be the death of him.

'Right you are, well I'm glad that we've finally got a signal –' he said briskly with false heartiness, and then pretending to talk to some imaginary other person in the mythical middle distance, called, 'Let me just take this call and then I'll be right with you – just two minutes – no, it is urgent – no, no, that's a great shot, I'm so glad you could spare us the time for the interview. Yes, really. We'll go with that –' and then more loudly to the phone, 'Who did you say it was again, only Mr Straw is a very busy man, Lesley?' All the while making a throat-cutting gesture with his finger.

Lesley pulled a face that implied incomprehension.

'Turn the fucking phone off,' Robbie mouthed.

Still Lesley did nothing, just stared at him, eyes wide.

'Turn the fucking phone off,' Robbie hissed.

'I heard that you miserable, adulterous, two-timing little bastard,' said a small disembodied voice on the line, just as Lesley finally got the message and pressed the off button.

Some instinct made Coleman hang back for a few moments, just long enough to see Maggie Morgan drive past towards the police station. He sighed; that woman was getting to be a real pain in the arse.

16

Maggie pulled into the police-station yard and sat for a few minutes in the car park trying to collect her thoughts, and also work out exactly what she was going to say once she got inside. The last thing Maggie wanted was for them to think she was hysterical or trouble or worse still plain crazy. She brushed her hair, took a mint out of her handbag and straightened her clothes so that she looked a little more respectable; more like a thirty-something schoolteacher on holiday.

She got out of the car, mouth set into a determined line, and headed across to the front door, her stomach churning, all the while running over what she planned to say, calmly and with confidence. Once inside, Maggie rang the bell for attention and waited, tying her fingers into an anxious knot. A few seconds later a hatch in the wall opened and a heavily set policeman smiled pleasantly.

'Good morning, Madam, and how can I help you?'

Maggie painted on a warm smile to match his. 'Good morning. A friend of mine was brought in a little while ago –' she spoke slowly, enunciating clearly, so that there could be absolutely no mistaking what she was saying, in the kind of voice she normally used for assembly. 'I wondered if it might be possible to see him, please. His name is Bernie Fielding.' Only now did Maggie hesitate. What if they knew that he was really Nick Lucas? 'A policeman brought him in a little while ago. The officer said that they were going to bring him here –'

The Duty Sergeant looked Maggie up and down. 'A policeman?'

Maggie nodded. 'In a police car. We were on the way back from Selworthy – I'm not hundred per cent certain what the name of the road is – and he pulled us over. Blue light – you know.' Maggie tacked the smile back on, trying very hard not to flounder or gabble in the face of the man's determinedly neutral expression.

The man nodded. 'Right you are, Madam, I'll just go and see what I can find out for you. What did you say your friend's name was again?'

'Bernie Fielding.' Could she risk saying that that was the name he was using – could she tell them that he was really called Nick Lucas?

'Bernie Fielding?'

Maggie nodded, while trying very hard to keep calm. 'That's right.' How hard could it be?

'And you say he was picked up in a police car?'

Maggie nodded again, this time not trusting herself to speak. It was not unlike having a conversation with her mother.

'And have you any idea what it was in connection with, Madam?'

'Well, yes, I have –' Maggie began, leaning closer and peering in through the hatchway, well aware that there was a part of her which hoped Nick would be sitting there, large as life, his long fingers cradling a station-house mug of tea.

In fact all she could see was a hessian-covered screen that obscured the view of the office beyond. 'He was brought in for his own protection; although there is a chance he's using his real name – which is Nick Lucas.' There. It was out now.

'Right.' The man nodded again, his face totally impassive, expression unchanging. If he knew anything about Nick he most certainly wasn't going to let it show. Maybe he just thought that Maggie was mad and was humouring her so that she didn't make a scene. As he spoke the sergeant flicked through a book on the desk in front of him and then, smiling helpfully, said, 'If you'd just like to take a seat I'll go and see what I can find out for you. Won't be a minute.'

Maggie sighed and sat down, feeling – as she had with the patrol man who had taken Nick away in the first place – that somehow, despite being unfailingly polite, the police officer was blocking her every step. Surely if Nick was there this man already knew – didn't everyone come into the station via the front desk?

Quelling further rebellious thoughts she waited. The moments tick-tick-ticked past and as they did Maggie could feel the tension building in her belly. She got up and then paced up and down, read the crime-prevention leaflets and every public-service poster in between, all the while trying very hard to remain patient and stay calm.

A couple of streets away, Nimrod and Cain were waiting, too, their car silent except for the beeps and crackles and stilted patois of the police frequency coming in over the scanner, and sounds of Nimrod sucking on yet another sweet. Outside, the sun shone, a light breeze scuttling cheerily through the trees and rifling through the leaves on a hedge beside them. In the car it was hot, the air as charged and live as the prelude to a summer storm.

Nimrod stretched and let out a long slow breath – he was working on stilling his conscious mind. He glanced across at Cain who seemed to be having no trouble at all stilling his.

Crouched in the back seat of the car, Bernie waited, too; the constant nagging fear making his heart pitter-patter, pitter-patter in his narrow chest. Nimrod had put the childproof locks on the rear doors and locked the electronic windows so that Bernie couldn't get out or open them for a breath of air, which made him feel sick and horribly claustrophobic.

Bernie had already decided that it wasn't worth trying to escape – by the time he had broken a window and clambered out over the shards of glass he would be history. It didn't take a psychic to guess that the end was nigh and Bernie was busy thinking about not if, but when, his two companions planned to shoot him. A trickle of cold sweat ran down between his shoulder blades.

Surely this wasn't what was meant to happen when you did the right thing? He'd been trying to save Maggie, surely that had to count for something, didn't it? It wasn't fair, he never had any trouble at all when he was being a complete bastard. Bernie closed his eyes and swallowed hard, all the while making all sorts of rash promises to various deities to change his ways and turn over any number of new leaves, if only they could get him out of this alive.

A little further up the road Robbie Hughes and Lesley were waiting, too – they could just make out the car where Bernie was sitting without being in a direct line of sight. Robbie was still a little shaken up after the phone call from his wife, although he hadn't said anything to Lesley; it didn't pay to let a woman know exactly what you were thinking, because inevitably they would take it down and use it in evidence against you later.

His wife had already told him several times that if she ever caught him playing away again she would leave him. No discussion, no excuses, no second chances. She would take the kids, the cars, the house and then screw him for every penny she and her lawyer, the Rottweiler, could get their sticky little paws on. Oh, and while she was at it she would sell her story to the tabloids; the real inside story behind TV's Mr Squeaky-Clean. It didn't bear thinking about. Robbie shivered. He'd never work again.

Robbie took a deep breath. What he needed was a good alibi. What he needed was film – some really good footage of Bernie Fielding doing something dodgy, preferably illegal, preferably something spectacular – to prove that he and Lesley were away on a shoot. That was it – perfect. Get the film in the can and all would be well.

It would be a terrible shame if he ended up homeless and wifeless because of this bloody fiasco. God, he hadn't even slept with Lesley, well at least not on this trip. If he was going to go down in flames Robbie would rather it was for something a little more noteworthy than a sleepless night in a narrow single bed over the kitchen, while little Miss Map Reader here had sulked in his suite and run up a bill on room service.

'What did that bitch from upstairs want anyway?' he asked casually.

'From the studio? Nothing very much – she just wanted to know how I was and where we were – well you heard that bit – and then she just said that as soon as we get back she wants to see me in her office. I'm not sure what about exactly – and she did say that she didn't want to go into details on the phone –' Lesley looked towards him, obviously expecting some hint, some clue as to what might be the reason behind the Royal summons. Not that Robbie had any idea but there was no way he was going to tell Lesley that. Instead he made a non-committal noise and looked away. Madam was probably going to give Lesley the old heave-ho though he certainly wasn't going to say so. Serve her right.

He could see the thinking behind it; Lesley wasn't a real team player and if he was honest she didn't have quite the right attitude for the whole *Gotcha* set-up. He would be sad to see her go but then again the perky little brunette in reception was at least five years younger than Lesley and there was no way she looked like a graduate. They could probably pay her half as much as what Lesley was getting and she would still be grateful. Oh yes, he could see the sense in the decision;

sensible use of the company resources. Shame, but there you go.

Beside him, Lesley picked up the video camera. 'So are we going in then, Robbie?' she said nervously, peering through the eyepiece.

Robbie shook his head. This was exactly the kind of thing he meant. 'And film what? Three men sitting in a car picking their noses? No, that's not the kind of TV we do at *Gotcha*, Lesley. No, what we need is some action; something special. No, we'll just sit and see what it is that Bernie and his little friends have got planned.' Robbie screwed up his eyes, staring hard at what little they could see of the silver-grey car. One thing was for certain, if Bernie Fielding was involved it wasn't likely to be anything philanthropic. Robbie just hoped that they were in at the kill.

Now that Coleman knew exactly where Maggie Morgan was, he drove round into the police car park, tailing a neat, unmarked navy-blue transit van that drew in ahead of him and then backed up slowly towards the rear doors of the police station. He had already radioed in to head office to let them know he had arrived – and also to request that someone inside the station take Ms Morgan to one side and keep her out of the way until they were done with Mr Lucas. Everything was in place. A transit van was hardly a coach and horses, but as a getaway vehicle it wasn't bad, and after pissing them about Nick Lucas couldn't afford to be too choosy.

Inside the police station Maggie was getting increasingly impatient. There was nothing else to read and no sign of the policeman coming back. Maggie stared at the closed doors of the enquiry hatch, willing them to open. Nothing. But as she turned away she did notice, through one of the windows, the arrival of a shiny navy-blue van, and watched as it indicated and pulled into the yard. It was being driven by what looked like two policemen in plain clothes – and some part of her instinctively knew that they had come to take Nick away.

Turning quickly Maggie headed for the great outdoors and just as she did the little hatchway on the front desk slid open.

'Excuse me, Madam. I've put a call through about your friend – one of the detectives will come through and have a word with you, if you like. He shouldn't be a minute – if you'd like to come this way and wait in the office –' said the Sergeant, opening a door through into the main body of the police station and indicating that she should follow him. He pointed down the corridor. 'If you'd just like to go through those double doors on the right. He shouldn't be very long. Would you like a cup of tea or a coffee while you wait?'

For a few moments Maggie was rooted to the

spot, torn between the persuasive and now very personable policeman and the arrival of the blue van. What if Nick was somewhere inside the station, safe and sound after all, just sitting there waiting to be rescued? What if she had got it all wrong? Maggie heard the van start to reverse up towards the building. What the hell, if Nick didn't get in the van then she could always come back and take the Sergeant up on his kind offer of a sit down and light refreshments.

The Sergeant opened the door a little wider and said, 'He's on the phone, but he shouldn't be more than a couple of minutes; if you'd like to come this way.'

Maggie had a sense of the soft but increasing pressure. 'Okay – but I just have to go and get something from my car,' she lied, and before he could say anything else, she turned and hurried towards the door. Maggie had barely got over the threshold before she clapped eyes on Coleman making his way over towards the van, and alongside him one of the men she had seen earlier in Blenheim Gardens, still talking into his lapel. Her stomach lurched.

In what felt like slow motion, Maggie ran across the tarmac towards them. Coleman looked up at the sound of her footsteps approaching and to her total amazement smiled.

'Well, well, well, if it isn't superwoman herself, come to save the day,' he said. Any amusement didn't creep high enough to defrost the ice in his eyes.

Maggie squared up to him. 'Where the hell is Nick? I know he's here somewhere –'

Coleman looked down at her.

'What have you done with him?' she demanded furiously.

'Done with him?' said Coleman, the smile not fading. 'Nothing, at least not yet. You know, Ms Morgan, you've made my job very difficult.'

Her eyes narrowed, 'What do you mean not yet?'

At that moment the back doors to the police station swung open and there, framed in the doorway, stood Nick.

'Nick?' Maggie called out to him, and he looked up as he heard her voice. 'Are you all right?' He didn't look all right, he looked pale and scared and dishevelled and as their eyes met, Maggie's heart went out to him. 'I just couldn't leave you here on your own –' she began.

'Go away,' he shouted. 'For God's sake –'

Maggie turned to look over her shoulder; surely he couldn't mean her?

'What?' she gasped in amazement.

'Please Maggie, get out of here before it's too late.'

'Why?' she said. 'What do you mean, too late?'

'It's too dangerous,' Nick snapped. 'If anything happens to you –'

She was about to step forward when Coleman stepped into her path, blocking her way. 'No,' he growled in a voice that would have cut through sheet steel.

'What? Why not – he's not under arrest or anything, is he?'

The smile on the big man's face dropped away. 'If you stay, Ms Morgan, then he'll die here,' said Coleman coldly. 'That isn't what you want, is it?'

Maggie felt the pulse double in her ears, not quite able to believe what she had just heard. Was there something that she and Nick didn't know? She looked round anxiously to be met by the stony face of Coleman's companion.

'Of course not. But surely you're here to protect him, aren't you?' she gasped.

Coleman snorted. 'We do whatever it takes to square things away, Ms Morgan, whatever it takes – but it doesn't always work out quite the way we plan it,' he said, and then he laughed.

It was an uncanny sound. A cold finger tracked down Maggie's spine.

'You want to stay and watch your new man killed, do you, or are you going to let him go?'

Maggie stared at Coleman, trying to make sense of what he was saying. It sounded like total gibberish, and she still couldn't work out whether he was a villain or a hero. Whichever it was, the enormity of what Nick was involved in hit her in the stomach like a clenched fist. She felt sick as she examined Coleman's face for some clue, some inkling of what was going on. Was Nick really likely to die if she didn't go? And then as Nick clambered up into the back of the van Maggie realised with horror that he was handcuffed.

'What has he got those on for?' she hissed. 'He hasn't done anything.'

'Of course he hasn't, but we can't have him running away from us again now, can we, Ms Morgan? Although maybe without you here to encourage him he'll behave himself. Anyway, we can't hang around, we've got a meeting to go to. Go – bye-bye,' he waved her away.

Maggie took a step back, mind reeling. 'What the hell are you on about?' she snapped, regaining her composure and making a beeline for Coleman and the back doors of the van.

But this time the man in the smart suit blocked her way and an instant later Nick vanished into the shadows and the van doors were slammed shut.

Once they were all in the back of the van, Coleman flicked the switch that would turn on the radio mike in his lapel.

'Hello, this is Coleman here. I want the plod to nip out and pick our Ms Morgan up and hold her until this thing is done and dusted.' There was a voice of protest at the far end of the line but Coleman really was in no mood for negotiation.

'I don't give a tin shit what your objections are. We don't want any witnesses other than those people with an engraved invitation, understand? No civilians, no onlookers, no trouble. Capiche?' The voice twittered again.

Coleman sighed; it had been a long day. His feet hurt now as well as his head. The helicopter ride had made his ankles swell. 'Look, to be perfectly honest I don't care what they pick her up for, they can get her for jaywalking, loitering with intent, being a nosy little cow, I don't give a fuck as long as she is out of the way. Have I made myself clear?' On the far end of the line someone coughed. It was all the acknowledgement Coleman needed.

Once he was done with the radio Coleman pulled out his mobile phone and tapped in a text message before looking across at his wheyfaced passenger.

'Well, Mr Lucas, it seems as if you're about to pay your dues. Any last requests before I call in the wolf pack?'

Nick paled and dropped his face into his hands. Coleman smiled and pressed Send.

'Don't you worry, son,' he purred. 'It'll soon be over.'

Nimrod heard his phone beep, once, twice. Pulling the mobile out of his jacket pocket he read the message and then, smiling, his eyes alight with fire, said, 'Apparently our services will be required after all.'

Cain looked up at him. 'Meaning?'

'That Mr Lucas is about to be delivered straight into our hands. Seems that our man is a lot better connected than we thought. Give me the street map, will you, Cain – unless of course you can help us, Bernie?' he said, turning to look over his shoulder at their hapless passenger.

Maggie stood with her heart in her mouth. She knew that she had to do something but didn't know what; she couldn't quite fathom what was going on, or why. The sense of impotence and the memory of Nick's fear was almost overwhelming. Cursing under her breath, Maggie hurried around to the front of the police station and ran out into the street. The blue van was already heading away from her up the road; there was no way she could catch up with them now. Maggie pulled out her car keys, but guessed that the van would be long gone before she was on the road. She still had to try. Her mind raced. Who could she call, who could she trust? The van accelerated away. Damn, damn, damn – Maggie was so preoccupied with watching the transit disappearing into the distance that she barely noticed the silver-grey car pull up alongside her.

'Well, hello there, Maggie, something the matter, sweetie?' said a low reptilian voice. Maggie swung round only to come face to face with a pair of the palest blue eyes she had ever seen. Their owner was in his mid-thirties, lightly tanned with cropped, bleached-blonde hair, broad shoulders and a face that was as handsome as it was cruel. Alongside him the driver was dark-haired and tanned, with cheekbones that wouldn't have looked out of place on a fashion model. They were both tightly sprung and as sleekly muscled as alley cats. Hunched in the back seat Bernie looked almost reassuringly out of shape, not to mention very pale and interesting.

Maggie froze. 'Who the hell are you?' she began, although she had already guessed. These were the men she had seen with Bernie in Blenheim Gardens, these were the men that had been sent to kill Nick.

The man in the passenger seat got out of the car, every movement unnervingly fluid, his expensive suit emphasising his long, lean physique. He exuded an air of quiet menace.

'Nimrod, Nimrod Brewster –' he said, offering her his outstretched gloved hand. Instinctively Maggie drew back as if he had offered her a live snake. He smiled, revealing a row of perfect pearly white teeth. 'Why don't you just get in, sweetie, and we can introduce you formally to the whole of our merry little crew,' he said.

Maggie stared at him. 'Why on earth should I? We're outside the police station; all I've got to do is scream and half-a-dozen coppers will be out here to see what the hell all the fuss is about. I can't imagine that you would welcome police attention.'

'Oh my, aren't we the cocky one?' The man smiled. 'You can scream all you like, sweetie. But before you do I'd just like to point out that we know where your friends are taking Nick Lucas.'

Maggie stared at him, wanting to know more while every instinct told her to run away while she still could.

Nimrod looked Maggie up and down; he could see the wariness in her eyes but he could also see the fire. He wasn't much into hostages but her presence would be a bonus if the going got tough – a nice little ticket home. No one in their right mind would ever use Bernie as a bargaining chip – there would probably be lots of people who would pay to see him suffer – but Maggie Morgan might come in very handy if things went wrong. And if things went right? Well they could just drop her and her ex off on the motorway and pick up their flight home courtesy of the Invisible Man. He had assured them that if the plans went belly-up he'd get them back to Spain on a private plane from a secluded little airfield in Kent, although if he was perfectly honest Nimrod would have preferred the ferry.

*   *   *

As Maggie hesitated the man caught tight hold of her and pulled her closer to him. 'Now let's get in the car, shall we? There's a good girl,' he growled in an surly voice, his gloved fingers tightening around her wrist like a wire snare. 'This is not a request stop, sweetie, and we really don't want any fuss, do we? Or you'll never find out what happened to your precious Mr Lucas.'

Maggie winced as his fingers bit into her flesh.

Bernie looked up at her from the back seat with haunted eyes, and for an instant she saw just how afraid he was.

'Run, Maggie,' he shouted as their eyes met, but as she turned Nimrod jerked her closer still.

'Don't even think about it, sweetie. Just get in the car. Now. Or else –'

He pulled open the back door and pushed hard, his hand on top of her head. Maggie was in and sitting alongside Bernie before she really got a grasp of what was happening.

'You can't do this,' she protested.

'Oh, I think we can,' said Nimrod as he clambered back into the passenger seat. 'We can do anything we like. Now – we have to get to Quay Street – are you going to tell us where that is or do we need to get the map out?'

Maggie blanked him, her heart ripping out a rhythm in her chest, the beat echoing in her ears.

'Please yourself,' growled Nimrod.

'I know where it is,' said Bernie, in a tiny voice.

'We have to head back into town.' Then he turned to Maggie. 'I'm sorry about this but maybe if we cooperate –' he left the rest of the sentence blank for her to fill in. She sighed, trying to guess what bonus Bernie could possibly imagine these two wolves had on offer.

From the front seat Nimrod turned round and smiled. 'Well done, Bernie, that's the spirit,' he said.

'There they go again,' said Lesley. 'Time to rock and roll –'

'What?' Robbie was still fiddling with the radio, still trying to work out what it was the men in the car were listening to.

'Bernie Fielding – he's on the move again – and it looks as if they've picked up someone else as well,' Lesley said as she screwed up her eyes, peering through video camera eyepiece and working the zoom lens backwards and forwards looking for a sharp image. 'Oh my God. I don't believe it. It looks like Bernie's ex-wife,' she said in surprise. 'Surely that can't be right.'

Robbie snorted. 'Who can say what's right with this mob,' he said. 'All seems a bit bloody inces-tuous to me.' He turned the key in the ignition. 'What the hell is going on here? Make sure you keep the video camera handy, Lesley. I'm depending on you.'

Lesley nodded, her hand cupped through the

strap and under the body of the camera. Robbie pulled out and they turned back towards town and the throngs of holidaymakers. Robbie sighed; surely it couldn't be much longer now?

Maggie stared out of the car window at the holidaymakers milling round on the Avenue, totally oblivious to what was going on. Cheeky tee shirts, ice cream and souvenirs of glorious Minehead were in sharp contrast to the atmosphere inside the car. Her spirits sank lower with every passing second; no one else in the world knew where she was or what she was up to. Even if Maggie didn't ring home it might be days before her mother thought about raising the alarm. What the hell was going to happen to Bernie, to her, to her boys. And to Nick? Surely if Coleman was on the level he ought to have whisked Nick away to a safe house miles away from Minehead, not have driven him back into town. What the hell was going on?

Alongside her Bernie was still hunched over, and so pale that his skin looked almost green. He had his eyes tightly closed and appeared to be praying.

17

In the back of the van Coleman looked across at Nick, his eyes as glassy and unreadable as canal water. 'So, Mr Lucas, here we are at long last – the grand finale. I did warn you not to audition for *Blind Date* but would you listen? Oh no.'

Nick shook his head in disbelief, Coleman's dark humour lost on him. 'What is this? Are you passing the buck? Come off it, Coleman, the TV thing was down to you and some cock-up at Stiltskin. That camera crew had nothing at all to do with me. I'm not crazy, whatever you may think – your computer's at fault. This is ridiculous –'

'Now, now. Don't go getting yourself all overwrought, Mr Lucas.'

'Overwrought?' Nick hissed. 'For God's sake man, what the hell do you expect me to be feeling.'

Coleman shrugged. 'I don't know. It's been a very long time since I've found myself in this position. This, my friend, is the end of the road as far as you're concerned. Nobody expected that it would come to this, but then –' He lifted his hands in a gesture of resignation. He sounded tired, his voice so low that the tone was almost hypnotic. 'What can I tell you? Needs must where the devil drives.' He paused thoughtfully and then added, 'You know, my mother always used to say that to me when I was a kid – I've got no idea what it means.' Coleman took a hit from his nasal spray and sighed.

Nick looked away, swallowing hard, his heart racing, palms slick with sweat. 'How long have you been planning this?'

'Does it really matter that much to you? This kind of solution is not something my employers take lightly, but it was, it is, always on the cards – if our friends Nimrod and Cain didn't get you then this was the last line of defence.'

'You?'

Coleman, tidying the cuffs of his crisp white shirt, nodded. 'That's right, Mr Lucas. Me. The Stiltskin team have suspected for a while that there was someone working on the inside. How shall we say it? Oiling the wheels of the information highway over your case, they just didn't know who it was.' For the first time since he had got in the van Coleman looked uncomfortable, not that Nick had a great deal of sympathy for him.

'But they will after today?'

Coleman shrugged. 'Maybe, maybe not. Who knows, it depends on how fast we can get the job done – I know that they have their suspicions.'

Nick swallowed again, mouth dry.

The inside of the van was getting increasingly hot and airless, and what air there was left was perfumed by a hint of diesel oil, the combination adding to Nick's growing feeling of nausea. He struggled discreetly against the handcuffs, the metal rubbing into his wrists as he tried to turn them around and slip free.

'Relax,' purred Coleman. 'No point fighting it. It will all be over soon.'

Nick closed his eyes, trying hard to quell the wave of panic that threatened to overwhelm him. How the hell had he got himself into such a mess in the first place? Had Coleman known what was going on from the start? Had the whole thing been a complex set-up from day one to get the two of them to this point? Had everything else; Maggie, Robbie Hughes, the trip to Somerset, all been a complicated smoke screen? Rerunning the events of the last few days over in his head, although it wasn't impossible, it was highly improbable – it seemed far more likely that Coleman had been pulled out of the woodwork as damage limitation when things had gone wrong.

Nick screwed his eyes tight shut; his head ached, his mind flickering with one thought after another like a candle flame in the wind. The only good thing to come out of the day was that at least Maggie was safe now. He had heard Coleman on the radio requesting that she be taken into custody at the police station, until it was all over. All over? Nick's stomach did another back-flip as he held off the idea of it being all over and instead allowed the sound of Maggie's name to conjure up an image of her that filled his mind.

If he concentrated he could see her clear as day. Standing there, all wound up and ready to go in the hall of her cottage, hefting a baseball bat up to shoulder height ready to whack him right into the middle of next week, her face a mask of determination. Her eyes bright with fear and panic. It seemed like an age ago, a memory already tinged with the patina of years, not a matter of days and hours. It was the kind of story that under other circumstances they would tell over and over again. Even given his present predicament Nick found it hard not to smile; Maggie Morgan really was something else. It was amazing meeting a woman like her now, when it was too dangerous, too unlikely and far, far too late to do anything about it. Fate could be such a bitch at times. His heart ached for lots of reasons but most of all for the might have beens, the things he was never going to share with Maggie.

The van swung round a sharp bend, shaking him out of the warm, dark thoughtful place. Nick, unable to steady himself, slithered along the seat.

Struggling to regain his balance he heard the engine slowing, then stop, felt the gears bite into reverse. Across the van everything about Coleman's body language announced that they had just arrived at ground zero.

For an instant Nick glanced down at his watch. It was a stupid thing to do under the circumstances, but he couldn't help wondering just how much longer he had got left. He closed his eyes and prayed that it would be over quickly, and that meanwhile he could manage to hold tight to the last shreds of self-control that were keeping him from screaming. Along with the fear was a disturbing sense of unreality as a part of his brain struggled to convince him that none of this was really happening.

Nick bit his lip; it was the part of the mind that eased the pain at the dentist or the fear as they wheeled you into the operating theatre. It was some sort of big chemical 'there, there', that put your consciousness out of its misery, making you an observer and not a participant in whatever was going on. Nick fought the feeling; he wanted to be there, not drifting into some anaesthetised state fuelled by his own terror, however tempting a prospect it was. Trying to shake the dreamlike sensation, Nick pulled the handcuffs tight, the bite of metal bringing him squarely back into the moment.

It struck him then that he couldn't get away

even if he wanted to, not while he was wearing cuffs – and with Coleman's companions watching him like hawks, the odds were close to impossible. And even if he could get away, where in God's name would he go?

As another wave of nausea rolled up through him, Nick pressed his body back against the cool metal side of the van, savouring the vibrations going down his spine, relishing the warmth of the breath in his chest – relishing the sensation of still being alive. And at that moment the engine cut out.

'So where to now, then, my lovely?' said Cain, looking back over his shoulder towards Bernie as they got to the next road junction.

'Left,' said Bernie, pointing to add emphasis. 'And then right at the end of the road, and then left onto the Esplanade. We're heading down towards the seafront. We need to head up to the old part of town – along and then up there.' He waved and pointed towards the broad shoulder of North Hill that sheltered Minehead's long golden beach.

'Whereabouts are we going again?' said Cain quizzically, as if they were all out on some Glee Club bus trip.

'We're going to skirt round the bottom of the hill, and then park up on Culver Cliff. It's out past the harbour – this big open space on the cliff top. There's a picnic area, and then there's a cliff-top path. It's nice – very quiet. It's where the South West Coastal Path starts, and follows the coast right round Land's End and then on to Poole Harbour in Dorset,' said Bernie knowledgeably.

Nimrod smiled. 'Well, well, well, so there we have it. It's like a trip out with Ray Mears. What a veritable fount of knowledge you turned out to be, Bernie. Although I have to say that I don't think we'll be doing the South West Coastal Path today; maybe another time –' He stretched, muscles rippling under his well-cut jacket, locking his fingers together in a basket and then bending them back like a piano player warming up. 'It sounds like our man has picked an ideal spot, though.'

'Ideal?' Maggie looked from face to face; she was under no illusion about what they meant by ideal; Culver Cliff would be an ideal place to kill Nick Lucas.

Cain, his expression almost jubilant, grinned. 'Perhaps we can arrange a nice little accident, one tiny-weeny little bullet hole, followed by a little trip off the cliff, high tide; a cliff fall and Bob's yer uncle – who would ever know? Who would care –'

Maggie bit her lip; she and Bernie would know but if Coleman was working for the other side she had no doubt he could cover their tracks. Although of course there was the chilling but all too real possibility that Nimrod and Cain didn't care what she and Bernie knew because they wouldn't be leaving the cliff top alive either. Maggie shuddered and tried to concentrate on staying calm and in control. She had to believe there was still a chance but knew that if she panicked that chance might be lost; surely there had to be some way out of this? It was summer, broad daylight in a seaside town, surely someone would come and help them?

In the front of the car, Nimrod, pulling the wrapper off another sweet, grinned at Cain. 'Dunno, we'll see when we get there, play it by ear. I have to say I would've preferred to have got there first really, sussed the place out, but then again yer can't have it all ways. It won't be the first time we've had to do a job on the fly, eh? Happier are you now, then, eh?'

Cain nodded. 'Yes, and I'll be even happier when it's all over.'

'Goes without saying but we're on the home-straight now. In and out –'

'And home in time for tea and buns,' said Bernie miserably from the back seat.

'Catches on fast, doesn't he?' said Cain, turning left.

Sitting beside Bernie, Maggie felt sick.

'Left, left,' bawled Lesley, waving the video camera at Robbie Hughes like a conductor's baton.

'All right, all right, there's no need to shout, I can see them,' snapped Robbie. 'It's a seaside town not the bloody Paris to Dakar rally.'

'Sorry, Robbie, it's just that I've got this really strong feeling,' said Lesley, turning to beam at him, her eyes wide and alight with excitement behind her glasses.

Robbie groaned; Lesley certainly picked her moments to go all hot and horny on him, he thought ruefully. 'I know, honey, it gets us all that way at times, but it'll have to wait until later, until we can find somewhere a little more secluded, when the job's over and done with. It's the excitement – the adrenaline – it goes with the turf,' he said, and then another thought struck him, 'or do you need a pee?'

Lesley's eyes narrowed down to angry little slits. 'No,' she snapped furiously. 'That isn't what I meant at all, Robbie, and you know it. What I meant was I've got a feeling that this is it. A hunch, an intuition. Whatever it is, it's about to happen. It's like I've got this really intense buzz deep down in the bottom of my belly.'

Robbie didn't like to tell her that he had one, too, but he had put it down to the dodgy burger they had had at the motorway services.

'There they go – look –' she gasped. 'Look!'

Robbie nodded. It was like taking a kid to see Father Christmas. Just who was driving who, he wondered, putting his foot down hard. Didn't she realise that Robbie was watching Bernie's every move? He needed the film more than Lesley did, the longevity of his marriage could depend on what they got in the can by teatime, but even so he was grateful that at least for the moment Lesley was back on side and showing willing. It would be far easier to work with her than without her – and besides, if she took the hump, even if she wasn't very good at it, who the hell could he get to operate the video camera?

Two or three vehicles ahead of them, the silver-grey car had slowed to a crawl, indicated, and was turning up towards the old part of town. Matching their change of pace Robbie dropped down a gear and with his eyes firmly on the car made as if to follow.

'Robbie!' screamed Lesley, but it was too late. Even before she had finished calling his name Robbie heard the furious blast of a horn, felt the thick dull crunch of impacting metal and then the recoil of his body being flung forward towards the windscreen, through which he could see something white moving in slow motion. It was a van – a white transit van.

'Look at that bloody moron. He's going far too fast in a built-up area, in a seaside town, for God's sake – there are kiddies all over the place.' Robbie began protesting his innocence even before the two vehicles had ground to a halt. A quick mind and an even quicker tongue were valuable gifts that had kept Robbie ahead of the pack for years.

'Mad bastard,' he growled, swinging round to Lesley as if appealing to the umpire. It didn't occur to him to check if she was all right. 'Did you see that? *Did you see that mad bastard?* He came out of nowhere. He must have been doing fifty – more probably. It wasn't my fault – the man is a total frigging maniac. He shouldn't be allowed on the bloody roads. He should be banned . . . He –'

Outside, the driver was already clambering out of his cab and heading round to Robbie's side of the car. He was small and thin with sparse ginger hair, a bright red face, and was built like a bamboo cane.

'What the fuck do you think you're playing at, pulling out of a junction like that without looking, you stupid old git?' he snarled by way of an introduction.

'What – what, do you mean *me*?' Robbie blustered. 'It was *you* – you were going far too fast. You must have been doing *sixty* –' the mileage and volume rose along with his sense of outrage. Little oik – did he know who he was dealing with?

The man had just jerked the car door open and was busy hauling Robbie bodily from the car when Lesley got out and said, 'I'm most terribly sorry. It was completely and utterly our fault.' Her voice was like pure silk and as smooth and unctuous as double cream. Robbie turned towards her and for the first time noticed that there was a little rivulet of blood on her forehead accentuating her pallor.

The man turned to look, too, then looked more intently. Lesley smiled at him, and for some reason the man, who had drawn back his fist to explain to Robbie the finer points of the Highway Code, stopped mid-stride and beamed. 'Oh, hang on a minute – I know you, don't I? I'm sure I've seen you somewhere before,' he said, still staring at Lesley. He was thinking so hard you could almost smell the rubber burning.

Lesley blushed and fluttered her eyelashes coquettishly.

'I know, hang on, hang on, don't tell me, it's on the tip of my tongue –' said the man, his face screwed into a mask of concentration. 'I've got it. You're on telly, aren't you?' he announced triumphantly. 'You're that girl who does that crime programme on ITV – I've seen you loads of times – I love that programme.' He began to hum the tune, gyrating thin hips to the upbeat opening music.

Robbie's head swung round and he glared at Lesley; those lines were meant to be for him. People had been recognising Robbie since before she was bloody-well born, the little cow.

Lesley's colour intensified; and Robbie started to wriggle furiously. Thanks to him putting a word in for her upstairs Lesley had done a little bit of on-screen work on the programme over the last few months. Not much, just read out a few readers' letters, answered some of the call-in stuff, but even so she was hardly Anne-frigging-Robinson.

The man still had a tight hold of Robbie's throat.

'Are you all right? –' he said solicitously, still looking in her direction. 'Only there's blood on your head.'

Lesley smiled bravely and pulling a pristine white hankie from the sleeve of her cardigan dabbed at the spot with just the hint of a wince. 'Don't worry, I'll be fine – it's nothing,' she said.

What a brave little soldier, thought Robbie malevolently.

'We're on a story at the moment,' she continued, all the while batting those long eyelashes of hers.

For God's sake, did she have to keep flirting with this ape, thought Robbie indignantly; had the woman got no shame at all?

'Lesley!' Robbie snapped, trying to get her attention. What in God's name was the girl thinking of.

The man, ignoring Robbie, beamed. 'Really? That's amazing. Something big, is it?'

Lesley nodded, and then pushed her glasses back up onto the bridge of her nose. 'We're just about to crack the story on a really big con man – he's responsible for all sorts of scams.'

'Really? So you pair are a bit like, what? Starsky and Hutch, then?' the ginger man said, although at least he had the decency to redden and then laugh self-consciously at his own lame remark.

Lesley appeared to glow under his attention. 'Actually we were tailing someone,' she said, waving in the general direction of the accident. 'Which is why we maybe weren't paying as much attention as we should be.' At which point Lesley glared at Robbie and then looking back at her red-faced, red-haired admirer, continued, 'I'm really very sorry –' She screwed her eyes and mouth up into what was presumably meant to be an expression of apology and contrition.

'Oh God,' said the man, 'and now because of me you're going to lose them. You should have said – and you should get yourself a better driver.'

'Thank you,' said Robbie, as he dropped to the tarmac like a stone.

'We'd better sort this out.' The man pulled out his keys. 'I'll move the van out of the way. My name is Dave – Dave Henderson –' He took Lesley's hand, shook it and then very coyly pressed it to his lips. 'Do you think your car is still drive-able? I could give you a lift if you don't mind roughing it.'

Her car? *Her car?* The bile rose in Robbie's throat.

Lesley peered myopically at the crumpled front end of the car and nodded and then pulled a seductive little look that implied she wasn't adverse to a bit of rough, given half a chance. The man reddened and Lesley said, 'That's really kind of you but I think it will be okay, actually – it only looks like the spoiler from here.'

'Oh and you would know, wouldn't you?' said Robbie sarcastically. 'The whole bloody wing is smashed, and look at the state of the headlights –'

Lesley smiled at Mr Henderson. 'If you've got a pen I'll give you our insurance details –' she said, reaching back into the car and dropping the glove compartment down to pull out a neat little packet of official-looking documents.

The man made a gesture of dismissal. 'It's all right,' he began, but Lesley shook her head firmly.

'No, I absolutely insist, after all, it was our fault –'

'It's only a works van, no one will know how it happened, or give a shit come to that.'

Lesley beamed. 'That isn't how we do things at *Gotcha*, Dave, and it was our fault, wasn't it?'

Watching the pair of them from the middle of the road Robbie wanted to throw up. Behind them a queue of traffic was busy building up.

'What about Bernie Fielding?' he hissed as Lady Bountiful wrote out her phone number for the Ginger Ninja.

'Their car went up Quay Street,' said Lesley, barely glancing in Robbie's direction as she tore the sheet off the notepad with a flourish. 'They can't come back out without turning round – it's a no-through road up onto the cliff top, we'd have seen if they had come back this way.'

The ginger guy was beaming. 'I know it's a bit of a cheek but could I have your autograph?' he said with a flirtatious leer.

'Of course,' said Lesley warmly. 'Would you like me to sign your dent as well?'

They both laughed. Robbie snorted. Bloody woman.

Someone came round to open the back doors of the van. Nick took a deep breath.

Coleman turned to him, eyes now as black as pitch. 'Time we went for a little walk, laddie,' he said in menacing voice.

Nick stared at him; what was there to say? Shivering as Coleman's hand closed around the top of his arm he stepped down unsteadily onto the tarmac, blinking as the daylight momentarily blinded him, all the while trying very hard to keep a tight grip on the fears that crowded into his head like wraiths.

'Steady,' said Coleman, but it was too late. Nick had started to shake violently, wondering if he could still make a run for it, his heart beating out like a war drum in his chest as they walked across the car park and up onto the broad expanse of grassy cliff top.

*   *   *

'Well, looky, looky, what have we got here? Seems to me like the heavy mob are all ready and waiting,' said Nimrod as their car pulled to a halt in the car park. 'There they all are – all wound up and just waiting for us to arrive.'

'The star turn,' Cain added, tidying his hair in the rear-view mirror.

Nimrod snorted. 'Yeah, you could be right. Touching, isn't it? It's a tough job but somebody's got to do it.'

At which point Cain giggled. High-pitched and manic, it was not a pleasant sound.

Maggie leant forward to try and work out what the hell was going on. She could see Coleman striding away in the distance, bundling Nick across the rough grass towards the cliff edge. Nimrod and Cain took a moment or two to compose themselves, and then in perfect harmony opened the car doors.

'Time to rock and roll,' said Nimrod, and then he was up and out of the car with Cain no more than a heartbeat behind him.

As soon as the two hit men were clear of the car, Maggie hissed, 'Get out, Bernie. Come on – now.'

Bernie stared at her blankly. 'What?'

'You heard me. Get out of the bloody car,' she yelled. 'Do you want to be here when the pair of them get back?'

'But the doors in the back are locked.'

'Oh for God's sake,' said Maggie in frustration, and wriggling quickly between the seats clicked open the driver's-side door and clambered out. The fresh air and the sound of the sea cleared her head instantly.

Bernie hesitated for a few seconds and then, more stiffly, he followed suit.

Maggie zippered her fleece against the breeze, looking round and trying to work out what the hell she could do. Coleman was already more than halfway across the picnic area with Nimrod and Cain loping after them like big cats about to bring down their prey.

Even though the day was bright there was hardly anyone around on the cliff top. There was a family or two, and an elderly man walking his dog, but certainly no one who could help, no one who wouldn't be a liability if they wanted to take the men on. Just other innocent bystanders waiting to get caught in the cross fire.

Infuriated by a great wave of impotence Maggie began to run across the grass towards Nick. She didn't know whether to call out, but in the end stayed quiet, afraid of the consequences.

'Where the fuck are you going?' shouted Bernie in astonishment. 'There's nothing you can do to help him.'

'But we have to do something,' she yelped, '– we can't just let them kill him.'

Bernie shook his head and something about the

gesture implied that it was too late. It made Maggie turn around and as she did she saw Nick running across the grass towards the trees. He had gone no more than two or three steps, when Coleman grabbed him. She spotted the gun in Coleman's hand, saw the flash from the muzzle, saw the recoil, heard the dull, sickening report of the shot muffled by Nick's body, watched as he shot Nick, once, twice – and then gasped in horror as Nick Lucas dropped like a stone onto the coarse green summer grass.

And at that moment everything stopped.

Nimrod and Cain froze mid-stride as the sound of the shots echoed off the cliffs and around the trees. Maggie felt as if she couldn't get her breath, as if the air around her had suddenly thickened to the consistency of cotton wool. From some-where close by she heard a woman screaming, and willed her to be quiet in case Coleman turned the gun on her. It took seconds to realise that the voice she could hear was her own.

'Fucking hell,' said Bernie, who was still standing close to Cain and Nimrod's car. 'He shot him. He bloody-well shot him.'

Maggie was too stunned to move. The scream faded into a horrible poisonous silence, while not more than a hundred yards from where she stood Coleman slipped his gun back inside his coat. A moment later he turned and walked back towards Nimrod and Cain, while his companion – the young man in the blue suit and shades – dropped to his knees and hunched over Nick, apparently searching for a pulse, while all the while talking rapidly into his lapel.

As he drew level with them, Coleman motioned towards the two killers.

'Hope you didn't mind, lads, but it was all getting a bit too messy,' he said in passing. 'We needed to square this one away before the local cops twigged that something was going on or Mr Lucas attracted any more attention to himself.'

Nimrod and Cain stared at Coleman in astonishment.

'But we thought this one was our shout?' Nimrod protested, looking over towards Nick's body.

Coleman shrugged. 'What can I tell you, boys? It wasn't my call – I just obey orders like the rest of us. As far as I'm concerned you can tell it any way you like. If you need another notch on your bedpost, it's yours. I'm certainly not keen on keeping score.'

Nimrod snorted and made as if to go over to the corpse but Coleman shook his head.

'I wouldn't if I were you. The local law are already well on their way. I'm pretty certain that they can be convinced they've found a nice tidy little suicide if you pair aren't around to complicate matters. Although if we can't persuade them then you're very welcome to take the credit.' He paused, eyes twinkling, 'And the heat.'

Nimrod smiled, his expression almost reptilian. 'That's very generous of you.'

Coleman lifted his hands in a gesture of admission. 'It doesn't pay to hold your hands up in my job. I'll be needing to cordon this area off in about –' he rolled his wrist over to take a look at his watch. 'How long do you think it'll take you boys to get back to your car and go buy yourself a hotdog?'

As Cain and Nimrod turned their attention towards the parking area, a big red car with a smashed front spoiler and dented wing screamed to a halt behind Coleman's blue transit van. Out leapt a small blonde woman and Robbie Hughes, who appeared to be busy brushing his hair. The blonde was wielding a video camera. Bernie Fielding took one look at the returning figures of Nimrod and Cain, denied their kill and heading back across the grass towards him, and scurried over to Robbie Hughes like he was his long lost brother.

'Robbie?' he said. 'Robbie Hughes?'

'Well, well, well, if it isn't the notorious Mr Bernie Fielding, at long last – purred Robbie. 'How very nice to see you.'

'I heard that you wanted to talk to me?' Robbie said, glancing nervously over his shoulder, white-faced and sweating hard.

'Indeed we do, don't we, Lesley?' said Robbie warmly. 'Keep that camera steady,' he growled as the blonde nodded enthusiastically. 'We've got a whole raft of questions that need answering.'

'All right,' said Bernie, with one eye firmly on the approaching hit men. 'If you take me away from here I'll tell you anything you want to know. Anything at all – sky's the limit. Do we have a deal?'

Robbie Hughes smiled broadly. 'You know, Bernie, I knew this day would come, I just knew it.' He turned to the camera and continued, 'And so here we are a long last on an isolated cliff top deep in the heart of rural Somerset. Faced with the might of national television, con man Bernie Fielding has finally given himself up. He knows that when he is dealing with the *Gotcha* team there is truly nowhere to run, nowhere to hide.'

From the blue van parked alongside Robbie's car, two muscular men in good suits were heading towards the dead man, carrying a stretcher and what looked like a body bag between them, but Robbie seemed oblivious to all but his prey.

'So, Bernie – where shall we begin?' said Robbie, moving a little closer.

'Anywhere you like, but can we go *now*?' said Bernie anxiously.

Nimrod looked back at Coleman. 'What are you going to do about those two?' he said, nodding towards the retreating figure of Bernie Fielding, and to Maggie Morgan, who was standing, still frozen to the spot, staring at them as if she was unable to believe her eyes.

'Don't worry, leave it with me,' Coleman said softly. 'It's nothing that you need concern your-selves with.'

From somewhere in the distance came the sound of sirens wailing. The hit men took a long hard look at Maggie and then another at the soli-tary figure crouched over Nick Lucas's body.

Coleman waved Nimrod and Cain away.

'Get going, lads, before the local plod show up – and don't worry, I'll take care of her and our friend Mr Fielding,' he said archly. The two men nodded and faded away back towards their car, moving as smoothly as tigers.

Maggie sensed rather than saw Coleman approach and realised that there was a part of her that almost didn't care what happened now. If she ran would he shoot her, too? Very slowly she turned towards him, her throat working over a great knot of fear and grief.

'Come to kill me, have you?' she whispered thickly, struggling with the conflicting sea of emotions in her chest, struggling to resist the temp-tation to run or cower in the face of his stony, unmoving gaze.

Coleman shrugged. 'No, no, you're safe,

Maggie. I did warn you that it wouldn't be pretty. You weren't supposed to be here, I asked the police to pick you up, keep you out of trouble. I suppose I should have known better –' He glanced back towards the activity around Nick's body. 'I did what had to be done, that's all,' he said.

Maggie wanted to spit in his smug, murderous face. 'What had to be done? You make it sound as if Nick was a dog that needed putting down,' she shrieked.

And as she spoke Maggie's mind spun. Who would ever know, who could she tell, who would ever believe her? Two more men were hurrying across to where Nick was lying. God, how long had they had this planned?

'It's time for you to go home, Ms Morgan, the show's over.'

Maggie stared up at Coleman. He sounded tired. 'Is that all this is to you? A show –' She swallowed back a sob, the emotions finally rising like icebergs in freezing water; there were things that needed to be said and it was now or never.

'Look, I've got no grudge against you, Ms Morgan,' said Coleman. 'I am just a solution to a problem. You have to leave –' he caught hold of her arm. 'I want you to go and get in the van and we'll get you home.'

'Do you think I'm crazy?' Maggie snapped, wriggling out of his grasp. 'I'm not going to go anywhere.' She pulled away from him. 'I want to see Nick –' and that said skirted past Coleman, who made only a desultory attempt to hold her back.

In the car park Nimrod and Cain were already climbing back into their car – eyes working back and forth across the remaining players before they drove back towards town.

'Stay back,' said the man in the blue suit as Maggie got close to the body. The body? *The body?* That couldn't be right, Nick couldn't be the body, her mind screamed, trying to make sense of what had happened and what she was feeling.

The man waved her away more ferociously. 'This is a crime scene, Ms Morgan. I advise you to stay well back.' Of course it was a crime scene, one in which they had all colluded in. As she took another step, Coleman grabbed her shoulder, and this time his grip was stronger.

'Not here, you heard what the man said,' he told her gruffly. 'We have to get going before things get messy. Go and get in the van, Maggie –'

This time his voice and grip were steely. Maggie spun round. 'Why in God's name do you think I'd do that, Coleman? You're a murdering bastard – you shot Nick down like a dog. You were supposed to protect him – you were supposed to be one of the good guys,' she yelled, almost hysterical now.

'Go and get in the van,' he said more firmly.

'No,' Maggie screamed. 'Do you seriously think I would go anywhere with you?'

She saw his hand lift, and an instant later felt a red-hot searing pain across her cheek as he slapped her. Maggie screamed.

His grip faltered and Maggie broke away and dropped to her knees in the grass beside Nick, her eyes filling with tears as she saw the blood pooling around his body as dark as night.

God, how could this happen. He was lying on his side, curled up and facing away from her, almost as if he was asleep. It was so unfair, so wrong. For a moment she thought that she might faint.

'Oh Nick, oh God, no – oh Nick, I'm so sorry –' she sobbed, feeling a great raw, angry wave rolling up through her like an earth tremor. Seeing him there hurt so much that it almost took her breath away. There was no way she had expected it to end like this.

'The bastards – oh Nick –' she gasped.

Behind her the two men from the van were pulling on white paper overalls and rubber gloves, arranging a stretcher, and beside it what looked like a huge suit bag with a zip down the front. Maggie let her tears flow as she realised that it was a body bag.

And then something very, very odd happened. As she watched, the man in the blue suit looked left and right and then tapped Nick gently on the shoulder. Very slowly he rolled over, his face splashed with blood, and then he opened one eye, and sighed. And then he grinned.

'What –' Maggie began, and as she spoke the world swam in and out of focus and she felt hot and cold, and then she felt herself falling forward, putting her hands down to save herself and meeting the cold sticky pool of blood under her fingertips.

'Maggie?' Nick said. 'I'm all right – it was a set-up – Coleman was using blanks. It's fake blood – Maggie?'

But even Nick couldn't bring her back from the dark place into which she could feel her mind slipping. She could see the concern on his blood-splattered face, felt strong arms closing around her and then the world went black. As the darkness closed over her like water she saw a stray thought scamper across the inky interior of her mind as bright as a shooting star. 'I have never fainted in my life,' she thought. 'This must be what it feels like.'

The next thing Maggie was aware of was the sound of someone throwing up and the realisation that it was her. She was sitting on a picnic bench with Coleman holding her head down between her knees.

He handed her a tissue. 'Nick?' she began, wiping her mouth, looking around frantically. Perhaps it had been her imagination, after all. Perhaps he was still dead.

'Take it easy, he's all safely tucked up in the van.' He nodded over his shoulder. 'Where you should be, Ms Morgan – I did try to tell you.'

Maggie looked at him, trying to fathom the dark unreadable expression on his face. 'So you *are* one of the good guys after all?'

Coleman snorted. 'Don't push your luck, Ms Morgan. The trouble you've caused me, to be honest I could have quite happily shot the fucking pair of you.' He handed her a bottle of water. 'The thing you have to understand is that we had no choice – unless Nick was dead those pair would never have given up.'

'Nimrod and Cain?'

Coleman shook his head. 'No, they were just the monkeys, not the organ grinders. No, I'm talking about their employers.'

'Miss Organised Crime and Miss City Slicker?'

Coleman nodded. 'As good a names as any, I suppose. Your turning up here was a pain in the arse but your reactions when Nick got shot helped to convince Messrs Nimrod and Cain that they really had witnessed an inside hit. Do you think you're up to the walk over to the van, only we really do need to be on our way.'

Maggie nodded and didn't resist as Coleman helped her to her feet and guided her over to the car park. 'What happens next?'

Coleman snorted. 'I think some of that is up to you, Maggie.'

She looked up at him. 'Sorry?'

He grinned and then shook his head. 'I have a feeling that Mr Lucas has something he'd like to ask you.'

Maggie looked him up and down and then laughed; Coleman was a strange choice for Cupid.

18

'So what's the food like in here, then?' Stella Conker-eyes said, letting her gaze wander very slowly around the interior of the prison visitors' room, all the while playing with her thick, freshly bleached, shaggy blonde hair.

Bernie Fielding shrugged. She smelt so gorgeous that he could hardly stop himself from drooling. 'What can I tell you? It's hardly Delia, but it's okay, a lot better than the last place I was in.' The room was painted battleship grey and was noisy, but in a repressed echoey way that always gave Bernie a headache. Some do-gooder or other had glued a bright yellow floral border around the room at dado-rail height. Its cheery little presence was more offensive than graffiti and made Bernie think that someone, somewhere was taking the piss.

Across the table Stella smiled warmly. 'You look better, too – settling in. That's good.'

He snorted. 'What choice have I got?'

Stella tidied herself and then said earnestly, 'I really need to talk to you, Bernie. Now that mum's passed on I've been thinking about the future. Considering what to do next – you know.' As she spoke Stella leant forward across the narrow metal table to reveal a great valley of cleavage framed by a pale pink angora sweater that struggled to contain the generous amount of creamy-white flesh.

Bernie groaned and looked away. 'Do you have to do that, Stella? I'm going bloody crazy in here thinking about you and that body of yours.'

Stella laughed and wriggled her shoulders to make her breasts all the more obvious. 'Oh, come off it, Bernie, I know you like a little look, you'd be disappointed if I didn't show a little bit of skin. Would you rather I wore a nice thick cardigan and covered it all up instead, then, eh?'

Bernie reddened. 'Well, no, I mean you can wear what you like. I was just saying how hard it gets –' His colour intensified as the double entendre registered and Stella lifted an eyebrow to underline it '– to have you sitting over there no more than three feet away and me not able to get me hands on you.'

'Oh you poor, poor thing, you. It's not that easy on this side of the table either, you know.' She glanced around the room. 'And besides, you don't really want me covering up, do you? All your friends always seem happy to see me.'

Bernie had to admit that amongst his fellow cons Stella was a very popular topic of conversation, as were her frequent letters. Two guys had already started a literacy programme on the promise of being able to delve into a photocopy of one of Stella's more graphic efforts.

If he was perfectly honest, Bernie really hadn't expected to hear from her again after his flit from the caravan at the Old Dairy. But – on a whim – he had decided to ring her on the off-chance just before they had come to arrest him.

'Why didn't you tell me you were in trouble?' she'd said, sounding more concerned than he thought plausible. 'You know me, Bernie, I wouldn't have turned you away, you should have said something. My old mum always said I was a soft touch, but I care about people – I really do. And besides, we're friends, aren't we, and what are friends for?'

Bernie had nearly choked. He didn't like to point out that they had known each other less than forty-eight hours when he had left for Somerset and his knowledge of her was mostly based on the anatomical rather than some deep spiritual connection. But apparently he was mistaken; it certainly gave bosom buddies a whole new meaning.

At that point Stella had paused and said, 'I saw that programme they did about you on ITV. You know – the *Gotcha* special,' she added archly in case he had missed the point. 'And I said to mum, God rest her soul, I said it all sounds a bit farfetched to me, Mum, he seemed like such a nice chap when he was here. Polite, considerate, the perfect gentleman. We had a lovely evening together at the Lark and Buzzard and he was chivalry itself, I said. And she just nodded and said they had to make it up to get the people to watch – just look at the Royal family and Coronation Street and that.'

And much to Bernie's amazement Stella truly seemed to believe those good things about him, something for which Bernie was immeasurably grateful and stunned by turns.

Stella tried to jiffle the seat forward until she realised it was bolted to the floor, giving him a clear view practically down to her navel.

'So, have you missed me, then?' she purred.

Bernie groaned again. 'What do *you* think?' he said. 'Hardly a minute goes by when I don't think about you.' Which, oddly enough, was also true.

She grinned. 'A girl likes to know where she stands.'

During the time he had been in prison Bernie had wondered at first if Stella was attracted to the idea of him being a little bit risky and dangerous, a little bit of rough on the side to add spice to an otherwise dull life. After all, life in a post office didn't strike him as being a hotbed of excitement. Worse still, he wondered whether

Stella had been taken in by Robbie Hughes's barely veiled suggestion that Bernie had a great stash of money hidden away somewhere in a numbered Swiss account for when he got out; the ill-gotten profits of his bad-boy ways. If only it was true. But whatever it was, since he had gone down for fraud Stella had visited Bernie regularly and written at least twice a week – every week.

In fact, Stella Conker-eyes's, wildly explicit letters were becoming legendary in prison circles, loaded with their double entendre and interesting and elaborate suggestions about what she planned to do to him once he was out and she could get her dirty little paws on his warm little body. For a postmistress, Stella had a very vivid imagination.

'I've been thinking about the future,' she said. 'You know, where we go from here –'

'Okay,' said Bernie guardedly.

'With Mum gone there's nothing keeping me in the post office really. I was thinking that maybe it was time for me to move on. You know, look towards the future.' Stella held Bernie's gaze and pouted suggestively as if waiting for him to comment. He felt his heart sink and wondered what she expected him to say. Was the next letter he was going get from Stella one that began, Dear John?

In the end Bernie settled for simple repetition. 'The future?' he said flatly.

She nodded and then giggled, her long earrings

jangling. 'Yes, Bernie, don't look so worried, honey. The future – our future.'

Bernie stared at her in astonishment. 'Our future? What do you mean *our future*?'

The giggle continued. 'Don't sound so stunned. A girl's allowed to dream, a little bit, isn't she? I've been thinking that perhaps we could set up a little business somewhere, you know, you and me. I quite fancied settling down somewhere nice and warm. I like the sunshine, me, and I've not had a decent holiday for years because Mum wasn't keen on flying. So what I had in mind is beaches, good nightlife, nice shops –'

Bernie waited, presumably there was more to this plan.

'I've brought you in a few brochures to have a little look at,' she said, hefting her bag up onto her lap.

As she did Stella signalled to one of the prison officers, who came over and checked the sheets of paper she gave him. He smiled and nodded and paused to check out Stella's cleavage at the same time.

Once they were given the all clear Bernie took the photocopied sheets and had a quick shufty through the various pages and photos before looking up at her in astonishment. 'Is this some sort of wind up, Stella?'

She shook her head. 'No, not at all. Why?' She sounded hurt.

'Because these places are in the Canaries; Lanzarote, Tenerife, Gran Canaria. They aren't bloody time-share, are they?' he asked anxiously, worried that his past might finally have come back to haunt him in the most ironic of ways. 'You haven't put any money down or anything, have you?'

'No, you're not looking properly, Bernie – they're mostly shops and little apartment complexes –'

'Are you serious?' he spluttered.

Stella smiled. 'Well of course I'm serious. I've been doing a lot of research over the last few weeks. Ringing round, searching on the Net, that kind of thing, and I've found this really nice little supermarket down on the front in Puerto del Carmen. That's in Lanzarote. There, that one there –' she said, pulling a wedge of paper out of the bundle. 'Three little studio apartments tacked on the side round a courtyard, good all-year trading figures, long lazy siestas, sangria on the terrace of a night-time. Just a four hour flight from London. How do you fancy a drop of that, then, Bernie?'

Bernie looked at her. 'Are you serious?' he repeated.

She nodded again. 'Of course I am. Only thing is it would all have to be in my name on every-thing, what with your record and that. And I need to have my accountant have a closer look at the figures – and until you're done in here I'm going to have to put a manager in – but I was thinking that maybe we could make a fresh start. You and me. Our own little place in the sun.'

Bernie let the idea run through his mind like a good tune, smiled for a few moments and then very sadly shook his head. 'I can't, Stella.' It was very tempting but it was time to let Stella off the hook. He had promised too much to too many gods up on the cliff top at Minehead to go back to his old ways now.

'Please, don't think that I'm not flattered, Stella, or ungrateful, but there is something that I have to tell you.'

Across the table he had her full and undivided attention. 'You're not already married are you, Bernie?' she asked nervously. 'You've not got another woman tucked away somewhere in the wings?'

Bernie laughed. 'No, Stella, you're all that any man could ever want. It's that the story about me having a pot of ill-gotten gold stashed away somewhere was just Robbie Hughes's over-active imagination. I'm flat-busted broke. When I get out of here my first job will probably be signing on.' He set the details of the supermarket back down on the table. 'I really am touched – believe me, it's a lovely thought, but I haven't got a bean, Stella, not a red cent. Nothing.'

Stella looked relieved. 'God, is that all? I

thought it was something serious. In that case, Bernie, you'll just have to work your arse off for me, then, won't you.'

He stared at her; remarkably, she was still smiling. It seemed that against all the odd the gods had taken notice of Bernie's rash promises and were rewarding him in spades. He grinned and picked up the agent's details again. 'Lanzarote, you say? I've never been myself, but it looks a nice sort of place.'

Stella nodded, and seeing his enthusiasm lifted up her handbag. 'It is. I've got loads of photos that they've sent me,' she said.

Meanwhile, tucked up in an enormous leather swivel chair in her new corner office, Lesley was flipping through her desk diary to check out the shape of the day. She was having a working lunch with the new *Gotcha* team, followed by a meeting with the Big Boss Lady upstairs at two o'clock. She was booked into the editing suite for a three o'clock session just to fine tune a few things for the evening's broadcast, then a full body massage and swim at five and, after the programme was aired, she had been invited to a celebrity fundraising supper at the Café Royal with Dale Winton.

Lesley stretched, cracked her knuckles and then pressed one of the intercom buttons on her desk. 'Could you bring me in a cappuccino, please? Oh, and some of those nice little Belgian biscuits if there are any left.'

'Certainly, Ms Jarman,' said a disembodied voice. 'And I have those letters for you to sign.'

'Good.' Along with a corner office Lesley had also finally retrieved her surname.

When Lesley had arrived back at the studios after her adventures in deepest Somerset with Robbie, and had got the call from upstairs, she had assumed – encouraged by Robbie – that she was most probably destined for the chop. But fortunately Robbie Hughes was about as good at predicting the moods and intentions of his boss as he was of assessing his current degree of popularity.

The boss was succinct and to the point. 'To be honest, we feel that it's time for a change, my dear –' At which point Lesley's heart had sunk like a stone; Robbie was right after all, she was getting the boot. 'Time that we dragged *Gotcha* kicking and screaming into the twenty-first century –'

The older woman had pressed her carmine fingertips together into a steeple and peered across the great expanse of grey slate desk, her dark kohl-rimmed eyes moving very slowly over Lesley's pale nervous face. 'We think it's time to bring some new blood and fresh ideas on board. We've been keeping an eye on you, Lesley, and we've been very impressed by your approach. You're thorough, well-organised and come across as warm, too. We have had several people ring in to say how much they liked your contributions to the show.' She picked up a piece of paper and read, 'Lesley Jarman is a real breath of fresh air –' and then continued, 'and you did very well in one of our recent viewer surveys.' She paused, letting the words sink in. 'We've been thinking that perhaps it's time you had a bigger slice of the *Gotcha* pie, Lesley. You're young – well-educated – obviously on the way up and yet you still have a certain, what shall we say? A certain untouched, rather charming naïvety without losing any sense of gravitas.' Lesley's boss turned her attention back to the single sheet of paper on her otherwise empty desk and scanned down over the contents. 'You scored very well with all our target groups – which, trust me, is quite rare.'

Lesley waited nervously, still not certain where this was leading, and then the older woman smiled, revealing a perfect set of shark-white teeth.

'Well, my dear?' she said, leaning back in her big black leather chair. Lesley smiled back. 'Are you excited?'

'Yes, of course I'm excited,' Lesley said diplomatically, still not altogether sure whether it was a trick question, or what exactly it was she was meant to be excited about, but far too nervous to ask.

The boss smiled again. 'As from next month I

have a feeling your life may well change forever. Enjoy your relative anonymity while you can – you have got an agent, haven't you? I can recommend one if you haven't. Fame can be a great servant but a terrible master –'

Lesley tilted her head on one side in what she hoped was a good listening position, as the head of the *Gotcha* production company continued enthusiastically. 'The plan is that we'll all be pulling together, working on the newly revamped show headed up by Lesley Jarman.' She tilted her head in Lesley's direction as if introducing her to an unseen audience. 'The team have been working the idea up for quite a while now, we just needed the right face, the right look to drive it. And now we've found it. You.'

'Me?' Lesley stared at her in astonishment as the penny finally dropped. Surely she couldn't mean what Lesley thought she meant. 'Are you serious?'

Meanwhile her boss was saying, 'Oh, and keep the glasses, I rather like the whole idea – it's got a kind of retro feel, a sophisticated female Joe 90; Michael Caine, Sophia Loren – Oh yes, very nice. And I've arranged for you to see the stylist about the rest of the look.' And so that was it. A week later Lesley had her own PA, a corner office on the first floor and use of the company gym and sauna.

As Lesley was about to get to her feet, trembling

with a mixture of disbelief and excitement, aware that her audience with God was almost over, she said, 'Excuse me, but what about Robbie?'

The older woman arched one perfectly plucked eyebrow and pulled a face that implied she had no idea who or what Lesley was talking about, and then, it seemed that she remembered. 'Robbie? *Oh, Robbie* – Robbie *Hughes*. You're very loyal, aren't you? I like that in an employee. The thing is, Lesley – and I'm trusting you to keep our conversation under wraps for the next couple of days, until I've sorted out the fine detail with our legal department – I'm not totally sure what we're going to do with Robbie. His contract is up for renewal at end of the year and the company's feeling is that he actually needs a new challenge. A new direction. We've been considering a sideways move into our satellite and cable division – growing market –' She paused to lick blood-red lips. 'We've been thinking lifestyle or possibly religious affairs. We've been working up a super little God-slot first thing on a Sunday morning that might suit Robbie down to the ground.'

'The one with glove puppets?' said Lesley, unable to keep the incredulity out of her voice.

'Oh, you've seen it?' said the boss with quite genuine delight. 'Clever girl – I like a woman who is au fait with the whole company image and keeps her eyes open. With that kind of attitude you'll go far –'

In a subterranean office on Colmore Road, Coleman was sitting at his desk looking at the CCTV screen. He was tracking the arrival and processing of one of the latest clients for Stiltskin's particular brand of magic, a small, pale, nervous-looking man with bottle-bottom glasses and a very bad hair cut.

Captured on the small screen the man pulled at his collar and coughed uneasily. 'I'm still not sure about this, Ms Heart . . .' he began. 'I know that you said that it would all be fine, but I –'

Before he could spill his fears and anxieties out all over the nice grey institutional carpet, Ms Heart nailed him with her icy blue stare. 'I'm sorry? Did you say something?' she growled.

The man swallowed hard. 'I'm worried about this – I mean will I be safe? With this Stiltskin thing, will I be all right?'

Her face rearranged itself back into what passed for a smile. 'We've been through all this before, our witness relocation plan is extremely secure. We operate one of the premier services in the world. Our record speaks for itself. A complete new identity at the press of a button.' She pressed a button on the keyboard to emphasise her point.

Coleman took this as his cue and stepped

through into the outer office. 'Just don't audition for *Blind Date*, and I'd steer clear of *Big Brother* if I were you,' he said jovially. 'I'm Coleman, Danny Coleman. Senior liaison officer on the Stiltskin team. You're high priority, trust me, you'll be just fine. Ms Heart here is my assistant.' He extended a hand. 'But from now on whatever you want, whatever you need, I'm your man.'

The smile on Coleman's face only warmed his mouth; his marble grey eyes remained resolutely cool.

The man swallowed hard. 'I'm still really not sure about all this.'

Ms Heart got up from the keyboard and Coleman took her place.

'So who am I now?' he tried with forced good humour.

Coleman looked up from the screen. 'Just hang on a mo', we'll have to wait for this to finish the run.' He glanced up at his assistant who was hovering by the door. 'Ms Heart, if you'd like to go into the other office and get someone to transfer all this stuff onto the new documents, please?'

She screwed up her face again and left.

The printer ground to a whining halt and Danny Coleman tore off a sheet of paper.

'Here we are,' he said, presenting the sheet to the man. 'This is your life.'

Coleman looked back over his shoulder into

the other office. Ms Heart was hunched over the photocopier peeling sheets of paper out of the tray.

He sniffed. He missed Dorothy Crow dreadfully, more than he thought possible, although Danny would never have said that to anyone. Too risky, too controversial. He pulled out a nasal spray from his inside pocket and fiddled with the top. Until Dorothy he had always considered himself a good judge of character and it worried him a little that he hadn't been able to see through to Ms Crow's dark little heart.

They had picked her up on her way to the airport, her jet-black hair tucked up and away under a blonde bobbed wig. Coleman didn't like to say how very sexy she looked. Dorothy must have guessed that she had been set up – after all, there were only a handful of people who knew exactly what was going on with Nick Lucas. What she hadn't known was just how closely each of those people were being monitored. He sighed and took a pull on the nasal spray; sweet relief flooded through him.

All those years of impeccable service, her spotless record all wasted. They had traced her text messages to Nimrod and Cain. They had found her new persona on file, all arranged by Stiltskin, although even now Coleman found it hard to believe that Dorothy Crow had sold her soul for a few hundred thousand, a small income for life and a place in the sun. But then again there was nowt so queer as folk, particularly folk who felt they had been overlooked at promotion and refused a department of their own just because they were a woman. Coleman had sent the hit men their final instructions by text message, his message rerouted via Dorothy's number.

He sighed and looked down at the latest set of personal details in front of him, remembering only at the last minute to paste back the smile – and wondered if, given the same situation, he might have done the same thing as Ms Crow.

While Bernie Fielding planned a new life in Lanzarote and Coleman was fitting a new witness with his shiny new persona, and out at Elstree Lesley was busy poring over her midweek schedule, an aircraft was landing at Heathrow. Aboard the aircraft two tall, good-looking, suntanned men in mirrored shades and expensive charcoal-grey suits waited for the cabin doors to open. Cain Vale tucked a newspaper into his flight bag.

'What d'ya think, then, Nimrod?'

Nimrod Brewster, sucking on a Minto grinned the cool even smile of a basking shark and glanced out of the window at the clear blue sky.

'No problems, my son,' he said in an undertone. 'In. Out. We'll be back in Marbella by tea time tomorra.' He mimed a sharp-shooter's draw with his index finger and then blew away a phantom wisp of smoke so real that he could almost smell the cordite.

They had had a lot of interest shown in their services since the Nick Lucas hit, under the noses of the local feds, had leaked out onto the grapevine. Nimrod – while not claiming any glory – certainly hadn't gone out of his way to disabuse anyone of the notion. He still had the press cutting tucked away at home somewhere. 'Tragedy as freak fall kills lone walker.'

Out in the aisle Cain cheered visibly. 'Right, so in that case can I have the window seat on the way back?'

Nimrod considered for a moment or two. 'I'll toss you for it. Afterwards.'

Cain stretched. As they got to the top of the plane steps ready to disembark, in amongst the noises and smell of the airport, was the hint of spring, all soft greens, the air ripe with all manner of possibilities. 'Nice to be back. Looks like a lovely day out here –'

Nimrod nodded. Shame they had to work really. He pulled on his coat and made his way down to the arrivals area.

On a long golden stretch of beach called Yorkies Knob, way up on the tropical coast of Far North Queensland, just a short drive from Cairns and God alone knows how many thousands of miles away from Minehead, West Norfolk and the rest of the crew, Mr and Mrs Nick Somerville were happily walking their dog, Bernie, along the water's edge.

Ahead of them their two boys – Ben and Joe, children from Mrs Somerville's previous marriage – ran around the weird circular patterns in the sand; intricately arranged traps baited by the little crabs that lived just below the surface. Laughing and playing the kids paddled in the water, picked up stray fronds of kelp and threw sticks for the dog, who barked enthusiastically, encouraging them on.

It was late afternoon, the sun already dropping in the cloudless blue-gold sky. Another half an hour or so and they would have to head back to get ready for the evening shift at Nick's new restaurant.

Evenings in the tropics weren't like those back home, night fell without warning, extinguishing the last rays of a fierce sun and leaving behind a humid midnight-blue blanket scattered with the twinkling stars of the Southern Cross. Deep in thought, Maggie stared out across the sea.

Nick liked to get the restaurant opened up early on a Friday evening, catching the customers high on that end-of-the-week feeling. His house special-ities were based on an imaginative fusion of ideas blending traditional Western food with Pacific-rim flavours, full of garden-fresh ingredients, herbs, subtle flavours and wonderful crisp, clean colours. They were already getting to be known locally as a decent place to eat – and that was all Nick needed. Word of mouth was better than almost any other advertising.

Maggie knew that she and the boys had to go home soon, but for now there was just the four of them, walking and talking and laughing and playing along the sea strand, relishing the rays of a fading day as the sunlight tipped the waves with shades of gold and bronze.

Maggie shivered, stuffing her hands into the pockets of her fleece and then grinned. It showed she was finally acclimatising. Heading into Oz's autumn she was feeling the first chill of the turning year, whereas the tourists on the beach were all stripped down to tee shirts and shorts and still too hot.

It felt like Australia had been a good choice so far. Cairns and the area around it was a great place to bring the kids to, a good place for Nick to open a restaurant, and far enough away for them to truly begin afresh. As far as Maggie's family and friends were concerned she had gone over on a teaching exchange. Only after her imagined year's contract ended would Maggie announce that she had found true love and would be staying on permanently.

Oddly enough, the one thing that hadn't caused her a moment's doubt was marrying Nick Lucas.

Coleman had arranged all the paperwork, a registrar, a special licence, and then shown up as one of their witnesses at a little family church on an estate, miles from anywhere that the guys at the relocation unit had hired for them, although Coleman had had to sign the register under an alias cooked up by Stiltskin.

So that was that.

Maggie had liked Australia from the moment she arrived, although maybe liked wasn't quite the right word – been receptive was a better choice. She had been receptive to the possibilities it offered. It struck her as still open and free and wild with loads of sunshine, fresh air, great food and – with a few notable exceptions – a warm tolerance of differences that often seemed missing in Europe. Not locked in by the old ideas of the class system all things were possible. It felt like a perfect place for a new family to start over.

The two boys had grown taller since they'd arrived and were already filling out. Both of them had settled down well into their new schools and seemed okay about the move. Not that there hadn't been teething problems for all of them, but they were the ordinary things associated with moving, rather than things specifically about emigrating to a new life with Nick.

It would take time for the dust to settle but Maggie knew instinctively that the four of them would do just fine.

She glanced ahead. Further along the beach Ben picked up a stick, chasing ahead with the dog while a balmy wind rolled in over the sea, calmed and subdued by the great protective arms of the Barrier Reef.

Nick slid his arm through Maggie's and pulled her close. 'Penny for them?'

Maggie sighed. 'Not sure that they're worth it – anyway, it's nothing new, you've heard it all before.'

'Ummm – you smell lovely, all sea and sunshine. You okay?' he purred, snuzzling his lips into the curve of her neck.

She giggled at the delicacy of his touch, relishing the little flurry of kisses and the wonderful feel of his body encircling hers while all the while still looking out at the clear blue sky and the heavenly blue water.

'More or less. Actually, and I know it sounds crazy, I was just thinking about the beach hut at St Elfreda's Bay. The sea always makes me think of summers down in Somerset. I don't suppose I'll ever see it again now.'

'Are you homesick?' he said anxiously, searching her face for clues.

She smiled and stroked his cheek; what they had between them was too truthful, too special for her to try and reassure him with a lie. 'Sometimes, sometimes I wake up in the middle of the night and wonder where the hell I am and what I'm doing here. And when that happens Cairns feels like a very long way away from home. I'm a Norfolk girl born and bred, palm trees and tree frogs and papaya for breakfast out on the veranda are way outside my frame of reference, Nick. And then sometimes – more of the time as the months go by – it's all all right and I know that given time this will feel like my home – and then I can't imagine being anywhere else on earth. I just need time to settle – let's face it, we all do.'

Maggie turned to face Nick, hoping that the warmth and affection she felt for him showed on her face and in her eyes. She had never loved anyone or felt more loved in her life than she did with Nick. It couldn't be any easier for him than her but it was always Maggie they discussed. Perhaps for Nick there had been less of a choice; he had had to go. But she and the boys had chosen to leave with him.

For Nick, the three of them were his fresh start, a ready-made family to cushion the blow of what amounted to banishment for life from everything he had ever had. Sometimes it seemed like a very big price to pay for a little justice; but then who was she to judge?

Nick, Maggie knew, was painfully aware that she had done nothing and yet had chosen to share his sentence, so maybe it was guilt mingled with gratitude that made him ask her.

Maggie grinned and pulled him close; curling

up against his body. How would she ever make him understand that while it was a hard choice it felt like the right choice – the only choice. Nick Somerville, nee Lucas, was the best thing that had happened to Maggie in years.

'So yes, I do love it here and I love being with you. It's just that some days it seems too big a thing, but I also know that it was the right thing. Do you understand?'

Nick lifted her fingertips to his lips. She let the grin linger. 'And you have to remember I lost you once – I still keep thinking how bloody awful that felt, seeing you lying there, thinking you were dead, feeling as if I had lost the chance to even begin. I don't ever want to do it again.'

The intensity of the moment was broken by Maggie yelping and jumping out of the way as their dog – an Australian Blue Heeler – charged between them, shaking the water from his sleek mottled coat, barking with excitement as he went.

'Bloody dog,' she laughed, picking up the stick that the dog had dropped at her feet and throwing it ahead of them into the white lacy-edged waves. 'And I suppose if it gets too bad I could always dye my hair, wear dark glasses and pop back for a holiday and leave you here to mind the fort. Assuming you wouldn't mind teaching my Year Six's next term?'

Nick grinned. 'I knew that you were something special the first day I met you, Maggie.'

She pulled a face and poked him teasingly. 'Oh please, Nick. I was actually just thinking how much easier my life would have been if I'd followed my first instinct and laid you out with a baseball bat the moment I clapped eyes on you.'

'There's still plenty of time for that,' he said, as she broke away from him and raced off down the beach, giggling.

Behaving Badly

Isabel Wolff

All men are beasts . . .

. . . or so Miranda Sweet believes. As an animal behaviourist, she can get inside the heads of deluded Dalmatians and introverted iguanas, but she can't work out why the men in her life behave so badly. Animals are braver, kinder and a lot more reliable, so Miranda's given up on love to open her own clinic and work her magic on neurotic pets and their grateful owners.

But can she keep the whole male species at bay for ever? Her best friend, Daisy, an incurably romantic weddingplanner, doesn't think so. When a delicious photographer comes on the scene, even Miranda starts to wonder if she's been a bit hasty. Then, just when she's letting her guard down, her past starts to catch up with her. Now she has to face up to her *own* behaviour, which hasn't always been as sweet as she'd like to pretend . . .

Acclaim for Isabel Wolff:

'Hilarious, moving, a wonderful story. I loved it.'

WENDY HOLDEN

'Warm, witty, romantic . . . Perfect!' *Express*

0 00 711862 7

The Devil Wears Prada
Lauren Weisberger

When Andrea first sets foot in the plush Manhattan offices of *Runway* she knows nothing. She's never heard of the world's most fashionable magazine, or its feared and fawned-over editor, Miranda Priestly. But she's going to be Miranda's assistant, a job millions of girls would die for.

A year later, she knows altogether too much:

That it's a sacking offence to wear anything lower than a three-inch heel to work. But that there's always a fresh pair of Manolos for you in the accessories cupboard.

That Miranda believes Hermés scarves are disposable, and you must keep a life-time supply on hand at all times.

That eight stone is fat.

That you can charge cars, manicures, anything at all to the *Runway* account, but you must never, ever, leave your desk, or let Miranda's coffee get cold.

Most of all, Andrea knows that Miranda is a monster who makes Cruella de Vil look like a fluffy bunny. But also that this is her big break, and it's going to be worth it in the end. Isn't it?

'Sassy, insightful and sooo *Sex and The City*, you'll be rushing to the bookshop for your copy like it's a half price Prada sale.' *Company*

ISBN 0 00 715610 3